Therina F.

Borealis

Original title: *Borealis*
Translated by Sara Mazzarello
Cover by Simone Matera

ISBN: 9798424755262

To my mother. She taught me to dance in the rain.

To my brother, my dearest friend.

Therina F.

"Nothing vast enters the life of mortals without a curse"

Sophocles

PROLOGUE

Every morning Mr. Cooper used to seat, fully dressed in one of his impeccable clothes, eating his breakfast with a huge napkin tied around his neck to protect his clothes from indecorous stains. In the meantime, he used to talk to his son with the same kindness that once his mother would have had for him.

Mr. Cooper's son, Elroy, known as Little Roy, used to listen to him carefully, with his blue eyes like sapphires wide opened. Little Roy had inherited his blue eyes from his mother Beth, native from Somalia, who used to observe them from the corner of the kitchen, slowly smoking a *Chesterfield* and puffing the smoke out of the half-open window. She loved that morning ritual that involved her dearest loved ones, deluding herself that time - in a certain way - could be frozen like in a Polaroid.

Towards the end of that fateful summer - before school started - Mr. Cooper called some workers to fix the roof shingles. The day turned out to be unexpectedly hot, while the workers had asked permission to spend their lunch break in the shade of the porch. Little Roy, with his brand-new toy, the accurate reproduction of a fighter-bomber - *Hawker Typhoon* more precisely - was running noisily throughout the garden. The workers watched him smiling, while he made the maquette perform acrobatic movements, reproducing with his mouth the sound of a guerrilla. He stopped for a moment to stare at the dusty blue dome that overlooked Folkestone, and it was at the same instant that he had the idea of using the metal ladder abandoned by the workers and leaning on the back, to continue the fiercest battle ever, at the closest place to the sky. On the rooftop. He got to the roof, but - as soon as he touched the first shingle with his foot - it fell and in a split-second Little Roy lost his balance and slid down to the ground.

That ordinary summer afternoon could have turned into a misfortune for the Cooper family. However, for a cosmic law unknown to most, that day turned into a very lucky day for Little Roy. A completely naked child saved Little Roy, supporting him with his frail arms, apparently without any physical effort. They were about the same age, and they both had curly black hair, dark skin, and blue eyes. Staring at the child in disbelief, Little Roy had the feeling that he had always known him.

The news made the headlines in local newspapers, allowing the workers - who attended the matter - to have five minutes of notoriety. However, they couldn't give themselves a logical explanation for what they had seen. The workers reported being dazzled by a bright glimmer light. After a range of investigations, the police found out that the mysterious child - renamed by the local newspaper as Angel Boy - didn't appear in the archive of the Register Office, he didn't have a name and not even a family. That unusual absence of a past ended up being handle in the most dramatic way.

That same year, the child was brought to Bristol, at the Müller Orphanage. After a few weeks of stir, the small crowd of local journalists, as well as other meddling people, finally disappeared in a snap. The institute shut its doors in 1958, as a consequence of the welfare rationalisation underway since the post-war period. Thereafter, the whole affair fell into oblivion. Nevertheless, Beth could never forget the frail naked child in her garden, so much like her son. She could never forget the moment in which Little Roy and his tiny saviour were sadly separated.

They both were aware that it was a farewell and had a completely spontaneous reaction: crying.

I

Wednesday, 22nd of November 2017

The churchyard in *Maddox Street* was covered with black umbrellas, while the melody of an organ came from inside, accompanying people leaving the funeral just celebrated behind closed doors. Arthur Murray - an estimated member of the *Slohan Oak* community - had left behind his wife Marta and their two children, Philip, and Alice. They were surprised to see the multitude of people waiting for the ceremony to end, and contrary to what those present expected, there would be no precession to the cemetery. The deceased - forward-thinking - had given written instructions about his own death, expressing the desire of a private function.

Marta - the mother of the two children - merely thanked those who attended, maintaining a strict composure. The eldest son, Philip, continued to look away, trying to hold back the tears in his green eyes. The youngest daughter, Alice, didn't let any feeling leak out. When people approached to her, she hinted at a smile of mere circumstance, trying as much as possible to avoid eye contact.

Mr. Murray had been found dead near one of the family properties, next to the small boat on Lake Hoarmere, where he used to fish. He was spotted by two children playing on the banks. He had died by drowning following a heart-attack that hit him aboard the boat, or at least, this is what had been stated in Coroner Richard Walsh's report. That death, violent and unexpected for everyone, upset the inhabitants of the small town of Wiltshire, arising mixed feelings: horror, dismay and even satisfaction for the passing of a man often respected but equally feared and despised. The funeral - celebrated behind closed doors - was the proof of the arrogance that had distinguished him while alive.

At the end of the farewells, the churchyard was left empty, and, at that precise moment, Alice lit up the first cigarette of the week - one of the *ciggies* as she used to call them. Although she was looking for the lighter in her coat pocket, and with the corner of her eye and under her long lashes, she noticed a male shape in the distance. She peered at the boy with curiosity, and since he did not avoid her gaze, she had the feeling of having already met him somewhere. Shortly after, Philip also came and reproached her - as usual - for the fact that she was smoking.

Alice hadn't been able to express her pain, although she was carrying the heavy weight of her conscience. That morning - while she was alone in her room - she had even tried to force herself to cry without succeeding. The absurdity of that fatal circumstance had aroused in her even more questions that she used to, and she had hoped - in some way - that that death would bring with it a plausible explanation, rather than merely nipping an existence. She no longer believed in anything, not even in the fact that after the end there could be a new beginning. She tried - just enough - to give herself comfort. Thus, the idea of a soul abandoning the body to re-join the cosmos probably represented the only concept that she considered admissible and capable of giving her comfort.

Alice put her packet of ciggies into the bag and looked around hoping to see the boy who had unintentionally caught her eye. However, as he had disappeared without a trace, she thought she was wrong and kept on pretending nothing.

Marta organised a reception at home. Only a few carefully selected people from a large circle of friends and acquaintances were invited. Yet, those who were excluded came claiming the right to take part in that event. The only relief was the Mayor Timothy Brickenden's absence and that of his wife, whom Marta kindly detested. The Mayor and his wife - while travelling around Europe - thoughtfully sent Murray family a wreath of white flowers with a note expressing their deepest condolences. Unlike her husband, Marta wasn't into public relations, although she had been forced to take part in many charity events, galas, inaugurations, notable weddings, and funerals. The Brickendens - who usually organised those social events - were disliked by her, simply because they represented the least favourite aspect of her marriage to Murray.

Marta was born in Italy, into a family of famous Florentine antique dealers, the Brunori. She had often thought of the first time she met her husband - almost thirty years ago - and of the way she was enchanted by his ocean eyes and his look of a typical tourist who goes for the first time to Florence and gets lost among all its beauty. Eventually, she had given him the information needed to get to the Church of Santa Felicita, which preserved - and still does - *Pontormo's Deposition*, a

Renaissance altarpiece depicting the Deposition of Christ, situated in the Capponi Chapel. He had thanked her and had invited her for a coffee, and it had all begun. Nevertheless, after a few years spent settling in the small English community - with the visibility of her social status - doubts about the real reason that kept them together in marriage had aroused, aside from their children and their love for art and antiques. That choice, over time, turned out to be a remorse. The more she looked at her husband - with his well-defined receding hairline and the signs of time on his face - the more she realised that she no longer nourished the enthusiasm and love that made her leave her hometown and follow him. Though, Marta was good at hiding her feelings, and whoever asked her how things were going - after catching a hint of sadness on her pretty face - she would answer "Divinely", but the only idea of having her children close was enough to cheer her up.

The Murray home, *Shelley House*, had been the birthplace of the two children's father. It is far from the downtown, and one must cross a portion of the countryside to get to it. The house looks like a lavish Victorian mansion, which can be accessed through a gate supported by white columns. In the summer, between June and July, when the blooming of the lavender is at its peak, Marta - helped by a couple of elderly ladies - collects honey from the beehives.

The two pregnancies, and her new status as a mother, had taken her away from helping his husband in his activities. However, even when the children were old enough, instead of taking part in auctions and antique shops, she engaged herself in helping in the dog shelters and in the cultivation of lavender. The latter - combined with the honey harvesting within the vast Shelley House property - produced a profit that was barely enough to pay the wages of the assistants, although lavender honey was popular among the local people. Since they were younger, Marta's children played near the beehives, not at all afraid of any bites. They used to play under the watchful eyes of their mother who strictly educated them, demanding obedience but providing them unconditional love. Since Marta was often alone, she was the only one that educated the children.

Mr. Murray, accustomed to the hustle and bustle and to his hobbies, had never changed his habits, not even after the marriage and the fatherhood. Grew up in a wealthy family as an only child, both Mr. Murray's parents had passed away before he was twenty-five, bequeathing him the antique shop which, however, he had thought of getting rid. Thus, he had decided to invest in the purchase of an auction house, first in London and later in Passy, the Parisian neighbourhood, where he had the opportunity to meet a lot of people. All those who met him were enchanted by his personality: he was educated, at time almost erudite, with a typical education of the upper middle class. However, the cheerfulness with which he dealt with business, his always proactive and optimistic way of doing things made people detest him, even though no one had ever expressed such feeling. In contrast to his innate business attitude - that made him earn a huge amount of money - he had empathy for less fortunate people. Among the various donations he made, he financed the reopening of the Slohan Oak shelter for children in need, which was renamed *Poppy Field Refuge*. For years, people had talked about that act of great generosity, and Mr. Murray enjoyed being the benefactor of that small community. Although he had no known enemies, many had ended up wondering how he could make such a fortune just selling the antique shop. His death was unexpected, however some people maliciously thought it was predicted; a sort of punishment for the luxury life he had. Himself had the feeling that he no longer had too much time to live - and perhaps for this reason - he decided to spend the last two weeks at Shelley House with his family, before the misfortune happened.

Alice couldn't take the reception any longer, wishing for it to be over. It was a sort of farce for her. She looked carefully at the guests, all well gathered around the buffet, which - by the way - wasn't enough for all those invited. However, she couldn't understand how people could be hungry after a funeral.

Since she was a child, Alice had developed a tendency to questioned herself, even about the most obvious things, and she didn't mind standing on the sidelines observing how people behave. She was sceptical in considering the world and the society. However, Alice talked several times to his mother about it, who saw in her daughter a certain resemblance to herself and was almost pleased with it.

Alice approached her brother in her oversized coat.

"Eventually, the presence of the guests will be good for mum. She will have time to enjoy solitude. Unfortunately" – Philip said.

Although they were completely different, both in appearance and personality, the Murray brothers were very close. It could be said, of Philip, that he was a bit know-it-all. He thought he was aften right, not out of arrogance, but because circumstances had often been on his side. He always had the final say, whether it was politics, fashion, or simply the weather. But not with his father. In fact, he had always suffered his father's personality. As he grew up, he had found in his sister a valid support, and even if she was four years younger than him, the bond became more and more solid and authentic. They attended the same prestigious school, the *Kingstone*. Once, Philip was even suspended for defending her by slaps. But things had changed since he was admitted to *Cambridge*, and Alice had begun to isolate herself even more. In a certain way, she felt betrayed, and her sense of emptiness couldn't be filled with Philip's occasional visits.

Following a couple of consideration about the attitudes of the guests, Alice and Philip found themselves discussing about the following days and Philip leaked some comments on the possible benefits of leaving Wiltshire for a while. There was clearly an expression of sadness on Alice's face, who felt that his stay in Switzerland, this time, would last for a longer period. Their relationship could be said to be rock solid, but since her brother had moved - first for working reasons and then for love - Alice felt that the house was empty without him, and she couldn't get used to it.

"What day is your return flight?" – Alice asked Philip.

"We will leave tomorrow. Brunhilde is working on an important case and she has to go back to her office in Bern."

"Oh, are you leaving already? Mum is leaving too. She is going to Florence to visit uncle Lory. I wonder how long I will be alone."

"You won't be alone much longer. Urielle will arrive tomorrow. However, it would have been good for you to go to Florence with mum" – Claimed Philip.

Alice objected.

"I have to go to the plant nursery. Claire is sick and they count on me these days more than ever."

"Alice… why are you still into that nursery thing? You can do better. By the way, did you contact the architects for that secretary position? It would be a great job to start."

Alice winced and felt hurt. She didn't like the fact that her work was minimized. Unlike Philip - who had graduated with honours in quantum mechanics - her university studies were a bit tortuous. Once she finished her studies at Kingstone, with decent grades, Alice enrolled in Law studies at *Durham University*, by the will of his father. However, she dropped out after the first year to start working at the nursery. The mother had supported her decision, aware that her daughter had never liked studying, much less Law studies. In addition to that, she was aware of the fact that Alice was reluctant to live away from home. Thus, Marta thought that working at the nursery was a right decision. Nevertheless, Alice was now suffering from feeling abandoned by her family, feeling the need to stay alone and escape from that context. Thus, when she saw Brunhilde approaching to them, she took advantages of the situation to get away, calm down and take off her warm coat.

Alice was aware that during her way to the clothes-hanger someone would stop her to ask her how she was. On the other hand, her constant nodding had allowed her to slip away for unpleasant situation in which she had to say how good her father was, or everything that one is usually expected to hear after the passing of a loved person.

Suddenly, time stopped. The voices of people faded, softly creeping inside the ears. In that very moment, she noticed a young man, at the sidelines in the main hall, the same man she had glimpsed that morning. It could be said that the young man was incredibly charming. He had bronze hair, well-defined cheekbones, and deep blue eyes. He was still wearing his coat and sat in one of the armchairs. Suddenly, a sound of broken shards, coming from the kitchen, caused an unexpected silence. The strange boy - without missing a beat - remained indifferent as if he was a statue. It was only when their eyes met that he moved, bowing his head, almost embarrassed. Alice didn't know him and - feeling strongly enchanted by his enigmatic figure - finally decided to ask her brother. Alice met his eyes even when she was walking to the hall. She was confused by all that air of mystery. Pleasantly confused.

"Phil, do you have any idea who that young man sitting down there might be?" – Alice asked, interrupting the conversation between her brother, his girlfriend, and Mrs. Willow, who seemed not to appreciate such interruption. Philip, intrigued, leaned over his body to look at the guy.

"Oh, do you mean that guy? Honestly, I have no idea who he might be! I saw so many people this morning and it wouldn't surprise me if he crashed the funeral. Maybe he was a friend of our father" – Philip claimed.

Brunhilde - who had been given her condolences all morning - started talking again to Mrs. Willow, as if nothing had happened, although she looked a bit nervous. While she talked, she touched a blonde lock of her hair. Alice had always had the feeling that a treacherous personality was hiding beneath that innocent look. She blamed herself for those negative thoughts that were probably due to an unexpressed resentment of nostalgia for her beloved brother who had moved to Switzerland. She rarely had met her, but every time she did, she felt a sense of discomfort. Alice had also tried to talk to Philip about that, but he minimized it, telling her to be patience.

"Come on Alice, let's introduce ourselves. After all, he is a stranger sitting in our house" – Philip claimed while pushing her towards the mysterious young man, who was sitting in the exact same position and didn't reveal any emotions. He introduced himself in a formal tone, shaking his hand. The young man turned his gaze to his sister, saying that his name was Aleister Crowley. Alice - cheerful and cordial - introduced herself and asked him if he knew her father, but the only answer she got was "Not really."

Silent fell within seconds, putting an end to the brief conversation they had. Philip got nervous, and then he left. He said he would join the guests, but he actually wanted to avoid the sight of the mysterious guest who seemed able to exert his charm even on him. Alice unable to manage such situations felt completely embarrassed and, to get out of that uncomfortable situation, offered him a cigarette. However, that proposal wasn't very successful.

"I think that I have to go. Sorry Alice." The guy stood up with a firm step, until he reached the entrance door, leaving her speechless.

That night, while she was in her bedroom, Alice thought about what happened during that day. She heard her mother moaning, who was finally by herself; the pain had reached its peak in the afternoon after the burial of her husband.

"Poor mum" – Alice thought. Shortly after, Alice remembered that the following morning her mother was going to leave for Florence, and she started wondering if being away from home was the cure to relieve her mother's pain. Thoughts thickened, and in the middle of the night, Alice found a way to fantasize about Aleister and the controversial attitude he had reserved for her. She was looking at the waxing moon, on that

22nd of November, thinking that in almost twenty-four years, she had never felt so alone in that room as she had on that night.

II

Thursday, 23rd of November 2017

The direct flight Rennes-le-Château - Southampton was an hour and a half late due to a sudden illness of one of the passengers.

Marie Urielle Blanchard - known as Urielle - had been forced to sit with her seat belts fastened, waiting for the plane to finally take off, while the man next to her squirmed on that uncomfortable seat nestled between the seats of that low-cost flight. The man moved as much as a boat does at the mercy of the waves, pushing her with his massive shoulders. The young woman found herself leaning towards the corridor to avoid his contact. However, people incessantly walked along the corridor to go to the toilets, and Urielle - at the end of that annoying journey - cursed herself for having taken a low-cost flight.

Urielle was going back home after attending a small convention of emerging young writers. She talked about her latest book *The power of the unknown and the modern subversive movements*, which - after being translated into French - achieved success in France, especially in the Aude region.

Urielle often travelled back and forth to Europe, but after the news of Mr. Murray's death, she had finally decided to take a little break from work. She was born in Nantes, her father was French, while her mother was a native from England. Life immediately reserved for her a bitter future: she found herself orphan at the age of four, after losing both parents in a tragic accident. She had grown up with her paternal grandmother, Yvonne, with whom she had moved to Slohan Oak following the tragedy, living thanks to her parents' savings and bequests. Since childhood, Urielle had shown unique skills, so that her grandmother had thought her to accept life by looking at it with a different perspective. Urielle could see people's halo and - in addition to the variety of perceived colours - she could hear the voices of the undetectable presences, among which people lived unaware of. After the menarche, the phenomenon - which until then had appeared very mildly, almost dreamlike - had become more intense, and not only during the night. That ability made her precious and unique in the eyes of her grandmother Yvonne who believed in mysticism despite not having any mediumistic skills. Her grandmother explained her that - with some practice and meditation - she would be able to channel the flow in the right direction to prevent the spirits from intruding her at any time of the day or night. Since no one would have been taken that gift seriously, they decided to keep it secret.

Over the years, the study of the occult - in all its shapes - kept Urielle very busy but allowed her to prepare herself for that condition with which she had to live. She published the first of her three books at the age of nineteen, attending numerous conventions. Thanks to that *power* - she aroused interest in teachers and researchers of paranormal field from all over Europe. Although she was known all over the world for her works, she preferred to be anonymous in everyday life.

In town, only few people were interested in her working achievements, as they were suspicious of the reasons that made her move from France to that small county of Wiltshire. In fact, she was still considered a foreigner despite she had been lived there for many years. Locals had often wondered why Mr. Murray was so much interested in Urielle and her grandmother to the point of paying for Urielle's studies at Kingstone School. Indeed - since her arrival in Slohan Oak - Urielle had gone to Shelley House, as Yvonne had agreed to work for Marta, firstly as a worker for the lavender harvesting and the beehives, and later as a housekeeper. Marta had welcomed little Urielle as a daughter, while Alice and Philip as a sister. They had even insisted on having one of the two guest rooms used as Urielle's personal room, having the walls repainted a soft lavender colour. Urielle, exactly like the locals, had wondered what that generosity was due, thinking that she could never repay that favour. At the beginning, Urielle thought it was a gesture of altruism, but over time she had realised that Mr. Murray loved to exert power over everything and everyone he met, including her.

That morning, the idea of going back home calmed and destabilized her at the same time. Urielle and her grandmother hadn't shared much with Arthur Murray. They rarely spoke to each other and had few opportunities to show him their gratitude. After all, Mr. Murray didn't mean to take on the role of Urielle's father, unlike his wife, who had provided her with maternal love. Urielle didn't know exactly how she would deal with Mr. Murray's death; let alone what words she would say to ease the family's grief. Death seemed to her the natural consequence of life, and she knew that sooner or later his spirit would go to visit her. Of this, she was sure.

Urielle asked the taxi driver to stop a little far from the entrance gate. Walking that short distance would help her to clean her mind. Marta was waiting for her at the entrance, wearing her favourite wool cardigan; the same cardigan she was wearing the day she planned her trip to Italy. She looked tired, and her brown hair made her look paler than usually. However, Marta welcomed Urielle as best she could, silently hugging each other. Marta told her that Alice was upstairs, sleeping in her room, while Philip had gone out to run some errands.

Urielle avoided asking about the funeral, she just listened to what she had to say. However, the truth was that Marta talked little about the funeral and showed only a strong resentment towards all those heartless people who had - nevertheless - turned up uninvited. Then Urielle headed for Alice's room which she found completely in the dark.

"Alice, it's time to get up" – She said, opening the shutters of the window to let in the daylight. But, as Urielle opened the first shutter, she found her friend sitting on the bed. "Have you become a vampire?" – Urielle asked.

Initially, Alice tried to realise who came in, but when she recognized Urielle's voice, she decided to play along.

"Can't you see that I'm not lying in a coffin?" – Alice replied.

Realising the circumstances, they both fell silent for a moment.

Alice - who until then had thought that what happened was a dream - had finally realised that it was real. Her father had passed away, that was a fact. However, Alice became aware of that only in the night, and that morning she became even more conscious of that. The night before hadn't helped her, nor had it eased her feelings of guilt. But Urielle's direct and almost peremptory behaviour calmed her, feeling a sense of cheerfulness, despite the situation.

As soon as she saw the time on the alarm, she swore. It was past ten, and time, not caring about her feeling, pressed on. Urielle just smiled and - given the situation - that smile turned out to be very important.

Alice got out of bed, and with her ruffled ginger hair, and wrapped in a warm duvet, she headed towards the bathroom. Urielle - waiting for her friend to come out - started to snoop around Alice's room, which she knew like the back of her hand. Some charcoal sketched were chaotically placed on the desk. On the lower shelf, Urielle could notice some old Polaroids. An almost faded photo was hung on the wall. The picture portrayed Alice and Urielle both with toothless smiles and smiling eyes, unaware of what the future had in store for them.

"Alice" – Urielle said, "I thought we could have lunch at the Whitebird Café."

"Okay, sounds good. I don't really want to eat yesterday's leftovers. By the way, how was your trip? Was your flight much delayed?"

"Well, it was as always. I realised that travelling in economy has its pros and cons. Let's start from the cons. I thought I had booked the most isolated seat, but it turned out to be on the way to the bathroom. So, there were lots of people passing by. I wonder why they don't force people to make a *pit stop* before embarking…"

"And what about the cons?" – Alice asked.

"Well, the ticket costed me only forty pounds."

Alice got dressed in a very short time. Then she checked her phone and found numerous messages, mostly from acquaintances expressing closeness and the usual condolences. She put her phone in her pocket, avoiding replying to the messages. She thought that those messages were intrusive and dictated only by the circumstances. By the way, "not replying" was her habit.

Philip had just returned home after having an initial meeting with the family legal counsel to discuss about the bequest. He had also managed to see the marble worker, to whom he had left his mother's dispositions, hastily written in an old notebook page. Philip wondered how the addition of ornaments on a marble plaque could make his father's the stay in the cemetery more pleasant.

Among the disadvantages of being the new man in charge of the house, there was also the responsibility of boring bureaucracy, which, however, should relieve the pain of grief.

Urielle found Philip sitting in the kitchen, planning his weekly commitments while sipping a cup of tea. The young man, thinking that his mother had come into the room - kept on thinking aloud, with his head bent to read on his agenda. "I have to call Betsy! No, I'll call her later. Better yet, should I call her as soon as we land or right now?" Philip turned his head and saw Urielle. At that point, it was almost impossible for him to hold back his enthusiasm. There had always been a strong alchemy between them, which led them to kiss once the year Philip moved to Switzerland. The last time they had seen each other was about two years earlier, during the Christmas holidays, before Philip met Brunhilde. At that time, he had the tendency to hang out with several girls. For Philip seeing her was a glimpse of light, and when he hugged her, the death of his father took second place.

Urielle asked him how he was, although the dark circles under his eyes spoke out. However, Philip - exactly as his mother and sister had done - changed the conversation.

"So, how is life going in France?" – Philip asked Urielle.

"I think the Country bored me, and this is not good. You know, I'd like to travel as much as possible and to get lost among the beauty of the world."

"And you *Riri*, you're more and more beautiful. You look like a goddess!" – He said frankly, calling her by the nickname his mother had given her when they were younger.

Then, as if the circumstances had not been so dramatic, they began to talk about this and that, current topics as of the Brexit one. Time seemed to rewind like a videotape and, as soon as Alice reached them, they felt they went back at their childhood, fifteen years earlier. They told each other stories and happenings, recalling moments as they sat together on the peninsula kitchen. But soon they were interrupted by the noise of a car coming from outside announcing the return of Brunhilde.

That moment of hugs and greetings was longer than expected, and Marta, as a typical Italian mother, made a series of recommendations before leaving Shelley House.

"The copy of the main key is near the doormat, under the wisteria. If you lose that too, there is another spare in the safety box", and "Make sure you always close the railing and double lock the door. The alarm is broken, and the technician hasn't call me back yet".

Finally, after that long incessant list addressed to her daughter, Marta said to Urielle "And please! Make sure she eats something. She hasn't eaten for days", then looking at both, she concluded "Girls, if you need something, call me."

Alice nodded to all those recommendations. While looking to the taxi, she noticed that Brunhilde hadn't go out of the car to say hallo. She was neatly seating in the back seat and waved an almost haughty greeting. She found her behaviour rude. However, the fact that she was about to leave for Switzerland, away from her, reassured Alice.

Once back in the house, Alice took the keys from the pocket emptier and - seeing the empty armchair in the living room - the memory that had kept her awake at night aroused in her. *Aleister.*

The two friends, taking advantages of the good weather, walked to the *Whitebird Café*. The Whitebird is a retro style place famous for its breakfasts. The sign - on a green background with two white wings - immediately catches the eyes, and it could be said that it is one of the most popular *Café* in Slohan Oak. Once, the club was full of employees of the small factories of the county. They often organized gatherings during the day to discuss about economic matters as jazz music played on the background.

Nowadays, it's not easy to find a seat, as the Café always crawl with people. However, Urielle managed to glimpse a table and walked towards it. She took off her crossbody bag and placed it to the back of the chair and - feeling particularly hot - she took off also her coat.

Alice looked at her astonished, jokingly asking her if she was on the threshold of menopause. Impassive at that joke, Urielle said that she had felt a sense of discomfort for a few days.

Afterwards, they went on talking about what became the main theme of the morning: Brunhilde Richter.

"She's very weird, sometimes" – Alice said. "I can't understand how it comes that my brother likes her. Brunhilde is even older than Phil and she doesn't even know how to relate to people!"

Alice quickly scrolled through the menu of smoothies and noticed that the smoothie of the day was that with citrus and beet.

The young waiter passed by smiling and took the orders. Urielle, as usual, ordered a hearty breakfast, while Alice ordered the citrus and beet smoothie, ignoring her mother's recommendations on keeping fit and eating consistently. It wasn't the first time she fasted and sometimes, it sounded like she was protesting. The rude behaviour in which her brother's girlfriend had left Shelley House had annoyed Alice enough to make her loose her appetite and make her forget about her mother's recommendations. Nevertheless, she didn't care much about *Hilde's* attention - the perfect girl born in Lucerne. What prevailed was perhaps the influence she was exerting on Philip, making him a puppet on Brunhilde's strings.

"Maybe you should talk to him about that" – Urielle claimed.

"I don't think it's a good idea. Since the night of my accident, I feel that something in him has changed."

"You still have blackouts since that night, haven't you?"

Alice nodded.

Urielle tried to comfort her by holding her hand, realising that Alice's hand was as cold as ice. Urielle would have preferred to avoid the topic, but Alice didn't allow her. She knew that all those feelings would only take her attention from her real problems. It seemed to Urielle that the matter of Brunhilde was just an excuse, even if no one had ever seen her laugh. For this reason, Alice often mocked Brunhilde asking her family "Has anyone ever seen her teeth? She never smiles!"

The waiter approached, giving a turn to the situation, which was slowly becoming melancholic. He had a clear prognathism and an expression typical of a playboy. He served an Hawaiian toast on a large ceramic dish - engraved with the headletters of the Café - and the smoothie in an opaque green glass with a note on it. He left only after smiling at Alice.

Drink me.
But if you want, call me.

A phone number was written on the back of the note, which was signed by *Dan*.

Alice felt embarrassed. At that very moment, she would have preferred to hide herself among the fences outside the room, rather than making eye contact with him or even his smile. She prevaricated for a while, drank the smoothie almost in a quick gulp and then cleared her voice and talked to her friend.

"I met a guy yesterday at the reception" – Alice said.

"Oh, one of the crushers? And...?"

"His name is Aleister Crowley. I don't know anything else. But I think I had already seen him somewhere."

"*Aleister Crowley*, like the esoteric writer?"

Alice reported that he knew her father, or *not quite*. She made a sort of wince as she remembered it. She immediately became serious as soon as she realised of his lack of grace and his need to leave Shelley House the day before.

"I must say the circumstances are unusual. What's the first impression you had of him?"

"I don't know. I'd say resolute and odd-mannered… he had a deep look. He intrigued me."

"Do you think you'll see *Mr. Resolute* again?"

"Why should I? I barely know his name. He left suddenly."

When Urielle asked her if she and *Mr. Resolute* would see each other again, Alice shaken. Afterall, the possibility of meeting him again in Slohan Oak was not to be ruled out. There weren't many inhabitants, "caryatids and children" as Philip would say. The only certain thing was that their meeting had awaken her soul, as she - over time - had turned indifferent to life. She was strongly attracted to him, but she didn't want to admit it even to herself. In the past, someone had blamed her of indifference, and her behaviour had been defined as elusive.

Although Alice was unfamiliar with love, she knew that after the first phase of attention received, she inevitably became less interesting. For this reason, she avoided getting too involved in relationships since the beginning. Her old relationships could be counted on one hand. However, they were short-lasting relationships and with feelings of indifference. Ethan Carter was the only one to make it through the year, although they split up shortly after he moved to the United States to go to the University. Although they both were sceptical of that long-distance relationship, it was Alice that decided to break up. At first, she was considered as the numb and Ethan as the broken-hearted boy. That was, until one day, his heart was healed by the sudden appearance of Melany, one of Ethan's many classmates in finance. To avoid any possible misunderstanding, Ethan had called Alice in the middle of the night, to give her explanations. He insisted that he was overwhelmed as he had finally found pure love, asking Alice to go along with that.

Alice, who accepted the consequences passively, was aware that the only conflictual relationship she would ever admit, would be the one with herself. Her life had always been an unsteady balance, made up of rare moments of calm, that most of the time ended up becoming doubts and insecurities. She didn't know what she was looking for in a love story, but after all that time, she had finally realised what she no longer wanted: compromising.

"Do you have plans for tonight? I have to go to the bookshop. I haven't been there for a long time. Do you fancy a dinner together?" – Urielle asked Alice, in the hope of being able to spend more time with her.

"It sounds good. Let's dine at my place. We can order Chinese food. But I have to tell you, I can't stay up late. Tomorrow morning, I'll work."

"Perfect! I'll pay for the breakfast. You better leave the Café, or Dan, the waiter, will ended up inviting himself to have dinner with us."

The clock tower marked that it was three o'clock. The light began to fade, as the colder hours were approaching. Alice and Urielle separated after Maddox Street. Urielle reached the bookstore which, unfortunately, was closed, while Alice made her way to the cemetery for *some unfinished business*.

The walk along the avenue was accompanied by the echoes of some children's laughter coming from the courtyards of the houses and some barking - most probably belonging to small dogs. The office of Alice's father is located on the second floor of a white building overlooking the main road. Mrs. Beans' flower shop is on the right side, and about ten meters further on, there is Kingstone School. Alice considered how familiar Slohan Oak was to her, to the point that she could walk down its streets with her eyes closed. She thought that she would have even reached the cemetery in a blink of an eye. Slohan Oak Cemetery - or *Hades*, as Philip used to call it - had been partially rebuilt after the end of World War II. The cemetery was built upon the Italian architectonic style but on a smaller scale. In fact, its structure reflects the most impressive Christian cemetery located almost everywhere in Italy. Unlike the Anglo-Saxon cemeteries, paved with soft green grass, the Slohan Oak cemetery has porches, tunnel vaults, tombstones of different varieties, gravel, and corridors along which there are niches, while some steps allow people to move from one area to another. It is located on a hill outside the center adjacent to a small oak forest. The gate is guarded by two sculptures of angels, placed on top of the two columns. One holds a sword, while the other seems to point to somewhere. Up ahead, on the right, is situated the guardhouse, where once worked the guardian Edmond - known as *Cerberus*. Edmond used to get lost in readings, and - although those who didn't know him might think that he was often distracted - Edmond was, actually, an attentive observer.

Alice's arrival at the cemetery didn't distract him from his readings. Although Edmond had always known her family, he welcomed Alice with those traditional words he spoke to anyone who went there in the afternoon. "I remind you that closing time is scheduled at five o'clock."

The sunlight stretched the shadows of the weathered grey statues, hinting that closing time was close.

After passing the gatehouse, it is necessary to walk through the *White Corridor* - known as the Children's Wing - to reach the West Wing, where Mr. Murray was buried.

Since they were younger, Alice and Urielle had spent entire afternoons stealing flowers from adjacent graves "For a worthy cause", as they used to say. In fact, they used to place such flowers on the gravestones of those who had prematurely passed away. It was the feeling of compassion that led them to take care of those children, as none of their loved ones were alive anymore to do so.

After the White Corridor, there is a series of stone steps which lead to the noble chapels. The most sumptuous chapel belongs to the Attenborough family whose last heir is the well-known Mayor Brickenden. The West Wing - the end of that labyrinth - is very obsolete, as it was almost intentionally made. The only remarkable aspect of a cemetery is the majestic marble statue of a winged genus crouched on a sleeping lion. The grave of Alice's father is located right down the West Wing, more precisely on the left wall. At that moment, the burial niche was still unadorned, covered only by concrete and topped with recently bought carnations. Alice carried with her a letter which she would have liked to read. Yet, decided to place it - quietly - in the middle of the white flowers. There were so many things she would have wanted to say to him, much more than she would have said if he were still alive.

"One day, maybe, we'll meet again" – Alice thought.

The bell of the main chapel rang twice, making it clear that shortly thereafter the cemetery would be closed as had announced. While she was staring at his father's grave, a familiar voice called her name. It was Aleister. Incredulous as she was, Alice wiped her wet eyes with the sleeve of her coat.

"Aleister! I didn't expect to see you here" – Alice said.

"I passed by to leave these" – He had shown up holding a bunch of gerberas in his hand. He stared at the surface of the niche and in the meantime, he tried to place the bunch of yellow flowers among the carnations. "Should I place them here, shouldn't I?" – He asked, pointing to one of the possible places.

"Let me help you."

Alice, while grabbing the bouquet, touched Aleister's warm hand. They stared at each other for a moment, but they immediately looked away of embarrassment. He sweetly smiled at her, and everything seemed to get back to normal.

"I guess, I owe you an apology for running away yesterday" – He said timidly, and Alice found it difficult to know exactly what to answer.

She lowered her gaze, thinking of how he had left the day before.

"Don't worry."

"I knew your father, or at least, I knew his name, although I don't think he could say the same about me" – He said, not caring about Alice wincing in doubts. "Years ago, your father helped my uncle with his testament. When his parents died, he wasn't eighteen yet. Thus, he lived with different curator. The last one seemed to be about to cheat him. Luckily, thanks to your father, my uncle managed to solve part of his financial issues linked to the *Falkenberg* property" – He pointed at Manor, situated at the highest point of Slohan Oak, and resumed. "My uncle is a very private person. He doesn't like to show himself up in public situations. For this reason, he didn't show up at the funeral, but I assure you that your father's death has deeply affected him".

Alice nodded and changed the subject. "So, you live in Manor with your uncle?"

Aleister nodded, smiling at Alice, and managed - even if partly - to answer the questions that had gripped Alice up to that moment. Only few people had been able to meet people from the Manor, and with that new certainty she calmed down.

From the end of the corridor, a croaking, reproachful voice interrupted the conversation. It was Edmond making sure all visitors had left the cemetery. He reminded Alice of closing time, and at the sight of Aleister, he paralyzed.

"*Cerberus!*" – Alice thought. "We better leave" – She said to Aleister.

Right after they left the cemetery, the lamps on the street lighted up. They slowly walked with their hands in their own pockets. Side by side, in a pleasant silence. Only the sound of the birds flying towards the nests and that of their steps could be heard.

Alice thought that Aleister was good company.

The boy walked at her pace and - observing him secretly - Alice noticed his blue eyes sparkling. After a few comments on Edmond, and after a few words of circumstance, it was time to say goodbye.

There was a moment of embarrassment, and once again, it was Aleister who brook the ice.

"How are you getting back home" – He asked.

"I came here on foot, I love walking."

"I hope you won't go through the woods."

"I will! It's the fastest way home." Then she added, "I'll see you around then."

They took different paths and suddenly, he called her name, making Alice turn around.

"Alice…"

The girl realised she wanted his attention, and the proof had been just that: wait for him to talk to her again. But that call was followed only by the silence.

Aleister wasn't there anymore.

Alice picked up the pace. She felt a presence behind her, as if somebody was following her. However, despite the darkness of the wood, she felt safe.

III

Friday, 24th of November 2017

That day, the weather forecasted rain. The night fog - typical of that period - had slowly disappeared, as an icy wind from the east blew on the plain, anticipating the arrival of the rain.

Alice stared the condensation on the window, as she sipped a hot coffee and ate some honey biscuits. On the counter in the kitchen there were leftovers of the Chinese dinner they had ordered the night before. Thinking back at that night, she could only smile at the thought of her friend's indigestion of steamed dumplings.

"How many of them has she eaten?", She thought. *"Right! A minimum of fifteen!"* Alice was about to laugh.

Urielle slept over in her room, the one with the lavender-coloured walls. She had spent the evening complaining about having binge. "I won't eat Chinese food ever again!" – Urielle said running to the bathroom in the grip of a stomachache. Eventually, Alice came to her aid with her mother's home remedy: the notorious *canarino*. It was a sort of Italian herbal digestive brew made of lemon peels and bay leaves. At first, Urielle had firmly refused to take it, but then, after her friend's insistence, Urielle drunk it. Urielle unintentionally produced a resounding liberating burp, making Alice laugh.

As always, they helped each other out.

Alice wisely decided not to wake her up, so she could healthily rest. Thus, she decided to leave Urielle a message on the kitchen blackboard.

I'm at work. See you tonight.
XOXO, Alice

Leaving Shelley House behind, Alice follows the path under *'the low, heavy sky weighs like a lid'* as in *Baudelaire's Spleen[1]*. The ticking of the rain on the umbrella reminded her of the little steps of the sparrows on the windowsill, and as usual, she started jumping from puddle to puddle in her Wellington. She still remembered Urielle and her funny expression of dismay at having burped. Alice chuckled.

Her good humour, however, soon disappeared by the sight of some beheaded crows near the stables of the Adlard brothers. On the ground, there were only the mutilated bodies of the birds, at the mercy of the weather. Their rotting reddish and orange entrails resembled small succulent fruits. Those macabre executions had been taking place for a while, and in the village, people blamed a small group of local thugs.

Since childhood, Alice had been fascinated by road deaths, and for this reason her most spontaneous reaction was to stop instantly to observe them. Looking at them a little longer, Alice had the sensation that the dark plumage was about to come to life; some worms peeped out waving, and suddenly she heard

---

[1] Referring to Baudelaire's poetry "*Spleen*" from Flowers of Evil.

a wheezing in his ears. It was at that point that Alice stepped back in horror and fear, thinking that it was the carcasses themselves that had spoken to her.

Alice walked towards her work. After having walked few yards, she reached the dog shelter and the *Gladi* fountain which is rectangular based and characterized by the statue of an angel gripping an unsheathed sword. Over time Philip had found more ways to rename it, and all the nicknames alluded to those young people who stopped there to smoke weed. Alice knew that even he had smoked some joints from time to time, although he had never explicitly told her so. Thanks to that name, she could identify the beginning of those stuns and the end; "Two hits of gladius" - during the early years at Kingstone, and "The fountain of the drug addicts" at the end of the school, before going to Cambridge, as if to take distances from that adolescent experience. In the last four years, that of the fountain became a peaceful zone. No one stops there.

Alice reached the old nursery - *Robins Garden* - in just over an hour, four miles away or six thousand seven hundred paces (we can say with certainty as she once counted them). The majestic Ginkgo Biloba tree stands at the entrance. Such a tree - the emblem of that place - was now bare and almost disturbing. The plant nursey had always been her tiny paradise and being back at work could have alleviated her grief. Alice realised that it wasn't going to be a busy day, as she had noticed that there were only three cars in the parking lot.

Her colleague Justina was at the counter, arranging ceramic vases inside of wooden boxes while muttering to herself. They said goodbye to each other, then Alice suggested to Justina to have a cup of tea.

"My dear, how are you?" – Justina asked with her cerulean eyes wide opened. Then put her tiny harms around Alice's shoulders.

"I'm better now, thanks."

"I'm sorry you had to get back at work this soon! But you know, Claire is ill and if you hadn't come here, we risked total anarchy! However, tomorrow we'll be finishing one hour earlier, luckily! We're being so busy these days!"

Alice looked around puzzled, noting that there were no costumers that day.

Justina continued. "Have you seen Marvin's new *toy*?"

"You mean the grey van outside? I wondered who it belonged to."

"Yes, that's it! And guess what? He said that once I'll finished working, he will take me out for dinner!"

"By van?... So, between you two... Has something happened?"

Alice didn't want to be indiscreet. She was certain that it would be the first date for Justina, who had long waited and desired for that date with Marvin Brown, the handyman at Robins Garden.

Justina began to talk to Alice about the previous days: about the amount of work, the sudden changes in weather, about *Rommie*, a stray tabby who wandered around. She talked about the new orders and how sweet and caring Marvin had been in those days and blah, blah, blah… Justina concluded her boring speech with an exclamation about Claire, the owner, who - still feverish - would have returned at work God knows when. Meanwhile, she had never stop gesturing, accompanying each sentence with significant facial expressions.

It had sounded strange even to Alice that a man like Marvin Brown had decided to invite a talkative person like Justina out for dinner. Nevertheless, life is full of surprises, as well as her colleague Justina.

"Do you mind dealing with these?" – Justina asked, pointing out to a pile of topsoil bags leaning against the side of the counter. It seemed that Justina was waiting for someone who could do the job of taking them to the shed and number them. Alice nodded and left her colleague dealing with something else.

Portering, in contrast to her slim body, was certainly not new to Alice. The job there - at the plant nursery - was slow rhythm. Some days there were only few tasks to be performed. However, it had never happened that somebody remained idle, even if they wanted to. Despite that, *someone* would always come up with some tasks. In total there were four of them working at Robins Garden, dutiful workers with a great sense of initiative. Alice got along with everyone, except Claire, the authoritarian and meticulous young owner. It had taken Alice a while to get used to the working rhythms, and - accustomed to growing a few small plants at home - working there hadn't been easy at the beginning.

From time to time, she looked at the sky from her waterproof brim hat, distracted by the dark clouds. She paused to observe the small drops on the plants that tried to defy gravity and then fell to the ground. The sound of the water calmed her, especially during working hours *"It could rain forever"* – She thought. While she was working on the thirty-fifth bag, Alice briefly said goodbye to Marvin - who was tidying up the greenhouse - and for the first time, he winkled at her. Alice ignored it, thinking that Marvin Brown wasn't her type. He was a macho and his black sideburns smelled of vetiver aftershave.

If she had been her colleague, she would have turned down that date. It had been at least three years since the last time Alice had been invited out for dinner, and - according to her brother's statistics - for a young woman of her age it was a long time. However, Alice wasn't the kind of person who takes advantages of the opportunity, she let others seize the moment.

Once the harder tasks were finished, Alice returned to the entrance, breathing a sigh of relief. Then, Alice called Justine, but suddenly stopped, widening her tired eyes. Her chattering colleague wasn't at the reception desk anymore. Instead, there was Aleister, who cheerfully said hello to her. At the sight of his *rare* beauty, Alice almost fainted of the embarrassment. She immediately remembered that she looked shabby, her hair was soaked and her fingernails dirty of soil. Nevertheless, Alice waved back at him ashamed. Trying to hide her nervous, she asked Aleister if he needed anything. Aleister, quietly showed a receipt attached to an unclear handwritten note. Only Alice's eyes could have deciphered Justine's hieroglyphs, which could be - by the way - considered scribbles.

"*Ausmas Roses*, right?" – She asked, and the young man nodded.

A little over two weeks before, his uncle had reserved an Ausmas arrangement. The plant nursery had competed for multiple editions at the Wiltshire horticultural competitions with such a variety of flowers, winning for four years in a row as the best cultivation. Robins Garden hosts a great variety of Ausmas Roses, and they were so well known that the demand had increased exponentially year by year.

The conversation about that reservation ended as soon as Rommie, the stray cat, got agitated and annoyed. Alice asked

Aleister if he had a pet, such as a dog, as this would explain the cat's unusual behaviour.

"A mare named *Epos*" – He told her. "You can see her from time to time at the Manor. My uncle prefers to keep her free, but she never goes further than she should."

Alice glared at the cat, as if she was begging him to stop. The more the boy talked to her and got close to her, the more the cat got upset.

"I didn't know your horse roams the woods" – She replied.

"She knows the risks", and shortly after resumed, "She doesn't dare to go beyond the wood. She roams around, but she's always supervised."

Aware of the previous day's recommendations, Alice wondered why Aleister was afraid that someone might approach the clearing. Although it seemed absurd to her. Alice decided to put her thoughts aside and invited him to follow her towards the rose garden.

The rose garden can be reached by crossing the *Floris* greenhouse, which was named after the nymph of Roman mythology. The rose garden is located about ten yards from the entrance. It is one of the few glass structures in Robins Garden that houses a variety of plants, transforming everything into a rainbow. There are flowers whose colours go from the brightest ones to the most delicate shades. The variety of colours aroused interest also in Aleister, who complimented the arrangement of the plants and how they were enhanced in their ornamental pots. At the entrance, the colourful Amaryllis caught the eye, followed by winter Jasmines, and a long row of red Poinsettias. They were Alice's little creatures - treated with care and dedication - and when someone appreciated them, she felt satisfied.

"This *Hydrangea macrophylla* is wonderful!" – He exclaimed, pointing to a majestic indigo Hydrangea with cold shades. "And this one… It must be a *Damask rose*, mustn't it? – Aleister asked pointing out to the bright pink plants in the adjacent flower boxes.

Alice nodded and smiled. It had never happened to her to meet someone so young who had such a mastery with the scientific names of plants. Not even Claire or Justina who, from time to time, merely named the colours of the plants "The yellow and orange flowers", when they referred to the Narcissus, and "The bluish flowers" for the Bluebells, just to name a few examples. More than a human, Aleister had seemed like a living botanical encyclopaedia. However, his attitude wasn't an excuse to show off his knowledge. Instead, the way he observed and pointed out the flower boxes suggested he was genuinely amazed. He looked like a child who, intrigued, asks questions in front of things he sees for the first time. In a certain sense, it could really be said to be the first time.

Walking along the greenhouse, he finally revealed to her that he had never seen a flower in his life, except wildflowers. No botany courses, nor books from the most prestigious school have aroused interest in Aleister, but only some evening readings, including Latin.

"How did it come that you plant Ausmas Roses?" – He asked suddenly.

"It's a strange story… Officially, the owner's great-uncles started the plantation. However, the truth is that Claire wanted this type of Ausmas Roses because she's obsessed with a science-fiction saga, *The Chronicles of Argo*. Have you ever watched it?"

"Never. What is about?"

"It is set in the future, in which the Earth has disappeared because of the pollution. Constant power struggles take place between space legions and imperial families for the supremacy of the Ausmas Rose, the only terrestrial life forms left."

"So, you have already watched it, haven't you?"

"Not yet. I've only read many times the trilogy. Yet, everytime I end up wondering, why *roses*?"

The reserved Ausmas were set near a row of pots ready to be delivered. They were decorated with *blue* ribbons, Alice's favourite colour. It was the signature she affixed every time she was commissioned to take care of a composition. She tore off the piece of paper written in her colleague's usual incomprehensible handwriting, dusted the bottom of the vase with her hand and smiled at the thought of having - without her knowing it - prepared those roses for him. Then, when Alice asked if he needed anything else, he looked at her calmly and shook his head.

Silence fell again. It was the kind of silence that annoyed Alice and any other reserved person. Alice preferred to stop asking questions, as it would have meant continuing the conversation. After having handed over the Ausmas arrangement - both embarrassed - they greeted each other by hinting at a smile. At this point, there wasn't anything left to work on. Thus, Alice sat down next to the row of vases, in the shade of the rain-stained glass window, plagued with thoughts. At first, she thought she was disoriented by Aleister's sudden appearances, but soon she realised she liked them.

Justina - certain of having entrusted to Alice an ordinary portering task - remained at the reception. However, as Justina didn't see Alice return from the shed, she began to worry. She knew that Alice couldn't have gotten too far away. Justina-wandering around the plant nursery, called her persistently, as she would have done if she wouldn't found Rommie taking a nap on the desk.

Justina finally saw her.

"Where were you?" – She asked surprised. "I thought you were gone. What's wrong with you?"

Alice promptly got up, dusting off her trousers, and tried to explain herself to avoid answering those questions.

"I'm fine! I was just taking a break" – She said upset. "I just handed over the vase of Ausmas Roses you wrote down. Aleister collected it."

Nevertheless, the colleague - instead of just nodding and get back to her duties - look at Alice and asked her if Aleister was the boy she had just seen out. "If so…" – Justina said, "His beauty has enchanted me, like light enchants moths."

IV

Saturday, 25th of November 2017

Money would never have exerted any charm on Urielle, although she enjoyed notoriety as a writer. A simple life - without any vices and made up of small satisfactions - seemed to be enough for her daily well-being. When her grandmother had passed away, she had decided to leave the *Suburbs* of Slohan Oak to move into a three-room apartment, in the downtown, above the esoteric bookstore. One thing was clear: Urielle had never felt alone. In that small apartment - old-style furnished - she used to talk to the previous deceased tenants. In particular, she familiarized with the spirit of Major Edward Roder, who loved to tell her war tales.

The Major's ghost - trapped in a dimensional limbo - had no desire to move beyond that dimension. The ghost always ended up telling her how he had won the battle at Alma during the Crimean War. Urielle had heard about the story so many times that she would have been able to list the reprisals and ambushes in detail.

In the middle of that morning, Urielle went back home and unexpectedly found a small basket on the doormat, with a bottle of liquor in it. It was a gift from Mr. Orpeco, the owner of the house. Urielle had expected it in a certain way, as he used to act like that, generously but discreetly. In a note, he congratulated Urielle on her new milestone, inviting her - once again - to celebrate together in the following days.

Wallace Orpeco owned several properties in Slohan Oak, and *Roots of the Mistery* bookstore was taken over by one of the family businesses. That place seemed to be a hobby, rather than a source of profit since there were no occasional nor regular customers. Women used to look at the shop window but never came in, as if they were intimidated by the attractive but austere owner. He could live comfortably thanks to the income deriving from the apartments he rented, included the three hundred pounds apartment Urielle had rented.

Orpeco and Urielle had met before she moved to France, when Yvonne - probably the only regular costumers - used to take her young niece with her at the bookstore, after picking her up from school. Even today, the Roots of the Mistery is located on the corner beyond Maddox Street, overlooking the churchyard. It is built on two floors: the ground floor and a basement - used as a warehouse - where old objects and artifacts are stored, as well as other bulky objects that "Sooner or later someone would have got rid of". There has always been smell of dust and withered flowers in that bookshop, and Urielle often felt nostalgic for what she considered a perfume. She also missed the long conversations she used to have with the man, when they used to spend the evenings sipping tea or drinking liquors.

She hurried out of the apartment, holding a copy of his latest published book, impatient to hand it over to Mr. Orpeco. She found him standing on a ladder, tidying up some books. He had already distinguished Urielle from the shop windows, through the lenses of his funny *pince-nez*, but he had continued to place the books on the shelves "First the duty!" – He would have said.

Urielle, standing on the doorsteps, scolded him "Don't you know that it's dangerous to climb the ladder like that?"

"Not for a youngster like me!" – Mr. Orpeco exclaimed. He went down the ladder, paying attention not to lose his balance, and got close to Urielle, happy to see her again.

"Just in time for a hot cup of tea" – He said cheerfully, "Or would you rather have some *Alchermes*?"

"I have no choice. I can't turn down one of your liquors, not now that we have something to celebrate for!"

The girl anxiously handed him the book she wrote, as a girl would show an *A* in math test to a parent. However, instead of grabbing the book, Orpeco told her to put it on his desk, saying that after the toast he would have taken a look at it.

Mr Orpeco's attitude was unique. He has always avoided physical contact, whether they were hugs or shaking hands. Once, he had let it slip that he had been adopted, but he had never talked about it again. In fact, as always, he had returned to focus on matters that didn't concern his own life. Urielle tried to explain his lack of confidentiality by blaming the abandonment he had suffered when he was just a child. Even so, it was difficult for her to understand his personality. Orpeco was an attractive man who looked younger than he was, despite he wore his funny glasses. He had unique interests, and as Urielle said, he was "A man of other times". Still unmarried, he had no children. Mr. Orpeco had devoted his life to knowledge, and he knew about the archaic world, beliefs, myths, and folklore. Despite that, he was reluctant to talk about himself and his past. He gave the impression he had no past. However, what intrigued Urielle was that she couldn't grasp the nuances of his halo, as if he hadn't one.

"How was coming back to Slohan Oak?" – He asked, sitting on one of the armchairs near the entrance to the basement.

"I don't know how to define it other than complicated. You know, my family… I mean, the Murray…"

"How is your friend doing?" – Orpeco asked. That simple and straightforward question made her suspicious. During her stay in France, Urielle had told him by fax about the sudden death of Arthur Murray. She wrote him only a couple of lines, as she would have told him the rest of the story in person. Nevertheless, Urielle was almost certain that the man was only interested in knowing about Alice, as he had even forgotten to ask her how she was doing, as well as asking about the other family members.

"Alice will be fine. As always" – Urielle replied mildly.

"And you, will you manage to get by?"

"I will. Surely."

"Nice! Now tell me more about the convention" – Orpeco asked, returning reserved.

The conversation went on for an hour. They talked about Masonic origins and Celtic mythology. Orpeco had even asked for her opinion on some books that he had placed in bulk with some others in the only free shelf. In particular, he asked for an opinion on *Valiant people and lost myths*, written by an American author. He had mistakenly bought three copies of that book, by clicking on an online bookstore advertisement. Orpeco asked the girl to come back to the apartment only after having taken a copy of that book. *IT* wasn't really his thing, as well as order, although he struggled to admit it. He had always said that it was a question of appearance as the proven *Dewey* method allowed him to store the books perfectly.

The only thing Urielle could be sure of, was that books written by modern authors were placed on the central wooden shelves. She knew that because its layout had remained the same, and those books were perfectly recognizable by their glossy covers and bold highlighted titles. Anyone's eyes would have been caught entering the store. Apart from that, each shelf seemed to be a copy of the one next to it, covered with *sui generis* books.

Suddenly the old-fashioned bell rang, announcing the entry of a young man, who - without saying much other than "Good morning" - walked towards them. Urielle thought she had never seen him before. He had bright eyes and a piercing gaze, and just like Orpeco, he didn't have the halo. She began to doubt his own gift, believing that over time the ability to perceive it would be reduced, a bit like what happens to night visibility in the fog. Mr. Orpeco dispelled all doubts and introduced him as his grandson.

"Grandson? That's weird" – She thought.

Politely, Urielle stretched her hand to introduce herself, but the boy didn't reciprocate. Thus, Urielle turned her gaze towards the man.

Urielle noticed a strange glow in their eyes, both in the boy's and in the one who turns out to be his uncle. They were apathetic, not at all happy to have seen each other again. Urielle felt confused and slightly embarrassed and kept wondering why Orpeco had never mentioned his grandson in all those years.

The man - pointing to the free chair - invited his grandson to sit down and join them drinking some *Alchermes*, but he refused. Orpeco raised his brown eyebrows, and waving his hand, asked his grandson to follow him to the basement to talk in private. He said nothing more.

Urielle thought they were arguing because of some disagreements or some family issues. The door was left ajar. Urielle could have had eavesdrop on the conversation, but her common sense prevailed over her curiosity. The sound of a broken shards suddenly came from the stairs and the volume of their voices turned up unexpectedly. The man's disappointment echoed upstairs. At that point, it was impossible for her not to listen to their conversation.

"That's enough!" – Orpeco yelled, "Stop this nonsense" – He added.

It was the first time Urielle had heard him addressing someone in that way, even though she didn't know the reasons of that reaction, she was sure she was in the right place at the wrong time. Shortly after, both of them climbed the stairs, and the boy - flared up - left without saying goodbye, slamming the door and making the bell ring.

Orpeco emerged from the basement as if nothing had happened and didn't provide any explanation of that matter. It was a clear signal that invited her not to ask questions; questions to which he certainly would not have answered. His furrowed brow relaxed again, and with an apparently calm, he adjusted his *pince-nez*. After that brief *incident*, Orpeco resumed the conversation exactly from where they stopped.

V

Generally, the working hours on Saturdays at Robins Garden were scheduled according to the "Let's start working earlier, so closing time will be anticipated". However, not always schedules are met. From time to time, it happens to deal with last minute customers; fastidious and undecided on what they want.

That cloudy Saturday, Alice's shift ended at three o'clock. After saying goodbye to her colleagues - anxious to go back home - she didn't even change her clothes. She left from the main exit. She walked along the usual path as she grew apart from reality by listening to music. However, unexpectedly, Alice saw Aleister sitting outside on a bench. The young man was panting, and his pale face became red because of the cold. He was trying to take his breath and - at the same time - to warm his hands by blowing on them. It was clear that he hadn't been waiting long, and it seemed that he had raced against time to cross the city.

"You ran!" – Alice stated looking at his tired face. "Why are you here?" – She added.

"Maybe, I've found the answer to your question" – Aleister said smiling, although he tried to hold back his restlessness caused by the cold.

"Which question?"

"That one about the Ausmas Roses in *The Chronicles of Argo*."

"So, you watched it!"

"No, I've read the books."

Alice opened her eyes wide out of amazement. Both enthusiasts, they started walking to Shelley House discussing about the trilogy. Aleister was pleased of having uncovered the old mystery, and - more than surprisingly - he had revealed that he had read all the books: two thousand nine hundred sixty pages and over four hundred and sixty-two thousand words.

Aleister explained the matter of the Ausmas Roses - debated several times by the characters - as a possible expedient to symbolize the love and the choice of man. The loss of those qualities was caused by the destruction of the Earth, which everyone craved and wanted to protect from the darkness. If all of this had really contributed to rise the fantasies of the Robins Garden's owner - who carried on the cultivation of Ausmas Roses as if it was a life mission - conclusions could be drew: personal beliefs that become fanaticism, influence the essence of life.

Aleister and Alice talked about science-fiction, classic literatures and about a book they both loved, *To Kill a Mockingbird,* by *Harper Lee.*

"How is it possible that you hadn't watched the film?!" – Alice asked sceptical.

"You say that, as it was a crime!"

"It is, more or less. Don't tell me you're prejudice towards black and white films!"

Aleister shook his head. "Actually, I've never had the opportunity to watch one. We have a VHS player which is still brand new."

Alice widened her eyes in amazement and listened to him, feeling a strong sense of tenderness. She hadn't heard of VHS since when she used to go to the Blockbuster every Saturday night to watch rented movies and eat pizza and popcorn. When the American company shut down in 2013, she almost cried like a child.

The Blockbuster store had been replaced by a laundry, and that was a blow. Although she was curious to know why Aleister and his family hadn't adapted themselves to the modern technology, she supported their wise choice of a VCR. She told him that she was a film lover, but not a TV one. Alice thought that by saying this, his dismayed expression would have disappeared.

Aside from films - which Aleister seemed to be completely uninformed about - they had more mutual interests than they imagined. They continued that conversation trying to slowly get to know each other better. Quite unexpectedly. Probably because Aleister didn't think he had aroused so much curiosity in her. So, he found himself explaining his days at the Manor. In the afternoons, he was busy in organizing manuscripts in the home library. He defined himself as a restorer of ancient books and a reading enthusiast. Encouraged by his uncle - who had hired him for that position - he was allowed to mix business with pleasure to please his thirst of knowledge. The rest of his time he used to meditating in Manor's wide garden, which overlooks Slohan Oak. Since he had moved to the Manor, he had been spending every day in that garden.

Art was another mutual interest of them.

"I like painting, especially in the evening" – Aleister said.

"Which artistic movement are you inspired by?"

"It's not easy to define, but I can tell you that in my works, the unknown vastness of the cosmos is the main subject." – Aleister stares for a few second at the sky, which was becoming more and more grey, as the evening was close. "It's all about perceptions. You know, from up there, each of us is only an infinitesimal part of the universe. However, from down here, the only thing that - *apparently* - separates us from the rest of the cosmos is that bright blue sky above us."

"You talk about that as if you had lived on a star."

"A star?" – He asked curious.

"Yup. Or even on an *exoplanet*" – Alice chuckled. "Light years away from Slohan Oak."

Their conversation on exoplanets and galaxies had made them loosing track of time. Back to reality, they realised that they had reached the Gladi fountain, which was surrounded by its usual silence. They talked about Wiltshire, the county and about Slohan Oak. The following questions concerned Aleister's life and family. Nevertheless, Aleister startled, and suddenly became austere, hesitating to answer to that question. He stated that talking about the past would not have made much sense "Where we have been, is important, but where we are heading is much more important". In a hasty way, Aleister told her that, after wandering aimlessly, his uncle home was a good destination.

Alice became worried. She wondered why he bothered to reveal her the mystery of the Chronicles of Argo, if then he seemed reluctant to open up with her.

Once at the yard in front of the dog shelter, Alice heard a familiar hiss. They suddenly stopped without saying a word, trying to hide their emotion that would reveal the awareness of a danger. The fright was a crescendo impossible not to be noticed.

"Did you hear it too?" – Aleister asked.

"Yes" – Alice replied. Then, she glanced at the shed. As if was on purpose, dogs started barking, one after the other. Medium-large beasts, purebreds, and mongrels - at first quiet - were now breaking the silence with their yelps and growls. The wind blew restlessly, crushing into the branches of sturdy trees, which bent to the ground, bowing to the world. Alice and Aleister became more and more worried and - since the night was about to fall - they hurried to Shelley House.

When the time to say goodbye came, none of them mention that event. Somehow, it seemed that they intended to forget about it. Before leaving, Aleister touched Alice's frail shoulder to say her goodbye. However, he changed his mind and took his hand off it.

"Be careful when walking in this place."

"Aleister?"

"Tell me."

"I was wondering why you always remind me to pay attention everytime I'm here."

"The wood is a dangerous place exactly like many others. Generally speaking, you have to be careful if you care about… your life."

Before leaving, he waited for her to get inside her home.

Alice thought about their walk constantly, and - trying to focus on Aleister attitude - she could notice only two behaviours of him: the way he cares about her and his uncommon reticence. Every thought of her revolved around Aleister, as if he had become the center of his mind. Thoughts on him have been part of the game. Thus, she decided that she would no longer try to interpret his mood swings, as they would have also influenced her ones. Alice convinced herself that it was only a temporary interest she had in him, like a seasonal flu that would have last maybe one or two days, and after those days she would be finally healed.

That mental haze caused her migraine and nausea. In the throes of hunger, she compulsively looked for something to eat in the cupboards. She soon realised that there was no food in the kitchen, not even leftovers. Since her friend had come back to Slohan Oak, she had been eating only take away food. The treasure hunt continued up to the basement pantry, but unfortunately, she found only canned food and old family photos. Alice would have eaten everything as long as it wasn't tea, which seemed to pop out of every cupboard. Alice went upstairs with a couple of binders dated *1994-2004* that she had found downstairs. Then, she placed a pre-cooked soup into the microwave. While waiting for the soup to be warm, she looked at those photos, going back in time. There were photos of her birth, birthday parties, as well as of her first day of school and other photos with her whole family on holidays. Alice became nostalgic, all by herself in that silent room. She felt nostalgic for those years when there was love and that typical children's light-heartedness. She remembered her mother's words, when on a spring afternoon she said, "We can never be happier than this". Although that expression was scored in her mind, it had always sounded nonsense to her. Nevertheless, that statement found answers the exact moment she found herself leafing through the photo album. The coming maturity of the children, as well as of the old age, were - somehow - taken for granted.

She felt weak at the thought that one day her mother and her brother might have preceded her in that inevitable destination. Even so, crying seemed impossible to her, although she was feeling sad and wrecked. She was aware that - sooner or later - she had to deal with loneliness, not by her own choice; it was a time matter.

Page after page, Alice bumped into a blurry group photo which was - certainly - mistakenly wind up there. The only discernible shapes were those of her father - who still flaunted his red hair - and a tiny blonde woman in a powder pink coloured dress, posing in three quarter. A date was written on the back, *1983*. Alice became curious, and - after rubbing one eye with the sleeve of her jumper - she went back to the basement to look for the photo album belonging to that same year. Nevertheless, there were only old junk, cans of wax for waterproof jackets and canned food. There was no trace of the photo album. Suddenly, the microwave timer rang, making her jump. She remembered of the dinner she had yearned for, and went upstairs, setting aside her researches.

The soup was hot, and after the first taste, she nearly burned her tongue. She would have resort to her mother's old remedy to eat the soup quickly, "four spoons of cold milk", although there was no milk in the fridge. She thus placed the dish on the windowsill to let it cool. Then, she went out into the garden and waited.

The dark cloudy sky covered the stars, revealing the arrival of the storm. Alice lit up her ciggies, looking at bare trees and imagining them wrapped in strings of colourful lights and covered with snow. She thought that Christmas would have been in exactly one month, and without his father it would have been different. She wondered how they would have celebrated, and that thought saddened her. She felt a sudden need to be hugged and to be told that everything would be fine, that things would return to its place like a piece that fits perfectly in a puzzle. A part of her would have sought her mother's comfort, but on the other hand, she would have liked Aleister to hug her, the boy from the *exoplanet* and with strange attitude. However, when she remembered how he had become grim by the end of that afternoon, Alice blamed herself to foolishly think about things that would never happen. She knew that the attempt to consider it as a temporary thought would be vain.

Alice took a puff of her cigarette and closed her eyes. She let herself be enveloped by the warm smoke, crossed by the drops of rain which fell synchronized with her heartbeat. Suddenly, a bright glare lit up the dark sky, and - in that very moment - Alice had a vision. The effects of that bright glare reached Alice's soul; she could feel it, as it was real. She slowly opened her eyes and caught his blurred features, getting lost in *his* deep and mysterious gaze.

The wind blew hard through the thin branches of the bare ash trees. The gust bent them over themselves, as to remind them who ruled.

Alice opened her eyes wide, realising she was all alone.

Then, she heard the annoying hiss. *That hiss.*

She run into the house to find shelter.

VI

Sunday, 26th of November 2017

The weather hadn't changed over the night and - with the first daylights - the thick blanket of fog got thinner, revealing the shapes of the houses.

Alice woke up with the usual annoying headache and thought about the almost real dream she had had. It was only a lucid dream, one of the many identical and sporadic visions she had been having in the past six months.

That morning, her mother called her from Florence at around eight o'clock, an unusual time for being Sunday. However, when her mother told her that a few hours earlier some puppies had been found gutted at the dog shelter, Alice understood the urgency of that call. Marta had been informed by one of the younger volunteers who - after the macabre discovery of about fifteen carcasses covered of dung, blood, and guts - had vomited and then fainted on the muddy terrain. The volunteers had found her lying on that mess, and believing her dead, they had called the police. The officers verified that the girl was only shocked, but still alive. Thus, they interrogated both the volunteers and people of the nearby houses to get some clarification. A lady of the neighbourhood had been awakened at around 5 a.m. because of the dogs barking as - even if she was used to the noise coming from the dog shelter - she was impressed by the intensity of those barks and decide to go to check. However, the silence suddenly fell, and she gave up that idea. The policemen - listlessly and horrified - were wandering around the scene of the "crime", and - after receiving a call from the Police Station - they quickly left.

The puppies had been deprived of internal organs - most probably devoured. Yet, it seemed that the incident wasn't seriously considered.

That news stunned Alice. Her mother claimed that the massacre was due to the return of the *Phantom Cats*, a breed of long brown-haired feline that were often mentioned in horror stories during bonfires. Alice thought of the beheaded crows she saw near the Gladi fountain, as well as of the rumours about the small group of local thugs. She would have expected someone to take measurements, as the situation was becoming an unprecedented crescendo of sadism. She calmed herself down at the idea of not having to walk along the usual path to go to the work. Alice decided to take advantage of that quiet Sunday morning to take a bath, a warm and restoring one, while listening to one of *Einaudi*'s melody. She decided to start reading *To Kill a Mockingbird* to avoid falling asleep in the tub, as the scented steam enveloped and relaxed her.

After having read a couple of chapters, Alice placed the book on the edge of the tub. She immersed herself completely in the warm water, which hided her from the world, removing all the bad thoughts of that morning. She stared at the ceiling for a few minutes and - at the sight of the condensation - she went in apnoea counting the seconds *"Thirty... Thirty-one... Thirty-two..."*

Someone rang the bell, interrupting her thoughts and that mental race. She had stopped at forty-six seconds, but she knew that she could do better. She quickly went out of the tub, stopped the music and - wearing only her bathrobe - she went to open the door, thinking it was Urielle. Alice saw a lady standing under the porch with a pair of sunglasses and her head wrapped in a silk scarf. Only few brown locks and a breathless face emerged. She was Mayor Brickenden's wife, dressed like a celebrity who want to escape from the paparazzi.

"Dorothy...?"

"Sssh, lower your voice... They don't know I'm here."

"They... who?"

The lady grabbed Alice's hand and gave her a little dark fabric bag.

"They could do everything to get it back. Beware of *Divum Deus*."

However, when Alice was about to ask her for some clarifications, the lady left, getting into the car without even looking back. In a few seconds, Alice's legs started to shiver and sweat. She could have fell, exactly like an apple falls from a tree. Luckily, as soon as she realised that her loved ones were far from Wiltshire, she calmed herself down and decided to call them. She ran into the house and tried to call both her mother and Philip. Yet, their line was busy. At that point, she panicked. Thus, Alice tried to call Urielle and - as soon as she picked up - she couldn't find the words to explain her what had just happened. She could only mumble disjointed phrases. Urielle - hearing her friend's almost hysterical voice - ordered her to leave the house and reach her as soon as possible.

Alice wore the first clothes she came across in her room and- with her hair still damp from the hot tub and panicked - she double locked the door and got on her *blue* car, a brand-new *Volkswagen*. Once seated, Alice opened the bag Dorothy had given her, which was - by the way- the reason that interrupted her Sunday rest. Inside the bag, she found an artifact: a metal egg, inlaid, while a hinge was placed in the middle of the object. Thinking that it was a copy of a *Fabergé,* she put the artifact back in her pocket, as she realised it wasn't as macabre as she had thought. Alice reached the crossroads in Maddox Street, getting stuck in traffic. There had been stir since Brexit opponents had occupied the Whitebird Café. The outdoor area and even a part of the street were used to collect signatures against Britain's exit from the EU. Such a matter would have been a big change for the Country, which would inevitably have led the United Kingdom to be more divided than ever.

Urielle would have never thought that her Sunday could begin in that way. She had planned to spend the first half of the day replying to the countless e-mail she received after the publication of her book. *"I express my warmest thanks, etc, etc."* that is what she would have sent to her faithful readers. However, there were some messages expressing only indignation, which - by the way - she would have elegantly ignored. After that - as she had planned - she would have had lunch on one of the benches in the old municipal greenhouse. To conclude - as her thick brown hair was turning into grey - she would have improvised a hairdresser and dyeing her hair, hoping of not getting her head dyed of some other colours. Yet, Urielle realised that her Sunday plans would have changed a little with Alice's appearance.

"What danger were you referring to?" – Urielle asked Alice after having opened the door. Still wearing her gown and with the TV on to the news, Urielle yawn and went to make a tea. She looked at Alice and at her wet hair and her worried face.

"Has the electricity gone out? If you needed a hair dryer, it wasn't necessary that you yelled into the phone" – Urielle told her.

Alice - breathlessly - sighed to put her thoughts back together. Then, she sat down on the Chesterfield sofa in the living room. The girl first told Urielle about the call she had received from her mother and the dog shelter massacre, then she talked about Dorothy's unexpected visit and about a Divum Deus who probably threatened her family to take back the copy of the *Fabergé* egg... Urielle interrupted her speech, telling her to speak clearly. Thus, Alice resumed the story over again. However, as soon as Alice mentioned Timothy Brickenden, Urielle told her: "Wait a minute! Dorothy Brickenden? She was on the news a while ago. The maid found the Mayor dead, lying on an armchair. There was a gun on the ground. You know...of those oddities of the silencer. A shot to the head and then... you can imagine."

Alice widened her eyes and put her hands on her mouth.

"Wasn't Dorothy there when it happened?"

"Apparently no. The police have already hypnotised that Timothy had started drinking alcohol again. However, this is only to not make people worrying. They are looking for Dorothy, she's gone too."

"When was she seen the last time?"

"Last night the maid saw her. And then you saw her this morning."

Alice put her hand in her pocket, and took the dark fabric bag, dropping the copy of the egg on the coffee table. Urielle observed it meticulously. The egg was made of silver and had some dents at its lower extremity. The artifact opened, revealing Mayor's initials, a mechanism, and a key. It was a spring-loaded music box and - once having turned twice the mechanism to wind it up - a lullaby started to play. Urielle rolled her finger up through her lock hair, passing it over between the index and the middle finger. It often happened to her when she thought deeply of something. She tried to find a logical explanation to that artifact, but she couldn't find one.

"Didn't she say anything else?" – Urielle asked.

"I think having warned me was enough. We should go to the police. If Dorothy were responsible for her husband's death, that would make me accomplice of her escape."

Alice - who was listing the pros and cons of that possible scenario - was interrupted by Urielle.

"Let's suppose that she killed him. She said that '*they will do everything to get it back*'. I have no idea in what the Brickenden got involved, but the less people know about your meeting with Dorothy, the less are the probability that we all must leave Slohan Oak. So, we won't go to the Police."

"Why should we ever leave Slohan Oak?" – Alice asked confused.

"To avoid any problem."

They thought that abandoning Shelley House was the only solution. Thus, they planned the following weeks which included Alice's stay at Urielle's apartment, until Alice's family would be back home. They would share the same bed, the same bathroom, and every space of Urielle's tiny three-room apartment. Alice would only have to go home to get her clothes as everything she needed for her work was in her *blue* car. Although Alice knew that the following days would have been alarming, she wasn't much worried.

Alice and Urielle felt that they could deal with all of that. If the Police learned about the artifact and Alice meeting with Dorothy, they would have denied the existence of the artifact to protect themselves. They would have acted like two ostriches hiding their beaks underground. They were sure that they would have solved any possible problem if they wouldn't talk to anyone.

Towards the end of the morning there was an unexpected meeting. While the two friends were about to leave, they saw Aleister sneak off the back door of the bookshop, holding some books. Seeing him aroused opposing thought in Alice: her face relaxed, her eyes seemed to sparkle, and her mouth opened in amazement.

"Aleister?" – Alice said

"Do you know each other?" – Urielle asked confused, looking at them. Thus, Urielle realised that *Mr. Resolute* Alice was referring to at the Whitebirds Café was the bookseller's handsome nephew. Although she didn't know many people with such a first name - actually, he was the only one - that situation seemed to her a singular coincidence. Although she had gotten used to the idea that the day would turn out to be full of unexpected events, she wondered about what other surprises that Sunday would have in store. Urielle thought of what happened in the bookshop that morning, as well as of the attitude of the young man who - at first glance - she didn't like at all. Following Dorothy's visit at Shelley House, anyone could have been a potential hazard.

Even a familiar face.

Even Aleister.

The young man seemed happy to see Alice. He said to Alice that he was at his uncle's bookshop to help him out. Then, Aleister looked at Alice and Urielle, noticing her imperturbable facial expression.

"Is everything ok, Alice?" – Aleister asked.

Alice thought about the dream she had the night before, that almost *real* dream. It was as tangible as the rain dropping on the roofs of the houses and then flowing on the windows.

She mumbled awkwardly as she couldn't tell what was going on. She was suspicious about Aleister's sudden appearances, which seemed perfectly planned. Alice's reluctance in answering was like that of the good weather in winter days in Slohan Oak. Thus, after all that hesitation, Urielle broke into the conversation.

"She didn't feel very well" – She said impatiently. "I asked her to come and stay at my place for a couple of days but now she has to go back home to get some clothes."

"Let me take you" – Aleister said looking at Alice, who was more astonished than ever and unable to give him an answer.

Urielle needed to know about Aleister's real intentions and- sure of the sensation perceived with her hand - she thought of a way to touch him. Considering the fact that the day before he avoided handshaking his hand, she thought that dropping her bag would be a valid solution, as the young man would have picked it from the ground. Only in that way she could verify his vibrations.

"Oh!" – Urielle exclaimed, dropping her bag. As expected, Aleister bent over the floor, set the books on the ground, and collected everything, gathering the spilled contents, as well as a purse, a mirror, and a set of keys. Urielle crouched and, when her hands touched the back of Aleister's hand, she found answers to her questions. The surface of the hand was warm, and she felt an unusual vibration that blinded her with a celestial glow.

They both stared at each other.

Instinctively, Aleister pulled back his hand. However, those few seconds were enough to make Urielle realise of the good intentions he had.

Urielle now knew it.

She agreed, letting Aleister go with Alice, aware that her friend was in good hands. There was something unusual in him, like if he went against any law of nature. A question arose in Urielle's mind *"Who are you?"* – She wondered. She was sure, the guy - whose appearances were unusual - belonged to the ancient world.

VII

Wednesday, 21ˢᵗ of June 2017
The night of the incident

Summer solstice has always been one of the most awaited celebrations in Slohan Oak, also due to the proximity of the town to the Stonehenge site.

Sunlight prevails in which is considered the brightest day of the year, corresponding with the beginning of the astronomical summer. From that day on, the sun will slowly set. People from Slohan Oak use to celebrating and thanking the spirit for the plentiful harvest and gave offers so that the harvest may be plentiful also in the future. During this day, every corner of the town is filled with sparkling colours and scents. Furthermore, people are used to preparing orange flower wreaths, and burning aromatic herbs as good omen to drive away the spirits from houses. People are used to attending gatherings arranged by ladies who cook currant cakes and *scones*. Children prepare branches of perforate St. John's wort and lavender, and they used to place them under the pillows before going to sleep. During the solstice it is possible to get the mystical strength that connect heaven and earth.

On the evening of June 21st, Urielle accepted the invitation to a party organized by Elizabeth Harvey, Alice's former classmate. Despite Alice didn't like that kind of parties - as she didn't enjoy herself - she appreciated the way the party was organized. After this period marked out by ornaments, decorations, and inexplicable optimism - which leads people to think "Maybe this time everything will be better" - she tended to regret having gotten involved. Although when she was younger, she took part in it several times, she considered that kind of celebrations as unhealthy pretexts of dissoluteness, where the music censored every form of dialogue. In her twenties she had turned down invitations making up last minute commitments.

That day, she wondered why Urielle - who was gifted with common sense - had ended up accepting that invitation, which was - by the way - made by Elizabeth Harvey. Elizabeth, known as *Lizzie*, embodied the typical student of the Kingstone. Born in a rich family - from her mother's second marriage - she used to spend her holidays in tropical destinations, while her relationship with her parents was adversarial. Her father, James - was owner of the *Harwey & Sons Steel Mills* - who remarried at the age of forty with Rachel - a former model of the 80s from New York - who had never accepted the passing of the time on her beautiful *wasp* face and who was part of the *Ivy League*.

Lizzie was the combination of her father arrogance, and her mother ambition. She was famous and infamous at the same time, but she stood out in everything, and she always had to compete for victory. Since she started attending the Kingstone, she had done everything she could to be in the spotlight. Indeed, she used to hang out with older guys, magnify her successes, smoke cigarettes stolen from her mother and drunk his father's alcohol. The word *failure* wasn't accepted in her life and - to appear as the only winner - she degraded people around her.

Alice couldn't put up with her. She had often complained about the contemptuous behaviour Lizzie reserved her in the locker room, or during lunches at the canteen and even during their tests. Philip felt pity for Lizzie, the *Diva* as he used to called her. He thought that she was a poor misunderstood soul, who desperately attempted to get the attentions of her absent parents. A sort of benevolent fourth *Gorgon*[2].

Urielle and Alice were still at Shelley House, and - in an effort to pass the dress fitting - Alice had the feeling that whatever dress she wore would end up making her look clumsy. She held the clothes-hangers in both hands and looked at her friend and at her clothes with a puzzled look, realising that her wardrobe was still old-fashioned. She was undecided between a floral flounced dress and a *Prussian blue* sheath dress. After having tried several dresses, looking at the mirror reluctant, Alice had decided to wear a pair of jeans and a t-shirt. She asked Urielle to remind her of the reasons that led her to accept that invitation and - above all - why Urielle hadn't talked to her before accepting. However, Urielle - ignoring Alice's sarcasm - reiterated that she had accidentally met Lizzie at *Penhaligon's* in Covent Garden, and that she couldn't turned down the invitation. After all, Lizzie always got what she wanted! Urielle also confessed that the real reason of that visit was because of the Harvey's library.

---

[2] A creature in Greek mythology. According to the Greek literature, two of the Gorgons were immortal (Stheno and Euryale), while only Medusa was mortal, who was slain by Perseus.

"I have to look for a book."

"What? Are we going to that horrible party only because you want to see a book?" – Alice said.

"It's not just a book, it's a first edition."

"Okay, that's different then!"

Despite she was disappointed, Alice had to surrender to that request.

When they arrived, the party had already begun. Alice parked her car near the wide lawn situated at the base of the house, where more other cars were parked. Many of those invited had attended the Kingstone, while Lizzie's friends and acquaintances were already drunk. Alice felt throwback to the days of the college, and once she crossed the door of the house, she tried as much as possible to avoid eye contact with the other guests. Although Urielle had never liked parties, Alice realised that her friend was enjoying it, exactly like everyone else in that house. Nevertheless, Alice couldn't understand how such a smart person like Urielle - whose Alice had always appreciated - could like that kind of parties. That was the only trait of Urielle's personality that she couldn't really understand in all those years of friendship. Unlike her, Urielle could adapt herself extremely quickly, placing herself on a higher level for ingenuity.

Urielle and Alice had to meet with Sue Ling - native from China and naturalised English - who was one of Urielle's close friend and Alice's acquaintance. Friendship between Urielle and Sue was unusual, based on common interests rather than on trust. They got along only because they shared a lot of knowledge and they both loved history. Sue Ling loved archaeology, travelling, and writing novels which dealt with Sumerian artifacts, even if she idolized Elizabeth. But that didn't matter to Urielle at all. She knew that Sue was an incurable romantic who - seduced by malicious people - had ended up laying from flower to flower with extreme lightness. Thus, after all her joyful and heart-breaking love stories, she had inevitably ended up becoming one of the Harvey's acquaintances.

Once they reached Sue amid the crowd, she suggested to join the rest of the people inside the house to get a drink. However, Alice turned down the invitation and waited for them outside. She sat on a remote swing and looked impatiently at her watch, waiting for that torture to end. From that point of the garden, she could see the dynamics of that party: the huge bonfire at the entrance that lit up the bodies of those who were dancing around it. On the left, near a hedge, there were those who - back then - formed the college's polo team, while far away, she could glimpse a couple kissing under a tree. Finally, she could see the unmissable August Lee, who - with his slimy ways - was flirting with a group of girls at the entrance. The only thing that could calm her, was that she was far from all that.

As soon as the atmosphere was quieter, Elizabeth made her entrance in a tight top that left no room for imagination. She waved her blonde hair, realising pleasant scent, although it wasn't enough to make the unpleasant smell of alcohol disappear. She had never called Alice by her name, as she always called her by surname. Thus, after having exclaimed aloud "Murray!", Lizzie confessed that she couldn't ever imagined that Alice would have come to the party. Then, Lizzie begun to ask her a lot of questions. She asked Alice what happened to her parents; she asked about Philip and her studies at Durham University. However, once Lizzie found out that all Alice was working at the plant nursery, she lost interest in the conversation. Therefore, she started talking about herself and her future, but Alice's lack of interest, annoyed her.

"Hey! Are you listening to me?" – Lizzie asked frowning.

"I got lost in your speech. Congratulations, Lizzie, for your achievements and for the future ones" – Alice lied, looking at the cloudy sky.

"You're such a boring person, Murray!"

At that point, Alice got off the swing to reach Urielle and Sue. "I didn't even want to come to this party. I'll catch up with my friends" – Alice told her, and suddenly it started rain. As soon as Alice mentioned leaving, Elizabeth looked at her anxiously, grabbed her wrist and unexpectedly kissed her.

"Don't' go" – Lizzie begged her, but Alice walked away.

"I like you since the first time I saw you in the classroom" – Lizzie tried to hold her by grabbing her hand and moving closer. Her sour breath was a presage of vomit.

"You made my years at the Kingstone horrible. I don't dare imagine what could you have done if you didn't like me" – Alice said, wiggling out of Lizzie's grip, then, she joined the crowd in the rain. She tried to understand what kind of feeling Harvey had hidden and given her astonishment, she decided to tell her friends only that she would be going back home. Nothing more.

Lizzie's behaviour of that night, after years and years of bullying, disoriented Alice. She got into her car, certain that driving was the only way to recover from that shock and then analyse what had happened. It seemed logical to her that Elizabeth had always been secretly in love with her, although she couldn't understand how Lizzie had managed to hide it that well. Alice realised that she was blind to the point that she couldn't get if someone liked her. However, she was certain that Lizzie's interest in her wasn't mutual. Thus, she decided to not speak a word of it with anybody, to protect Lizzie from narrow-minded people. After all, Alice was a good person, she would have never dare to put other people into unpleasant situations.

On her way home, Alice changed several times the radio stations and - for lack of signal - she had to opt for an alternative.

Paying attention not to astray, Alice searched through the CDs, finding one of the *Tears for Fears*, which belonged to her mother. As soon as the music played, Alice lit up a ciggies and smoke nervously. The windscreen wiper swept the pouring rain and - thanks to that hypnotic movement - Alice calmed down. The journey would have been long and linear. Although she was exhausted, she tried to stay awake. However, after a series of yawns, she fell asleep and lost the control of the car, which headed towards the clearing.

That night Alice could have been died in the accident.

The car had crushed, and fainting wouldn't have allowed her to escape from the explosion, triggered shortly thereafter by the leak of fuel and the cigarette butt still lit. However, when her destiny seemed to have been written, suddenly the air tense as if to form a bubble, and - for a few seconds - a silent explosion lit up the entire forest. Someone freed her by forcefully bending the car door and tearing off her seat belt. Then, he picked her up gently, holding Alice in his arms, and once he realised, she wasn't injured, he run as fast as he could to protect her from the blast. Alice slowly opened her eyes but cradled by the warmth of what seemed to her a dream, she fell asleep.

The following day, she woke up in her bedroom, having to provide a long series of justification to her family and the police regarding the discovery of the smouldering remains of her car. However, she couldn't remember anything of what happened, except for a strong glow.

VIII

Sunday, 26th of November 2017
Truth

Urielle knew she had little time available. Thus, she took advantage of Alice and Aleister's absence to question who was able to clarify all her doubts. She quickly climbed the stairs to reach her apartment. She was as tight as a violin string, and her anxiety made her slow down every single action. It took her a couple of attempts to get the key into the door lock. As soon as she opened the door, she ran into her bedroom and crouched in front of the rosewood trunk. She begun to search thoroughly inside, pulling out five white candles, a box of matches, a mirror, and a sprig of mugwort tied to a red cord.

"Let's start" – She thought.

Urielle got up to set the lighted candles to recreate the tips of a pentacle. Then, she closed the shutters of the window. She sat down on her knees in the centre of the pentacle and - holding the mirror in front of her, as usual - she pronounced some French words.

"*C'est moi qui parle[3]*" – She said. That sentence would allow her to get in contact with her grandmother's spirit.

After a few seconds, the atmosphere in the room became colder, and the candles suddenly blew out at the same time.

Yvonne's spirit shown up, answering in her mother tongue to avoid the possible awakening of unexpected presences.

"*Ma petite[4].*"

"Grandma… I have some question I hope you can answer. I sensed an ancient presence. His name is Aleister."

A flicker inside the mirror invited the girl to look at it. A series of frames of the boy's life were first sketched and then shown clearer. She caught a glimpse of a beam of light, of a bell tower in the rain in the middle of the night, a swarm of moths and a naked boy.

"Why hadn't you shown me it before?" – Urielle asked her grandmother.

"*You have never asked me the right questions, ma petite. Remember, what you had just seen was when it all began.*"

Then Yvonne slowly vanished, until becoming an echo, until becoming silence.

The candles suddenly lit up again, the mirror returned to reflect the girl's amber eyes, while the ribbon tied to the sprig of mugwort dissolved along with her grandmother's spirit. Each time they got in contact the ribbon vanished. It symbolised the indissoluble union that would rejoin them after death to prevent them from getting lost in the otherworld labyrinth.

Urielle felt dizzy, confused, and weak. She knew that she could asked her questions about the extra dimension to the only reliable person still alive: Orpeco. Before composing herself,

---

[3] It's me.
[4] My dear.

Urielle burnt the sprig of mugwort in a small brazier to purify the environment from any unwanted presences, which might have been mistakenly evoked. Nevertheless, she was sure that something sinister was about to happen, as she noticed that the malaise - she had had for a few weeks - wasn't gone yet.

Urielle went to the esoteric library in search of proofs. There, she saw the man reading a book, sat on an armchair. The young girl opened the door, and - when the old bell rang - he kept reading with his head bent over the book, unconcerned of Urielle's arrival. Somehow, it seemed that the man was waiting for Urielle. Her gaze dispelled all doubts.

"I was hoping that this moment would never come" – Orpeco said after a deep sigh. Then, he locked the door from the inside, closed the curtains of the windows and asked Urielle to follow him to the basement. His sapphire blue eyes looked at the archive, at the back of the room. Orpeco took a series of dusty binders containing folders and black and white photographs. He took one photo in particular - in which there were a group of children of different ages - and handed it to Urielle.

"This is me", – He pointed to a little boy - of about 5 years - with olive skin and brown hair. "This photo was taken in 1956 at the Müller Orphanage. A Swedish couple - the Falkenbergs - adopted me before the orphanage shut its doors. They were impoverished nobles and after the World War II - before they moved to Manor - little was left of the wealth they had owned in the past. My mother, Anja, couldn't have children, and my silent presence worsen her suffering. Shortly after my arrival, she began to suffer from nervous breakdowns, which led her to death after my twelfth birthday." They sat on two old armchairs, Orpeco placed the binders on the ground and the resumed. "The employees of the orphanage couldn't explain themselves my attitude. I was a child with great vitality and often ended up getting into trouble without realising the consequences. When we played outdoors, I got bruises and scratches and sometimes even deep wounds, but I didn't feel pain at all. All the wounds I got myself healed in a short time, even those that normally require hospital surgery. However, another question worried the employees: my body temperature couldn't be considered normal because was above the standards. The doctors had given me medicines for a long time, until they believed that the fever was a side effect of the therapy. They thought I was suffering from a rare disease, so they tried to treat me with questionable methods. With poor results, of course".

"I still don't understand" – Urielle - incredulous - didn't' grasp what the man wanted to tell her. Orpeco became sadder and sadder as he continued to tell the story. He leaned over to get another binder from the ground. This one contained part of newspaper headlines. He handed it to Urielle, who began to look through the newspapers.

'Angel boy, the child from the sky saves the son of Mr. and Mrs. Cooper. Investigations underway' – Daily Mirror, August 1st, 1956

'Mystery in Folkestone. A naked child without identity saved a boy of his own age. Investigations carried out by the local Police' – East Kent Gazzette, August 3rd, 1956.

The employees of the orphanage - once they knew that I didn't have a past - named me *Wallace Orpeco*, which my adoptive parents kept along with the name inherited from them, Falkenberg. My unusual last name is the anagram of '*Cooper*', and - as you can read on the headlines - the police found me in the garden of little Elroy Cooper's house."

"What happened to that kid?"

"We were separated since the first moment, since when I was generated on earth to save him from the fatal fall. I couldn't allow fate to be fulfilled."

"What do you mean by *generated*? Haven't you ever thought of getting in touch with him? If he's still alive, of course."

"Urielle, I think you need to know the rest of the story. Elroy is still alive."

"So, have you heard from him?"

"A mutual connection was created since the very first moment I was generated. As long as he's alive, I will be too" – Orpeco sigh. "Unfortunately, such a condition has its cons. If I died, the thread would automatically break, and he would die too."

"Is Aleister like you? What are you two?" – Urielle asked almost begging him to answer.

"We are *Altor*. We were originally pieces of exploded stars which orbit in the ether. We belong to *different hierarchical orders*. Each Altor is billions of years old. In contrast to what is the common belief, stars have evolved over time until developing consciousness. We have observed terrestrial beings and their behaviours over the centuries. We endure the randomness of events, spending a life of solitude in space. Until when - one day - the light of a terrestrial being dazzles us, leading us to renounce to our semi-immortality to save him from death. We are the materialisation of the desires of the human being, coming on earth assuming the age and embodying the strongest desire of the one we choose to protect. We come to this world in the form of humans, as it is the only one that terrestrial being can accept. We have even the navel - which is totally against nature – even if we don't come from a maternal womb. However, there is a difference between the humans and us, like a manufacturing error: the soul. We don't have one. It belongs only to human beings. At that point, our light vanishes and what attracts us is the purity of the one we choose to protect, for whom we feel a desire that goes beyond love. We learn the hard way that once we are generated on earth, the predestined person will have to give up half of his soul to give it to us. That's what happened to Little Roy: he received a second chance to live, but he was also deprived of half of his most important piece. He felt alone and I couldn't let his light vanish in that summer day. Nevertheless, I wonder if it was the right thing to do, to intervene in the existence and in the destiny of a person."

Urielle swallowed. She was confused and couldn't speak a world. However, she finally realised what questions she wanted to ask.

"I'd like to ask you some questions" – She said.

"Go ahead."

"First of all, what did you mean when you said *different hierarchical orders*?"

"Are you familiar with *astronomy*?"

"I would say that I only know about the planets of the Solar System" – Urielle answered with a hint of embarrassment.

"Well, let's start from the Sun, the hottest star in the Solar System. Beside it, there are much hotter and brighter stars in the Universe. When those stars explode, they realise their small fragments into the ether. I was part of a common star with orange shades. It wasn't much hotter than the Sun and its light was even less bright." – Orpeco stopped to drink some water. "Aleister was part of a rare bright star. Its light was bright blue, almost similar to the ultraviolet light. It was the hottest and brightest star of the ether, even more than the Sun."

"How rare?"

"Few Altor are like him. To make it clearer, if envy were a trait of our being, Aleister would be detested. However, there are pros and cons of this condition. The cooling process - in my case - took place progressively and without causing many problems. As for Aleister, only patience will help him. Besides that, he owns only theoretical knowledge, as he had long observed the humans. Thus, he now finds himself practicing."

"What kind of... problems?"

"Although the cold of the Earth influences him, his temperature is still hot. Obviously, it's not as hot as it was the first months, and not even as hot as a star. But he's an Altor and he could be discovered if someone become suspicious of his body heat."

"Okay, I think I understood it, so far. I have another question."

Orpeco nodded his head to invite her to ask that question and drank the water in one gulp.

"You mention semi-immortality before. What does that mean?" – Urielle asked.

"You know... when we look at the sky, we are only looking at the past. Parts of the lights you can see are exploded stars. So, what you see glowing in the dark night are the Altors. Life on Earth is much shorter than our life up there. Aleister renounced to his semi-immortality as a star fragment to take care of your friend, Alice."

"Wait... Alice Murray? What does she have to do with all this?"

"I thought you understood. Aleister is the result of what your friend needed. The night of the 21st of June - during the summer solstice - I saw Aleister naked wandering around from the windows of the shop. He was surrounded by moths, attracted by the light he was releasing, and which was slowly fading. He was staring at the church tower. I immediately called him, or he would attract attention. Imagine if anyone had seen him! When I asked his name, he declared *Aleister Crowley*, reading aloud one of the modern occultism authors' names. He seemed disoriented and his frightened gaze reminded me of mine when I arrive on Earth. So, I offered him a shelter and a home - where he could settle to watch over Alice - and I helped him to face the feeling of loss. Believe me, Alice wouldn't have survived the accident if Aleister hadn't saved her..."

"How can you be sure that Aleister had not generate himself only because he wanted to be part of the Earth?"

"My dear Urielle! No Altor would give up his semi-immortality for the whim to live in such a corrupted world. It would be a form of self-harm. Every action is due to an impulse stronger than love. It is the *Erheiur* effect, the feeling that goes beyond time and space. Aleister's task will be to protect her unconditionally and to manifest *Erheiur* at its peak."

"So, if your aim is to watch over protectors, and since you belong to an extra-dimensional space, are you the Altor fallen angels embodied in human beings?"

"I'd like you not to diminish our figure by considering us as religious legacies. The Altors have nothing to do with religion. We go beyond the human intellect... if you prefer, we are creatures of the *Volteya*, the brightest light of Borea. However, in

Aleister's case, he can still interact as an entity - even if for a short time - in the extra-dimensional space."

"For how long?"

"We don't know exactly. Mind you, we can never change our nature, we just adapt. The stronger the bond with Alice, the faster the process will be."

"What will happen to her?"

"She must never find out that. Exactly as happened to Little Roy, Alice's soul is now halved, as half of it was given to Aleister. Nothing irreversible will have to happen to them so that they can stay alive. It is called *absolute Entanglement*, and it is when one's life strictly depends on the other to the point that their actions can affect both. This phenomenon will influence their lives, it's the price to pay."

Urielle felt useless at the thought that her friend's life depended on someone else. Alice and Aleister had an immeasurable responsibility, which only Aleister was aware of. Every possible solution would have led Urielle to only a path, that of silence. Aware of the possible negative effects, she swore to herself that she would never reveal that truth. She knew that Alice wouldn't ever understand the meaning of those words. Thus, Urielle preferred to hide the truth from her friend. Urielle would have observed the powerful effects of the *Erheiur* as a spectator in a theatre, hoping that the end of the act would never turn into a tragedy.

Although Urielle had to go home, she felt the need to ask one last question. She asked why Orpeco had never let Urielle get close to him. The bookseller hinted at a smile and held out the back of his hand. As soon as Urielle put her hand on Orpeco's one, a bright glare illuminated his hand. However, Urielle realised that the light was less bright than that she could perceived from Aleister, which had reached her nervous system.

"We had to protect ourselves, Urielle" – He said. "We also know who you are."

Since the first time the young girl had come into the library, Orpeco had immediately recognized her unusual power, her *gift*.

IX

On her way to Shelley House, Alice didn't say a word, except for some comments on the weather. She was shaken, although she tried to hide every emotion.

The house seemed abandoned as there was no one livening it up, while the grey cloudy sky made it melancholic. As soon as he got out of the car, Alice looked around, and then tried to start a short conversation with Aleister.

"So, you and my friend Urielle know each other?" – She asked puzzled. She remembered having mentioned her friend who - by the way - had never said a word about knowing Aleister.

"I met her yesterday at the bookstore. I know that she and my uncle are good friends" – Aleister tried as much as possible to be ironic. "By the way, it must be almost impossible to bump into someone in this *joyful* town, which has just over four thousand inhabitants."

Alice smiled at him, thinking that it was foolish doubting of that guy. Nevertheless, when Alice inserted the key in the lock of the front door, she found it opened, and it was enough to arouse fears in her. She had double locked the door, as her mother had always told her to do; she was sure of that. The mere thought that someone had broken in her house upset her. However, she started doubting that – probably - her agitation made her forget closing the door.

"*Weird.*"

She decided not to talk about that with anyone, in order to avoid worries.

Alice and Aleister went upstairs, where every corner of the walls was covered by art. Aleister was amazed at the sight of *Yves Klein*'s blue canvas, hanged on the landing. *Blue…* that colour could dig deep inside and reach one's soul. Every single piece blended into one.

Alice, on the other hand, didn't even pay attention to that canvas. She had to leave the house as soon as possible, as she was afraid of any unpleasant meetings. She took some clothes from the closet, some clean underwear and a couple of sweaters, which she rolled into a ball and put them into her bag. She stopped only to look at her reflection in the mirror, realising that her hair was damp since that early morning. Alice tried to fix her hair up, tying it in a bun. However, that made her even more sloppy. Then, she grabbed her bag, immediately dropping it to the floor, as if she had changed her mind; deceptions made her feel uncomfortable. Initially, she mumbled something, looking down at the ground, but then, she decided to turn her gaze to Aleister.

"I have to tell you something."

"What happened, Alice?"

"I think someone broke in the house this morning. The door was opened when we arrived. I'm sure I had locked it before leaving."

"Why didn't you tell me before?"

"I didn't know where to start. There's a lot to tell. However, I'll tell you everything in the car."

Alice quickly went downstairs, and - out of the corner of her eye - she saw the binders and the photo she had forgotten the night before. She impulsively took the photo that portrayed her father and the woman with powder pink-coloured dress. Before leaving the house, she checked that she had double locked the door, which - by the way - didn't seem forced. She grabbed the handle to check that the door didn't open, then took a sigh of relief and walked to the car.

A rustle moved the leafy branch of the willow making them ripple. The guys silently observed that movement.

"Why didn't you tell me before?" – Aleister asked disappointed.

"How could I? we don't even know each other, and all this situation is surreal."

"You're wrong. I know you more than anyone else."

That statement surprised her. Alice tried to understand the meaning of that words, thinking of that almost real dream and of the visions she had been having in the last few months. She looked at him silently, wondering about his behaviours that seemed uncommon to her.

On their journey to Urielle's house, Alice told the story to Aleister, mentioning every single detail. She also told him about the dogs slaughtered, which was still a mysterious event to her. While she told the story, the image of the potential criminal who had tried to access her house came to her mind. That thought made both of them startled.

Aleister was aware that - from the moment he had arrived on the Earth - his life would depend on Alice. During the first months on Earth, he had to learn some rules, whose he eventually had learn to put into practice among the terrestrial being. Those rules could be followed in several contexts, and on situation involving Alice and her family. Until that moment, Aleister had always protected her without her knowledge, considering a form of threat only few events: sudden illness, accidents, and natural disasters. Aleister had forgotten the innate nastiness of the human beings and - the thought that Alice might be in danger - harassed him. He wanted to reveal the reasons of his protective behaviour, but he just couldn't. Thus, he resigned himself. The young man couldn't stop thinking that - probably - she didn't trust him, blaming himself for not having revealed to Alice his nature since the beginning.

Once they arrived at Maddox Street - and parked nearby the church - they noticed confusion near the Whitebird Café. They could notice a group of representatives of local entrepreneur seated under numerous banners unfolded along the sidewalk. They were expressing their disapproval to Brexit and invited passers - by to sign a petition to call off the upcoming referendum.

"For the safety of our Country" – Said a man in a winter coat and a wolf fur hood.

"And for the chance to face terrorism and international crime" – Another man added. Those representatives thought that Brexit would have an impact on the labour market, on customs duty and – consequently - on the whole import-export economy.

Aleister stopped to look at them, then he turned his gaze to Alice.

"I've read some newspapers. What's wrong with Europe?"

"Newspapers? Everyone and every news have been talking about that for months!"

The young man obviously knew little about that matter. He had only read a few articles in Orpeco's newspapers, which face the issue from various point of view. What he had understood was that - it didn't matter from which perspective that issue was faced, someone would feel betrayed. Reasons of such a feeling of betrayal went from past decisions far from the independence and choices that would lead the Country to greater autonomy from the European Parliament. However, Aleister still didn't understand what made Europe so charming to the point of leading people to protest for it or even reject it and ask to be separated from it. He was busy listening to the industrials' point of view, who - attracted by his presence - seemed to put their attention only on him.

Suddenly, the disorder took over, and everyone witnessed an argument between two people. The noise made it clear that the argument wasn't due to the exit from the EU, but it had to do with wounded prides. There was a man - Thomas Firth, a forty-year-old American in the real estate field, with a wrinkled face - who has spotted a naval engineer from Portsmouth. What unleash Firth's wrath was the hidden relationship between his wife Karen and the young naval engineer, whose existence had been discovered only when the young man had forgotten his underwear under the sofa. Thus, the petition had turned into a mob around Firth, who had started pushing the guy. Brexit supporters had also arrived and, having heard that hustle, they approached with curiosity. After that, Firth had covered the knuckles of his hand with his tie to punch his wife's lover. Luckily, the police had managed to stop him. Then, along with the policemen, he looked at Aleister and said, "May God be with us!"

Alice was stuck into the crowd, trying to wiggle out feeling trapped like a rat in a cage. Eventually, she managed to get away from the hustle, realising that Aleister was gone. He got lost among the crowd and - as soon as people became aware of him - they inevitably stared at him with a semi-contemplative look. That few seconds that Aleister spent in the middle of the fray had been enough for one of the demonstrators to push him to the ground hitting him from his back. Nevertheless, the guy realised that he had mistaken Aleister for another person only after looking at him.

"I'm sorry… oh no, what did I do? Again, I'm sorry" – The guy told him deeply embarrassed.

"So, these are what you call good manners?" – Aleister asked, dusting off his trousers, aware that - if he wanted - he could knock him out with a single punch. He walked among the crowd to reach what appeared to be a glimmer of light: Alice. As they moved away from the crowd, Alice slowed down and pressed her hand on her forehead.

"Hey, what happen?" – Aleister asked.

"I don't know. I think it's migraine… But your forehead?! You're hurt!"

Aleister touched his bleeding forehead. He had underestimated the gravity of that injury, until Alice worried and had told him to go to the hospital. He knew that - according to the *absolute Entanglement* - that fall could also affect Alice, but he tried to reassure her, telling her that leaving Maddox Street would prevent them from further trouble.

They soon reached Urielle, who was informed by Alice of what had happened in the last few hours.

"I need some bandages and saline solution. Aleister got injured during the demonstration" – Alice said.

Urielle had immediately saw the wound on his forehead, thinking back to Mr. Orpeco's story about the recovery process. Not knowing exactly what to do, Urielle took some towels and the first aid kit which was still wrapped in its packaging. She was unable to take her eyes off Aleister, and - inspecting at him - she realised how fascinating he was.

Alice told him to sit on the sofa in the living room.

"Don't move! Are you sure you don't have fever? Your forehead is too hot."

"No Alice, I'm super healthy. Tell me, where did you learn it?" – He tried to cross Alice's gaze by moving his head. However, Alice reproach him not to move.

"To do what?"

"To medicate."

Then, silence fell, followed by a sigh.

"School trip to Ben Nevis, in Scotland. All pupils had to attend a course before going to the mountains."

Before she applied the patch, the wound had stopped bleeding and was already healing. Even her migraine had suddenly stopped. However, she silently kept medicating his wound, while Aleister he pretended nothing was happening. He just thanked her for her kindness.

Urielle - who had witnessed the scene - turned her gaze to her friend, trying to send her away from the room.

"You'll get a stiff neck if you don't dry your hair" – She told Alice.

"Okay, I'm going to fix it up."

Alice left the room and headed to the bathroom. The noise produced by the hairdryer allowed Urielle and Aleister to speak.

"I don't know if it's the story of your arrival here that scares me more, or the idea that Alice is unaware of all this!" – Urielle said sarcastically.

"So, my uncle told you everything."

"Your *uncle*..." – Urielle smiled mockingly. "Yes, Orpeco told me everything about the Altors... creatures from *Volteya*."

"That's good. It's a relief to me."

"Oh really? I thought you would play it close to the vest for a while longer... if it had been for Wallace, he wouldn't have told me anything. However, the truth would come out sooner or later."

Aleister looked at her silently, with a puzzled look.

"Your halo, Aleister. You don't have it, and people like me can perceive it." – Urielle noticed that he suddenly looked at the bathroom. "Don't worry, Alice doesn't know anything about it."

"It's not easy not to tell her about it."

"I know what it feels like. I've always lived hiding my gift."

"Doesn't she know about you?"

"No, she doesn't. I should have told her, but everytime I tried, I ended up telling myself that our friendship would end. Alice wouldn't understand, and - in this case - I think that being silent is the right choice. I'm afraid she would detest me."

"You underestimate her. Alice is unable to hate."

"And so, is this the reason that spur you to save her life that night?"

"From up there, we can see everything. Money, lust, power… these are your human aims. Since the first time I caught her energy, it was like seeing the light in the dark for the first time."

Urielle looked at his eyes silently.

"Orpeco told me about the *absolute Entanglement*, and that you can still interact with the extra-dimensional space. Is that so?"

Alesiter nodded.

"For how long?" – She asked.

"I don't know the answer."

"You don't understand the seriousness of the situation."

"I would never do something foolish. Nothing that would endanger her."

"The *Erheiur* will not protect her. You belong to different worlds, and this one is nourished only by hate. If anything happens to you, Aleister, it would be the end" – She sighed. "You have to make sure she never discovers that."

They both fell silent to break the tension, while sipping a cup of hot tea. Since the very first moment, Orpeco had warned his nephew about Urielle's paranormal gift, but he wouldn't ever thought that she could doubt his loyalty. They were both aware of their nature, and that seemed to be annoying them.

Alice finally caught up with them, putting an end to that brief yet deep conversation. Her face was too relaxed for Aleister to keep looking at the cup of the grimy. Thus, they immediately changed the topic of the conversation, commenting on what had happened that morning.

They retraced every detail, from Dorothy's arrival at Shelley House, to presumed intrusion in the house. Aleister thought that the best solution was to inform the police. Urielle turned on the television to the midday newscast channel. A couple of commercials were broadcasted, and then the breaking news announcing the discovery of Mrs. Brickenden's corpse. The witness - whose name wasn't mentioned as she was a minor - reported to have noticed a black saloon car - with its door open - parked on the edge of the bridge that connects Slohan Oak and the neighbouring town. The witness said to have noticed the lifeless corpse only after leaning over the canal, immediately calling the police. At that moment, the Inspector Donovan Cole spoke about the events happened in the last twelve hours through a press release. He sadly expressed his condolences for the Brickenden's, who were model citizens and - above all - his close friends. The Inspector reported that the tragic death of Dorothy's husband had led the wife of the Mayor to moments of delirium, with the consequences of committing suicide.

Urielle turned off the television angrily.

"It's not possible!" – Burst out Urielle.

"After she had visited me this morning… how could it be a case of suicide?" – Alice asked worriedly.

Aleister looked at the music box as he hadn't looked it yet because of the conversation he had before which - by the way - was as essential as the one they had just started. He briefly observed how the mechanism worked, then turned the key twice and the music box played the usual tune, which stopped after a few seconds.

"What are you going to do with this?" – He asked both.

"I'll keep it with me" – Alice replied. "I'll stay here with Urielle until all of this has ended."

"And then? What will you do?"

"We'll see. I think that all we have to do is be patience" – Urielle said.

"It's not about being patience. It's about safety, and you aren't safe here. You could be the next ones, and Dorothy's death could hide something more."

Both Aleister and Urielle knew that he was also included in that matter. It wasn't about being selfish, but if Alice had been involved in a fatal situation, he couldn't have been saved. In that case, there would have been three victims. Aleister hoped that the hypothesis wouldn't turn into reality, making the headline in the Wiltshire newspaper.

"We don't have any other alternative. We can't leave both houses. Someone might become suspicious!" – Urielle replied.

Shortly thereafter, Alice got a call from her brother who questioned her on how things were going in their absence. She moved to the kitchen and - after a series of usual questions and answers - Philip revealed to her the real reason of that call: his intention to get married in the summer. Alice avoided mentioning the countless reasons why she considered his choice senseless. She didn't know if complaining about that to Aleister and Urielle was a good choice, or if it would have been better talking about it another time. Yet, she considered the second option, aware that it was strange that Philip was so yarning for getting married after their father's death. Moreover, Philip had always been reluctant to get involved in relationships, how could it be that he wanted to trap himself in a marriage?

That wasn't bad news only for Alice, as also Urielle expressed her disapproval from across the room. She couldn't believe that Philip was ready for that important event.

Aleister - who hadn't listened to that conversation - went to the bathroom to look himself in the mirror. He slowly took off the dressing and saw that the wound was already healed. The only mark left was a slight discolouration of the skin, as if nothing had happened. It seemed that a whitening ointment had been applied to it. Aleister remembered Orpeco's warning not to do nothing foolish, realising - again - that he was between the hammer and the anvil.

Alice joined him in the bathroom and - annoyed - told him about his brother's choice to get marry. Shortly after, Alice noticed that Aleister had removed the patch, realising that the wound was already healed.

Aleister stared at her eyes, before he could missteps, before she could ask anything.

"I must ask you to trust me" – He told her.

Alice didn't say anything. She thought once of that dream, which this time was a sort of memory. Aleister continued to be a mystery for Alice, who wondered if following her gut was the wisest thing to do.

"Okay" – She said. Then she blinked and repeated "Okay, I trust you."

"Good. So, I suggest you come with me to Manor Falkenberg until the situation will be ended. You and Urielle will be safe there; no one can see you there."

X

Very many people had had the chance to visit the outside of the Manor Falkenberg at least once in their life. Even nowadays it is considered one of the most prestigious estates in Wiltshire, once belonged to the Methuen dynasty, descendants of English Barons. A conceivable misfortune had ceased Lord James' dynasty, after his three daughters were born. After that event, the Falkenbergs had taken over and - although the name of the estate had changed from *Thistles* to Falkenberg - no one had never figured out how a Swedish family - sharing neither their roots nor the history - had managed to settle easily in the England, during the World War II.

Those latest events made Urielle surrender to Aleister's request, although persuading her to leave her apartment - even if temporarily - could have turned out to be a feat. Urielle didn't speak for the whole trip to Manor House, letting Alice and Aleister's voices - combined with the sound of the rain ticking on the window - filled the silence. She thought on what had happened in the last few hours and - as a consequence - she began to nourish a sort of hate for Dorothy Brickenden. Although she tried to think about something else, she was aware that - sooner or later - the police would find out about Dorothy's visit. Furthermore, she had become obsessed to find out the truth about the Altors. There was no certainty other than waiting for the storm to be over not to make any choice that she might regret in the future. After all, she thought that hiding the truth to Alice - her closest friend and sister by choice - was the only right thing to do. Never before she had regretted going back to Slohan Oak, a place that - until then - she had considered to be the quietest one of Wiltshire.

They arrived at majestic Manor House, which can easily be seen from the shrub. After crossing the gate, a gravel road must be travelled. The road leads to a wide clearing with a greenish statue in the middle, once was made of bronze and now oxidized by the weather. Several stone walkways branched off the main square, all of them leading to the impressive house.

"Go inside the house. I'll take your suitcases" – Aleister said to both, pointing out to the entrance. It took him a short of time to take the suitcases he had placed one on top of the other. Then, he supported them on his arms, certain that the effort wouldn't have aroused any suspicion. The bag on the top of all the suitcases belonged to Alice. She had brought with her only essential clothes, while Urielle seemed to have taken the stay more seriously, as she had brought a trolley and two suitcases full of books that would have allowed her to continue her research for her new essay.

"Are you sure you don't need help?" – Alice asked him. She couldn't believe that he had such strength. However, Aleister shook his head.

"As you can see, I can do it. Knock at the door, someone will open it for you."

The governess - wearing a spotless white apron - opened the door. As soon as she saw the guests, the governess looked at the young man amazed.

"Oh Aleister!" – She exclaimed, and - observing carefully the two young girls - she thought that their stay at Manor was like an essential breath of fresh air.

"Let me introduce myself. My name is Annette Dutrieux… please, come in… come in before you catch a cold! Please, give me your coats."

The governess was a native from France, although she could speak English fluently. One couldn't ever tell that she was French if it hadn't been for her last name, which was clearly not English. She had broad shoulders, the skin of her face was soft, but - above all - she had unmistakable maternal attitudes. She was a few years older than Orpeco, although the absence of wrinkles made her look younger. Urielle seemed particularly intrigued, so much so that she introduced herself. After all, it wasn't easy to take the eyes off her. Urielle had understood that she was a mere mortal. She had realised it in the moment she had naively shook her hand to introduce herself, and by the way she smiled when she had seen them. The governess had a bright emerald halo, which created an outline between her bun and the work uniform. She must have been a human, but did she know about Orpeco and Aleister's nature? This had become the question that Urielle would have asked herself every time she would have met someone who have interacted with the two Altors. How many people knew of their secret? Egoistically, she hoped that also the governess knew about that.

"Madame Dutrieux, this is Alice and Urielle. They will be our guests for a while" – Aleister said while he took off his coat.

"I'll go get the rooms ready, then. In the meanwhile, you can show Manor to our guests. I think it would be nice" – The woman said goodbye with a smile.

"Please, follow me. You can easily get lost at the beginning" – Aleister said, and then placed the suitcases on the floor near the entrance. Then he went on.

Manor Falkenberg welcomes its guests with a wide entrance hall, which the black marble and the red drawn a geometric pattern floor. The ceiling - covered with Baroque frescos - embellish each room of the mansion, although in each room there are portrayed different scenes of struggles between good and evil. Nevertheless, it's almost impossible to catch the details due to the height of the ceiling. On both sides of the entrance hall there are what once were the old parlours of Baron James Methuen and the Baroness, before the arrival of the Falkenbergs. Nowadays, both rooms are used as a cloakroom. At the entrance there is a pair of masonry arched staircases which leads to the sleeping area. In total, the mansion hosts fourteen bedrooms - of which six at the ground floor originally belonged to the servants - and the master room, as well as the guest's ones, were at the first floor. Each room is provided with a bathroom and a fireplace. The new owner installed the electrical system, while the water system was recently integrated. Over the staircase, there are the so-called *twin rooms* as they are adjacent to each other. They are known as *Cobalt room* and *Scarlet room*, which once were the music room and the painting room. Nowadays, only the second room is still used with the same purpose. Inside, in fact, there are canvases, easel and everything that could be useful. The *Cobalt* one, indeed, is still decorated with mauve coloured curtains and has become the tearoom. The pool room - on the left side - isn't used. Inside there is only the pool table used only to decorate the room. The studio and the library - the rooms were Orpeco and Aleister spent most of their time - are located next to it. Close to those rooms, a narrow corridor is set, which leads to the kitchen. Apparently, the kitchen looks like a medium-sized room, although the room is sunny thanks to the glass window recently added. The kitchen is connected to two dining rooms: one used during the winter and the other one for the summer season. The two rooms are recognisable by the friezes placed on the arches. Indeed, the winter kitchen is decorated with grapes and apple grains, while the summer one with wheat friezes. However, among all that beauty, what amazed the most Alice and Urielle, was the ballroom. The ballroom was located on the right side of the house, accessible from inside and outside thanks to a platform that surrounded it, forming a sort of terrace overlooking Slohan Oak.

"Are you girls hungry?" – Aleister asked after having reached the kitchen at the end the tour of the mansion. He was hungry and - if Madame had agreed - he would have brought the dinner forward.

Both the Altors felt the need to eat frequently during the day to keep up their strength and - for this reason - Madame Dutrieux's task was to go food shopping three times a week. The governess, indeed, made sure that the kitchens was always stocked. Since Aleister's arrival, she had noticed that he had to keep high his caloric intake, certainly because he had been recently generated. However, since she had known Orpeco, she hadn't noticed any major changes even in his diet. Indeed, Orpeco always preferred hearty breakfasts based on eggs, bacon, and crispy toast, almost as if it were more of a legacy that belonged to little Elroy Cooper rather than a habit of him.

In the cupboard there was always whole wheat bread, seasonal vegetables and fruit, and a great amount of red meat enough to feed a huge crowd of people. Everything was perfectly stored inside the refrigerating room or in the cupboard. The rest of the stocks were stored in a basement - accessible from the kitchen via a winding staircase - in which there were sausages, pickled jars, preserves, dried fruit, spices and other vacuum-seal stored food. The Manor would have cope with the longest and coldest winters only thanks to Madame Dutrieux.

"I'll make some sandwiches" – Aleister said while he opened the shutters of the cupboard, taking out a jar of mustard. Then he looked at Alice "Is it okay for you? Or do you fancy something else?"

"I'm not very hungry, but thanks anyway."

"I don't want to persist, but I think it would help you to eat something. You will be my guest for a while, and I'd like you to feel home."

"Okay then. The sandwich is fine. But no mustard please."

"Okay, a sandwich without mustard" – He kindly looked at her as he took the other ingredients: some leftovers roast turkey, tomatoes, lettuce, and boiled eggs. When the guy took off the package the first slides of bread, Madame Dutrieux suddenly interrupted Aleister. She began to wave her tiny hands over him, preventing Aleister from continuing making the sandwiches.

"Aleister, please. It's my job. Alice and Urielle's room are ready. Don't keep them waiting."

Then, the governess hazel eyes met Alice's ones, grabbing her hand excitedly. "Make me happy and please have a cup of tea. I will turn on the kettle while Aleister will take you to your rooms. Alice, your room is on the west side. What a thrill! It has been long time since the last time someone visited us!"

Aleister left Madame Dutriex making the tea, while he took the suitcases and went upstairs to show Urielle and Alice their rooms. Urielle would have slept in the corresponding room above the *Cobalt room*, which was wide and bright and equipped with a library. However, it was nothing compared to Alice's room. The room assigned to Alices belonged to Lady Catherine Methuen, the youngest of Lord James' three daughters. It was said that Lady Catherine Methuen feared the darkness of the night. Indeed, the room is in a convenient side of the mansion where the moonlight can easily reach the room. It seemed that the governess gave Alice a special treatment, probability because she had been told about the young girl.

"Has Madame Dutrieux been working for your uncle for a long time?" – Alice asked after having unpacked her suitcase.

"She has been working here enough to consider this place as home. She and my uncle had lived here since always. Annette's mother was the governess of the Manor too."

"After all it seems that she really cares about this place. She has a radiant and maternal personality; she puts you in a great mood. You are lucky to live with her; she cares about you."

"I've never thought about it, but you're right."

"Isn't she married?"

"Her story is very sad. The guy she was emotionally involved to, broke up with her because of an unwanted pregnancy. Her son disappeared shortly after he was born."

"Oh no! The social workers took him?"

"Not really. The wood brought him with it. That's what I've been told."

"The wood?!" – Alice asked incredulously, but no word answered her question. From the back of the corridor, Madame Dutrieux informed everyone that the tea was about to be served in the sitting room. Aleister knew only the mere essential about Annette Dutrieux's past; only what she had told him when she had arrived in the Manor. Nevertheless, his relations with those who lived with him in that house were singular. The young man didn't even have a traditional relationship with Orpeco, who - exactly like the governess - preserved the formalities. Or at least, this was Orpeco's rule. Indeed, Madame Dutrieux only amused herself in mocking his unflappable attitude. As usual, none of them were used to talking when there were no guests. Not a word of their extra-dimensional past has ever been said. In most cases they enjoyed spending time together, appreciating the silence. Madame Dutrieux - with her purely feminine and lively taste - was able to make the Manor a more cosy and less spiritual place. Probably, what connected them was that form of reciprocal respect that had intensified over the time.

After having unpacked their suitcases, Alice and Aleister joined Urielle downstairs. Madame, on the other hand, didn't take a cup of tea with them in the library, as she had decided to deal with her business. She had covered the coffee table with a white doily, silver cutlery, and *Rörstrand* crockery, the best Swedish porcelain. The sandwiches were served in blue dishes and illuminated by the light of the fireplace, which made them even more tempting.

"Aleister, you must compliment Madame Dutrieux. This sandwich is delicious!" – Urielle exclaimed with her mouth full of food, then she added "This sauce... Oh Alice, you have no idea how tasty it is. It's the best sauce I've ever eaten. Did you buy it at Mrs. Danton's store?"

"Well... Actually, Madame made the mustard. I think the recipe was originally from *Dijon*" – Aleister tried to keep his eyes on Alice, who - although she seemed having appreciated the meal - was particularly quiet. Until then, she had been told that the wood was one of the many dangerous places she had to watch over herself. However, that little information wasn't enough for her; not anymore. She wanted to know every single detail of that story; she needed to know it.

After three bites, Urielle had already finished her sandwich; then she stood up and began to look around. The fact that Orpeco hadn't tell her about all those volumes amazed Urielle. There were books of all kinds, from classics ones to scholarly essays, as well as old manuscripts still with their original binding. Urielle thought that she could have spent the whole day in that place, loosing track of time. After all, she realised that the stay at the Manor might have turned out to be more pleasant than she had expected. She grew apart from the conversation, looking to the titles of the books. Then, she took the copy of the apocryphal Gospels. She sat down in one of the armchairs - far from the lit fireplace - and isolated herself, loosing herself in that reading.

"So, it was the wood..." – Alice said whispering.

"Yes, as I told you before" – Aleister replied.

"What do you mean?"

"I don't know much about it. It might be that Madame has never accepted the premature death and that she's convinced that the wood took her son. The mind sometimes plays tricks."

"You always remind me to pay attention when I'm through the wood, and now you're talking about self-defence mechanism of mind… I don't understand why you're so contradictory."

"There are some legends about Slohan Oak wood" – He drank the hot tea in a gulp. "But they're only legends."

"Tell me about them" – Alice looked at him defiantly, so much that she would have left the room - and maybe also the mansion - if he didn't provide her with a valid explanation.

"We found ourselves in such a dangerous situation, why do you want to increase your worries with folklore tales?"

"For the same reason people read books. For the knowledge's sake, Aleister."

"Okay then. Let's assume that Annette's son wasn't wanted, and that her pregnancy was caused by odd circumstances. Now, let's suppose that there are unknown entities in the wood. The legend has it that those entities have taken him back from his cradle on *Samhain*'s night."

"You mean Halloween?"

"Yes. And I can see scepticism in your eyes."

"It's hard to believe it. However, this doesn't mean it has never happened."

Then Alice thought over the story, looked at Aleister, and began to believe in what he had said before that story. "Yes, you're right. The mind sometimes may play tricks" – Alice slowly drank her hot tea, looking at the flames sparkling in the fireplace, like dancing witches do around the bonfire of a Sabbath[5].

---

[5] Gathering of people who practice witchcrafts and other rituals.

Urielle spent hours reading until she fell asleep with the book open on her chest. Page after page, she had realised that love was what made people less rational. If someone had asked Urielle if she had ever been in love - or loved someone - her answer would only be negative. Since she was a child, she had believed in the existence of good and evil, but her mind was like a watertight container: she was incapable of giving and receiving. She was firmly certain that reside in one's head, not heart, which is just an organ that supplies blood, not emotions as literatures would have us to believe. Most of her relationships had been only about sex, without any emotional involvement. Only Philip had been able to shake a few bricks of that imposing wall that she had built around herself. All the other guys she had hung out with were only amusements who perceived her emotional void and tended to judge her. Alice, on the contrary, thought that her friend was terrified at the very idea of get emotionally attached to someone, and unconditionally trust. Her parents' early death - and the void left with that- had not healed yet. Probably it would have never been healed. Urielle couldn't be blamed for that; she had found satisfaction in readings and knowledge.

Orpeco returned to the Manor for dinner, as he usually did, and when he saw Alice and Urielle he became clearly puzzled. He would have appreciated if someone had informed him of the two guests, especially of Alice, whom he had heard so much about, but he had never seen her. Madame welcomed him on the doorstep, helping him taking off his coat. Aleister, took the opportunity to provide him brief explanations about the guests.

"Wallace, stop being childish! You have made specifically choices" – Madame said. "I disagree in impeding your nephew to live a normal life. Stop being a *grognon*[6], or you'll get wrinkles on your forehead!"

"I'll stop being a grumpy, Madame, but I want to point out that the girl is not aware of our real nature."

"She's lucky then!" – Madame said. "If I were her, I would never want to know of such truth. Especially if it's you to tell it."

Aleister - as he attended that quarrel - reminded himself that he hadn't been fair to Orpeco, the man who had welcomed him as a son from the first night he had arrived on the Earth; the man who had helped and educated him and - above all - had tough him to speak. If his bond with Alice had unravelled in a parallel life, it would certainly have been one of the many ordinary relationships. In that case, Madame Dutrieux would have been right, there would have been nothing to worry about. However, he seemed to have forgotten the real issue: that the laws that ruled his nature makes him precarious at any moment, because that bond wasn't ordinary at all.

Aleister and Orpeco reached the winter dining room, where Alice and Urielle were waiting for the dinner to be served. They sat facing each other, while Madame Dutrieux sat at the head to maintain control over the table.

During the whole dinner - despite the governess' attempts to avoid any quarrel - tension was palpable. Urielle savoured the food and made appreciation of all kinds, while Alice felt observed all the time. It was easy to guess what Orpeco was thinking about, and his thoughts would have been shared if everyone sat around that table had been aware of the secret. It wasn't Alice that upset Orpeco, although he continued to claim that it

---

[6] Grumpy.

was foolish to make her join that makeshift family at the Manor. After years and years of coverage to escape from a troubled past, he found himself facing an uncomfortable situation. He feared that the young man or the governess could unintentionally reveal something, as well as something dangerous could happen to his step-nephew. Probably, this was what he feared the most.

That agony only ended once the dessert was served along with an alcoholic cider, which was pleasantly appreciated so much that everyone took three shots of it. At that point, the tension between tablemates disappeared. During the evening, they talked about what had happened that morning, and even Orpeco wasn't able to provide explanation of the events that took place that Sunday. However, it seemed clear to everyone that living separately would only worsen the situation. Marta and Philip were also included in that; although they were completely unaware of what was going on, they were involved in that issue and thus they needed protection. Alice thought that extending his family's staying outside England would prevent them from possible danger. She didn't know when they would return but knowing that they were far from all those dreadful events would have made her worry less.

At eleven o'clock, the pendulum clock produced a sinister sound. Some of the tablemates went to their rooms.

Alice - who liked to stay up late as nocturnal animal - had laid on the canopy bed, observing its ceiling for half an hour. Her thoughts overwhelmed her, until recalling wide vineyards under a muggy summer weather. When she had trouble sleeping, she always recalled one of her holidays in Tuscany. Even so, that night she could feel her anxiety from her head to toe, so much that she couldn't managed to get relaxed. She got up resigned, stumbling upon one of Aleister's canvases, which were lit by the moonlight. It was a medium-sized painting - made by grey brush strokes and combined with white streaks - which she hadn't noticed that afternoon. Despite being a simple painting, it enchanted her, as if - deep in her soul - she felt that she had gone to the metaphysical space at least once in her life. She squinted to focus on that canvas and the total absence of defined outlines of those celestial elements, made her feel part of the work.

Shortly after, Alice sat on the sofa placed near the window, grabbed her coat, and took the music box off the pocket to listen to its melody as she watched the painting. The silver music box shone at the moonlight, which illuminated the silhouettes of the trees immersed in the darkness. Alice still couldn't understand the real intentions behind Dorothy's attitude, and the more she thought about it, the more she regretted the boring life she had lived until that moment. Then, she sensed that someone was at the door, as she heard the creaking of the wooden floor.

"Aleister?"

"I'm sorry if I woke you up. I thought you weren't sleeping yet" – He whispered.

Alice asked him to come into the room. Aleister was bewitched to see her in the darkness of the night and illuminated by the moonlight that stood out her pale skin. As soon as he sat on the sofa - next to her - he realised that she was worried. Then, he looked at the moon in the starry sky, and pointed it out, commenting on its brightness. However, Alice was completely absorbed in her thoughts.

"And so, you know me" – She asked cool. "Is it because of my father? Is this a way to be grateful to him?"

"What? No, it isn't. How can you think about that?"

"So what? You told me you knew me better than anyone else."

"I let myself get carried away by the situation."

"That's strange, but I'll make an effort to believe you."

After having talked about astronomy and astral conjunctions, they ended up falling asleep on the sofa which - by the way - wasn't comfortable at all. Suddenly, in the middle of the night, something woke them up.

The egg - which had been placed in a wrong way - suddenly opened. There was something underneath the mechanism that stopped the melody. They took apart the music box and, finally, they found a smooth white stone with a small engraving on it. That episode clearly worried them, to the point that they spent the rest of the night sleepless, thinking about that engraving. Part of their doubts were postponed to the following morning, during the breakfast. Alice and Urielle extended their stay at the Manor for the following weeks, living ordinary days as nothing had ever happened. However, Alice decided to go to work. Aleister took her both on the outward and return journeys, spending his time without her in a state of anxiety.

The streets of the town began to be adorned with lights and Christmas decorations. The snow fell, bringing the Christmas atmosphere all over the town.

XI

Saturday, 23rd of December 2017

At the kindly behest of Claire, the plant nursery would stay close until after the new year. Claire would have done the inventory, giving the employees a deserved rest. Justina and Marvin - who were now officially a couple - had planned a romantic trip to Letterkenny, to her parents' house. Alice, after having worked for two years almost non-stop (except for accident break) - would have spent her holidays at home. Marta and Philip would have gone back home that Sunday. Brunhilde wouldn't join them as she was busy with commitments of various kind. Better days were ahead at Shelley House which would made avoid Alice to spend more time at the Manor. According to the two Altors, Alice and Urielle's stay had had a positive impact. Indeed, Madame Dutrieux cooked every day with love appetizers and desserts, as well as the usual daily meals. She also did the guests' laundry, so that they didn't have to leave the mansion to get clean clothes. The house was decorated with flowers of all kinds brought by Alice as to repay the hospitality. As day went by, the environment of the mansion became more and more ready for the upcoming Christmas holidays. The sparkling anemones and chrysanthemums were replaced by mistletoes, poinsettias and decorations based on juniper and fir oak branches, and Christmas lights. It seemed that everyone has forgotten about the reasons why the girls had temporarily stayed at the Manor. Indeed, Orpeco's scepticism towards Alice seemed to have disappeared as he was contaminated with that joyful atmosphere, so much as he had almost apologised to his nephew to have hindered him. At the end of their stay, Orpeco had even asked Alice when she would return to the Manor. Indeed, he considered her a lovely person, one of those who could make one's day better.

"We'll come to visit you in following days" – Alice promised him on the doorstep, just before leaving.

Aleister invited her enthusiastically.

"I thought I could ask Alice and her family to join us here on the New Year's Eve."

The man expressed his disappointment hinting at a smile. The fact that they were lovely, wouldn't mean that they had to spend their time with other humans other than the two girls. Orpeco wondered why the boy kept making decisions without talking to him first. As soon as Madame Dutrieux joined them to say them goodbye, she expressed her happiness in spending New Year's Eve with them. Thus, Orpeco gave up and decided to take the events passively.

Urielle was annoyed with the idea of leaving the Manor, or rather all those books. She tried for a long time to find out the meaning of that white stone found in the music box. During her research, Madame Dutrieux often had kept her company sipping a cup of hot tea as she wrote down her thoughts on a sort of diary. Urielle - lost in her readings - had pretend nothing happened, but she had realised that the hazel-eyed governess stared at her. She had wondered why Madame was such curious, however she ended up getting used to it, allowing the governess to observe her.

That Saturday - even if they had tried to wake her up to tell her it was time to go home - Urielle stayed in bed until late. She got up at around nine o'clock and - after having said goodbye both to Orpeco and the governess - she thought that day she would change her routine. During her stay at the Manor, she had missed her loved ones. Thus, Urielle took the opportunity to greet Yvonne and her parents with a propitiatory ritual. She called a taxi and got off in front of her apartment in Maddox Street. Once she unpacked her suitcases and looked inside the chest, she noticed that all she needed for the ritual was almost finished. Urielle grumbled, realising that a stroll through the streets of Slohan Oak would be good for her. As she was very busy, she hadn't even noticed the Christmas decorations all over the town. It was like she had forgotten the beauty of Christmas, how the streets - decorated with sparkling lights - had come back to life. After the grey days of November, the Christmas decorations lit up the atmosphere. The sidewalks were full of people, while the atmosphere smelled of cinnamon. Mrs. Beans' flower shop was already full of customers since the very hours of the morning, and the employees were more busy than usual. Urielle went into the shop, certain that Mrs. Beans had all she needed.

"Urielle!" – Someone called her from behind. It was Sue Ling, wrapped in her winter clothes.

"It had been months since the last time they met. Looking at her, Urielle noticed that she didn't look joyful at all, despite the other residents. Her look was sad, and she was holding an arrangement of pink carnations. Urielle waved back at her, then looked at the flowers. The choice of a bouquet - discreet and funerary at the same time - wasn't to be casual under the Christmas period.

"Are you spending the holidays with your parents?" – Urielle asked to test the water.

"Yes. Like every year, we'll join the rest of the family in Beijing. We will leave in a few days."

"I guess you're happy to see your grandmothers."

"Of course, I am" – She said. However, after hesitating for a while, she told Urielle "Actually… I'm going to Lizzie's. Her father passed away a few days ago. The funeral was yesterday, but she preferred not to mention it to anyone."

Those words shaken Urielle. She thought of how Elizabeth Harvey might have felt in having to deal with the sad reality of abandonment. For a while she forgot how much arrogant she had been when they were at school. She thought that Lizzie was completely unprepared for all of that. No one can actually be prepared for when death come into their lives, but Elizabeth was – perhaps - the less prepared person to deal with the loss of her father. Urielle felt a strong feeling, similar to compassion. She imagined the struggle to organize a private funeral. After all, Mr. Harvey - as he owned the steel mills - provided jobs to many employees.

That conversation continued outside the shop to avoid getting in the way.

"Oh Sue… I'm so sorry for her. How is she doing?"

"As you can imagine, she is heartbroken. She has also to manage her father's huge inheritance."

"What about her mother?"

"Didn't you know? Lizzie's parents divorced shortly after the summer. Now, she lives in Florida with her new boyfriend."

"Ah! This is also terrible. I haven't seen Lizzie in a long time. However, Mr. Harvey had always seemed to be so healthy. What happened to him?"

Sue didn't answer, hesitating to talk about Lizzie's father's death, as if someone had forbidden her to. She simply invited Urielle to pay a visit to the Harvey's as in her opinion "Elizabeth would have liked it".

They walked along some paths still covered with snow, as the snowplough hadn't carried out his duty yet. On their way, they talked mostly about things of little importance and how they would spend Christmas holydays. Urielle realised that Sue was agitated, as she would have normally talked about Sumerians or archaeological finds o even about men. But, at that very moment, something must upset her.

When they arrived at the Harvey's, Lizzie herself welcomed them. Her face looked tired - typical of who hasn't slept in days - and she wore an old checked pyjamas, which belonged to her father. It seemed that she had appreciated her visit. After numerous pleasantries, and after asking how Alice was doing, Lizzie invited Urielle and Sue to sit on the armchairs in the living room, while she put the carnation Sue gave her in a vase.

It seemed that ages had passed since the summer party, but now, only Elizabeth's dejection echoed inside that sumptuous house.

"If I had to describe the relationship between my father and me, I would define it as a working relationship with one of his subordinates. He has never shown interests in our family life. A cold man... even icy. However, anyone who had seen him in the last two weeks would have noticed that he was out of his mind" – Elizabeth said. She got up and walked to the bar furniture, made of inlaid mother of pearl. She took a bottle of Brandy and some glasses, giving it to the guests. Nevertheless, they turned off that request to drink alcohol in the morning. Elizabeth resumed telling the story.

"He became obsessed and was delirious all the time. And, as if all that weren't enough, I found his dead body in his studio" – She started to cry, wiping her eyes with the sleeve of her pyjamas. Then, she drank all the remaining Brandy in one gulp.

"You said that he became obsessed. With what?" – Urielle asked her. She had known James Harvey, and had always considered him a classy man, however his way of speaking was bizarre, due to the conspicuous diastema he had found himself. Unfortunately, the way Lizzie had described her father's emotional detachment was more than relevant: James Harvey had never been a model father.

"He had locked himself in his room for days, without even say a word to us. Gregory brought him meals, but he didn't want anyone to be with him. Then, when he realised that he had to give us explanations, he left the studio and had only few moments of lucidity. He screamed '*Nothing is as it seems*'. We wanted to call Dr. Laurie, but he didn't agree. I thought there were issues with the steel mill… you know, an imminent bankruptcy of which we could be unaware. Thus, checks were made. It came out that the accountings were in order. The only possible reason could be my mother's selfishness. He felt abandoned. The truth is that we will never know, he brought the secret with him!"

Elizabeth stopped talking for a while to pour more liquor in her glass, while Sue tried to get her stop drink. However, she was completely ignored. "No written letters, nothing at all. He ceased his life hanging himself." She was aware of those sad circumstances and how Elizabeth's father took away his own life. Nevertheless, she had preferred Lizzie to tell Urielle the story. Sue would be even able to tell all the details of that suicide, and although it was already the second time, she had heard the story, she was shaking as if it was the first time.

Despite she had already dealt with such a matter, Urielle felt incapable of comforting her. She didn't want to diminish Lizzie's pain with words of mere circumstances. Thus, she preferred not to say anything.

"What will you do with the steel mills?" – Sue asked her, trying to change the subject.

"I will sell the shares of the company and then I'll move elsewhere. I have nothing here anymore. I'm not going to stay a minute more in Slohan Oak, it makes me feel sick" – She looked around herself. "Much of the furniture will go to charity. As regard the house, it will take me some time."

In that very moment, Mr. Gregory Lunt - the Harvey's butler - appeared holding some books. Urielle noticed the man's unperturbed look, thinking of the psychological effect of the events happened in the last two weeks. The man had always worked for the Harvey's family and having witnessed the decline of the head of the household must have shocked even him.

He walked close to them and politely interrupted Lizzie.

"Miss Harvey, where can I place these?"

"Please, place them close to the others. Thanks Gregory."

Soon after, Lizzie told Urielle and Sue that many of the books were going to be given to the public library. Then, she asked them to look if they wanted to take any book. As soon as she had known of her father's death, Lizzie had requested the butler to have everything packed. Her departure turned out to be a conscious choice, not only a mere thought. Elizabeth knew that nothing was worthy staying there anymore. She just wanted to run away from that place as soon as possible.

Urielle didn't wait for Lizzie to repeat it and looked at the book she might like. Her common sense made her consider that the book Orpeco had suggested her couldn't be taken on that occasion.

Sue and Urielle went to the home library, while Lizzie followed them. They checked the books, from classic books of the English literature to university ones. At some point, something caught Urielle's attention. Among all those books, she found one with an old binding. On the cover of that book, a white stone set in a metal seal was portrayed. She had already seen that stone. It was the same stone she found inside Mayor Brickenden's music box.

"If it's fine for you, I'd take this home" – Urielle said without even knowing the content of that book.

"Sure, take it. It's just one of my father's old junks. Take it and do me this favour."

The girls chatted for the following hour, even if Urielle couldn't stop thinking about that book. At that point, it seemed quite clear that Mr. Harvey - as well as the Brickendens - might have been involved in a sinister affair.

Urielle left the house, saying that she had a commitment and - as soon as she was outside the house - she began to quickly leaf through the pages of what turned out to be James Harvey's diary. She noticed that no names were mentioned, but only animals involved in some happenings. After a succession of events, nothing else had been written.

Util that day, Alice had hidden her stay at the Manor from her mother. The technician had never called back to fix the alarm system. Thus, Marta had known that Alice hadn't been there, it could be said that she would be in serious troubles. Alice was hoping that everything was at its place, exactly as she had left it. She spent the day at *Velvet*, the only shopping centre in Slohan Oak. At the end of that afternoon, Claire called from the plant nursery. Shakenly and indifferently at the same time, she asked Alice to go to the Robins Garden as soon as she could, informing her that a delivery man - driving rashly - had ran over Rommie that very morning. When Alice asked why she hadn't promptly informed her, Claire said that she didn't want to worry her, as she preferred to wait for Dr. Ward's verdict, the vet who had Rommie under observation. However, Claire had spoken clearly "Rommie couldn't be here anymore, and I can't take care of him. I have to many things to do", as if she had been asked to try to do something that was beyond her human intellect.

Alice wondered how Claire could run a business by growing plants, when her heart was completely arid. Justina would have certainly taken care of him, after all, she would have never dared to put her job before a needy pet. For such a reason, Alice - *cat lover* from the bottom of her heart - didn't flinch. Indeed, she went to the vet, both for Rommie and her colleague's sake, who was spending her holidays in Ireland.

Dr. Ward said that the cat needed to rest and to limit rush movements, although he knew that it wouldn't be easy to keep him at home as he was accustomed to living through the streets. Nevertheless, when Alice brought Rommie at home, he seemed to get accustomed to the new situation. He was collaborative and confident with the surroundings, as if he had always lived in that place. It was probably a sort of sixth sense that made him act in that way, as he seemed aware that he would have stayed at Shelley House until he was completely healed.

XII

Sunday, 24th of December 2017

"The highest form of disbelief that influence the human intellect by letting people roaming alone in the dark of the night can only be lit up by the moonlight. Be the very essence of the flare, Alice, be the moon, be light." And suddenly the darkness came. An endless leap in the void, that is what Alice 's dreams had become, steady dreams in the form of dark shadows. Her mind played tricks, she knew it, and every time she tried to sleep, she wished she wouldn't dream.

Eventually, she couldn't fall asleep that night. She had just doze off for a couple of hours. She has laid in bed motionless, staring at the ceiling until when the alarm rang at eight o'clock. She stretched her legs and then got out of bed with effort. That morning, she would deal with the preparation for that night's event. Thus, she took everything she needed from her father's studio: writing paper - the ones with the bluish watermark - and some ribbons.

As soon as she sat down, the doorbell rang three times. That insistence worried her. Luckily, it was Urielle, who made her noisy entrance.

"If Mohammed will not go to the mountain, the mountain must come to Mohammed" – Urielle said, still wearing her coat. "Alice, I've been trying to call you since last night! I thought something had happened to you! Ah, by the way, Merry Christmas" – Urielle handed her a bag full of presents that they would open that same evening. Although Urielle's voice was cheerful, Alice could notice a sense of annoyance.

Thus, she apologised for having- as usual - ignored the phone, which was left somewhere in the house.

"Why you're so much worried?" – She asked.

The bell rang again - only once this time. It was Aleister. Urielle, without saying anything - as if she wanted to mark her presence - used all her strength to slam the diary on the peninsula, whose noise echoed as if the diary was as thick as the *War and Peace* novel.

"What is that?"

"Jame's Harvey's diary."

"Who is he?" – Aleister asked, as he had listened to the conversation.

While Urielle was telling them what had happened in the last few days at the Harvey's, Alice noticed the white stone drawn on the cover of the book. Immediately, she tensed up and realised that the matter wasn't over yet. She asked Urielle numerous questions to which she had no answer. Alice became even more worried and - when she was told that in that diary no human name was mentioned - she felt even more confused.

"Animals?" – Alice asked. That moment of dismay was interrupted only by the reading of some lines of the diary, which had aroused Urielle's curiosity.

'From the union of the Fox and the Phoenix a bastard was born.'

'The Crow took an oath in eternal union.'

Urielle leafed through the diary and pointed at a line that seemed important to her. However, the disjointed statements seemed to hide other meanings. Alice and Urielle couldn't understand the reasons that had led James Harvey to write his thought down on a notebook. They considered all the writings as a product of Harvey's imagination, as if he had found himself mad and on the verge of death.

"They represent people" – Aleister said, after having listened carefully. Seven beasts were mentioned: the fox, the phoenix, the turtle, the owl, the crow, the horned snake, and the dragon. All of these were beasts that were often mentioned in the past in relation to the vices and the immoral conduct of men. It couldn't be a coincidence that the stone found in Mayor Brickenden's music box was exactly the same of that drawn on the cover book. Everyone in that room agreed that there had to be a link between their death and those stones.

"I'll go check out the Brickenden's house" – Aleister claimed.

"No, stay here. My mother and Philip will be back soon. It's Christmas Eve today, let's celebrate it in harmony" – Alice begged him.

"Also, breaking into someone else's house is a crime" – Urielle added sarcastically.

"There are too many strange anecdotes in this story, and I want to clear them up" – Aleister replied.

That quiet atmosphere was - nevertheless - only temporary like that unexpected clear sky on that Sunday in December. Just before lunchtime, the Murray family reunited. Marta-happy to have seen her daughter again - hugged her crying. However, she was sad for the misfortunes of the Brickendens and the Harvey.

Alice could only think about the list of animals mentioned in the diary, which were unpleasantly echoing in her mind. Wrapped in her mother's arms, Alice looked out the windows as she was thinking of Aleister. She hoped he could find answers to their questions, and that nothing dangerous would happen to him, as he had ventured into the woods.

The Altor walked quickly through the snowy paths of the woods. He felt full of energy and vitality, sensing that he was about to adapt himself as a human being. Aleister reached the Brickendedn's home - located near a clearing beyond the woods - in a very short time. As no one lived there anymore, the garden, as well as the roof of the house, was covered with snow. Aleister started the research in the garden, hoping of not meeting anyone. The chimneys came out from the snow, while a thin layer of ice covered the windows glass. He went to the front door and noticed that the police tapes had been torn, while the door lock had been tempered with. Someone else had come there before him, and he hoped that what they were looking for hadn't been found yet. Nevertheless - without making any assumptions - he went inside the house. The house was ice-cold, while some damp spots covered the corners of the walls. Overall, the house looked neglected and harsh. Silence reigned in that house, and the only noisy Aleister could hear was that of his own footsteps on the wooden floor. There were numerous

photos hung on the wall, along with other questionable ornaments. Their smiles on the photos contrasted with the gloomy
atmosphere of the house, and the dramatic events that had hit
them.

Aleister stopped to look at the armchair on which the Mayor
was found dead. He suspected that the Mayor's death was
caused by more dangerous events than those officially reported
by the press release. He went upstairs silently, heading to the
bedroom and the two private bathrooms. Aleister first went to
the bedroom and checked Dorothy's dressing table. There were
numerous nail polishes and reddish and pink blushers. Nothing
uncommon. Then, the guy inspected the bathrooms, differing
by their colours. Mrs. Brinckenden's one overlooked the garden and was white coloured, with some floral relief, which decorated the tiles until the tub. Next to that room, there was the
bathroom used by the Mayor. It was mint green coloured, and
a strong scent of aftershave came out from the drawers. Aside
from the stench of that aftershave *pour homme*, Aleister
thought that there was nothing uncommon both in the bathrooms and in their bedroom.

A sudden noise came from downstairs; the keys of a piano
were being playing, followed by a sinister meow; it looked like
a horror film. Aleister leaned out of the staircase and saw a
malnourish cat which - not at all scared - kept pressing the keyboard. The hinges stuck out from the keyboard cover and, as
soon as he noticed a sheet music lied on the keyboard and read
it, he decided to take it. It was a piece by *Franz Schubert*. The
passing of the years had turned the pages yellow, but the title
could be still read. It was THE CROW. He took the music sheet,
folded it, and put it in the pocket of his jacket to bring it to
Shelley House. When he left the house, he realised that the cat

was following him like a shadow in the snow. It seemed that it was a request of help. Aleister slowly got close to him to pet him, realising that he wore a blue leather collar with his name engraved on it.

"It's a pleasure to get to know you, Mabon" – He said hinting at a smile. Then, decided to take the cat with him. Before going back to Shelley House, he decided to stop quickly to the Manor to talk to Orpeco and Madame Dutrieux about the latest news of those events, as well as to ask them for some advice.

He walked quickly, cuddling Mabon in his warm harms.

XIII

The soft white snow contrasted with the warm colours of the twilight, while the branches of the bare trees were covered with thrushes. Aleister couldn't take waiting for Mabon anymore who – occasionally - got lost in the snow as if he wanted to slow Aleister down.

As soon as Aleister reached the Manor, he smelled a metallic scent that he had never smelled before. That smell annoyed him, as it could also be tasted from his palate to the throat, until becoming a real flavour. His human sense organs weren't fully developed, although they were very receptive. He tried to follow that smell, which he linked to the red colour. Indeed, he noticed blood stains on the ground. The worst scenarios came to his mind. He desperately looked for Orpeco and Madame Dutrieux in the garden. Then he went to the stables, where the stains became more numerous and spread over the snow. Orpeco was sat on a stool, next to Epos - the mare - who were lying on the straw, heavily breathing. Orpeco and Madame's latex gloves were covered with blood.

"Are you wounded?" – Aleister asked them both.

Orpeco stood up with effort, while Madame Dutrieux was speechless. Her tiny hands seemed to speak for her. She took off the gloves and washed her hands nervously, as if she wanted to get rid of something malevolent stuck on her skin.

"The poor Epos was attacked" – Orpeco replied. He had approach to her and caressed her dark muzzle, whispering comforting words, while Aleister observed her coat.

Epos was a Fresian, one of the oldest breeds on the continent. Both Madame Dutrieux and the bookseller loved the mare, although the latter had contributed to her birth ten years before, and had taken care of her immediately, as her mother had died during the delivery. Epos had never been riding, she lived free in the surroundings of the Manor without ever leaving the wooded area. She considered Orpeco and Madame Dutrieux as part of her herd. She wasn't really accustomed to living inside a stable, thus, she constantly moved her paws in an attempt to get back on her paws. There were lengthwise wounds, which became deeper near the withers and the jugular furrow. Nevertheless, it seemed that there was no major damage.

"We were inside the house" – Orpeco went on. "I heard two shots coming from the clearing. So, I run outside to see what had happened and Epos suddenly appeared. She started kicking and almost hit me. She was nervous and after trying to calm her down, I realised that she was bleeding."

Madame Dutrieux silently nodded in fear.

"This isn't a hunting area. Is it possible that she went to the clearing and got injured?" – Aleister asked.

"I think the injuries were caused by a small calibre weapon. The sound of the shots didn't sound like a rifle."

They arranged the stable so that the mare could comfortably get recovered there. However, they noticed that the more Orpeco got close to her, the more she got nervous. It was only when the man placed his head on her muzzle that she finally calmed down. After having arranged the stable, Aleister could tell them about the latest events. He told them especially about his visit to the Brickendens' house. Such a news caused concerns in Madame Dutrieux, who participated with spontaneous exclamations in French like "*Mince!*" and "*Zut!*[7]". Orpeco noticed the presence of Mabon only at a second time. However, he didn't agree to keep him, also because Epos - at the sight of the cat - became more shaken and breathed heavily.

"Get him away from here!" – Orpeco told Aleister, trying to calm down the mare. Then, the man looked at Mabon and shivered "Go away!" – He yelled at him with a withering look.

Although Orpeco had opposed, Aleister thought that it was necessary scouring the surroundings of the wooded area before returning to Shelley House. He walked softly along the snowy path through the woods, as not to make any noises. He noticed Epos' blood stains which suddenly disappeared. The sound of a broken branch made him turn around. He sensed an evil presence behind him, although there was no one. He felt his heart in his throat, then he swallowed.

Shortly after he heard a hiss. Then, his name echoed. It was a feminine and persuasive voice, which seemed to want to seduce him.

"*Come with me*" – The persistent and annoying echo was taking over his mind. However, the guy chased away that feeling.

---

[7] Damn!

"Who are you?" – He yelled.

Nobody replied.

Suddenly, he glimpsed a dark shape along the path. Then, a shot echoed, making the birds fly away, while Mabon fell to the ground. Aleister continued to walk into the snowy path undaunted, keeping his eyes on the shape which was stealthily falling back into the woods. Then, he shot again, luckily missing Aleister. He thought that a single shot could have been enough to kill him. Then he turned around and saw a little fawn lying on the ground bleeding. He realised that the animal couldn't be saved, even if Orpeco had treated him. The killer - even if Aleister though it was something more evil - had pulled the trigger and shot the poor animal right to his throat. His gaze seemed to beg Aleister to put an end to that agony, as the blood was flowing to the ground, turning the snow red. Without thinking twice, the guy grabbed his head and - with slight movement - ended that suffering. For the first time in his life, Aleister - down on his knees - found himself dealing with death. Sorrow run through his chest like ink spilled on a page, overstepping the fear the had felt. Even so, he was certain he had done the right thing. The glint of the bullet caught his attention. Aleister noticed that there was an engraving on the rim: two head profiles looking at opposite directions and joined in a single body. He picked it up with his shaking hands and went to the Manor to show it to Orpeco.

"I've already seen this symbol engraved in some epigraphs of ancient Rome" – Aleister told Orpeco.

"I fear you're right Aleister. This is the Two-faced Janus also known as *Divum Deus*, a polytheistic god dating back to the ancient world" – Orpeco stared beyond the clearing and noticed a dark sign hovered in the air. "We're no longer safe in this place. I sense a dangerous and creepy evil coming out into the open. Look what had happened in such a short time. So many creatures have died. Evil is among us, and it seemed to be hungry for death."

After all those tragic events, no one should have left their houses, and Aleister thought that Orpeco was right: they weren't safe anymore. That evil was different than the one they know about. It could be said that it was more ruthless. Aleister realised that the human being was easily gullible, and that the desire of power and revenge run through his vein.

"You must go back to her" – Madame Dutrieux told him.

"What will happen to you two?"

"We can take care of ourselves. But you must go. Time is running out."

"Find the origin of this evil and get rid of it as soon as possible" – Orpeco wisely recommended him, looking at the wooden area.

XIV

A glow of soft lights coming out from the house could be seen from the garden of Shelley House. The Christmas lights wrapped and lit up the hedges, making them look like stars in the dark sky. A huge holly wreath was hanged on the main door, while smaller ones were placed on the windows on the ground floor. Marta's retuned meant that every corner of the house aroused joy for the long-waited Christmas period. Every single light would have distracted everyone from bad thoughts. However, everyone - including Marta - knew that it was the only way to move on from the emptiness that death had caused.

Aleister, as he had promised, returned to Shelley House before dinner time. As soon as he arrived, he couldn't even take off his coat as Urielle and Alice reached him out. Alice grabbed his arm, then immediately stepped back, realising that the reaction was too impulsive. She saw Mabon - standing between Aleister's legs - who promptly sneaked inside the house.

"And so?" – Urielle asked. "We don't have much time to talk about it. Marta and Philip went to the cemetery. They'll be back soon."

Aleister didn't know exactly where to start the story. He had gone into the woods alone and came back with the Brickendens' cat. Given the circumstances, he tried to briefly tell what had happened, after having asked Alice to bring a bowl of water for Mabon. Then, Aleister showed the bullet he had found, although he didn't tell them the whole story. He thought that if he had told them about the shape that tried to kill him, they would be worried. Thus, he decided to omit some details carefully selected.

"Someone chased Epos, and I found this bullet soon after. If you look carefully at it, you'll see the portray of the Divum Deus. James Harvey was the third victim." – Aleister said.

He decided not to tell the rest of the story - at least for that moment - although it could have been crucial.

Urielle glared at Mabon, who had scraped himself against the guys' legs, except hers. She didn't like him at all and tried to stay away from him as much as possible, exactly as Orpeco had done. Even Rommie seemed to dislike his fellow, as he scrutinised him from under the furniture, straightening his fur and tail.

"What if Mabon is cursed?" – Urielle exclaimed noticing Rommie's reaction "Look! Not even Rommie likes him!"

"Don't even think about it!" – Alice said, grabbing little Mabon and letting him curl up on her knees. She petted his fawny fur on his back which had become skinny.

"I don't trust that furball" – Urielle reported.

That discussion would soon turn into an argument. Aleister - aware that a quarrel wasn't really necessary at that moment - decided to show them the music sheet.

"Would one of you like to perform?" – He asked showing the sheets. He could have played himself the piano as he had learned how to do it over the centuries.

"What is this?" – Urielle asked.

"I found it at the Brickendens'. THE CROW by *Franz Schubert*."

Playing the piano was one of Alice greatest skills, but she let her friend playing it. Urielle got up from the armchair and went sitting on the stool. She stretched her fingers and began to play the notes on the music sheet. At the middle of the melody, she suddenly decided not to play anymore. Her faced became pale and took her hands off the keyboard. Mabon quickly jumped from Alice's legs and sneaked into the studio.

"*Merde*[8]..." – Urielle whispered. Then she turned around. She asked for the music box to be played. The composition of that little music box was the same she had just played on the piano. Impulsively, Urielle took James Harwey's diary and read "*The Crow took an oath in eternal union. I think it refers to the marriage of Timothy and Dorothy.*"

Silence fell. Never before she had felt such fear, enough to destroy all her resolutions. Urielle feared death and thought that the three deaths were only the beginning of troubled times. "*Maman*[9]" – she thought "*Maman*, I wish you were here with me" – She thought of her mother, sad of not being able to find comfort in her arms.

The sound of a car engine announced the return of Marta and Philip, and Alice got nervous at the idea that they went back home earlier than expected. Although Philip had already

---

[8] French exclamation used to express displeasure or embarrassment. It is the equivalent of "Oh, shit".
[9] Mum in French.

met Aleister the day of their father's funeral, her nervous made the introductions less relaxed than she thought.

Aleister made efforts not to make the same mistakes as the ones he made the very first time. First, he introduced himself with a firm handshake. He handed them the bottle of *Chianti*[10] wine, as a gift prepared by Madame Dutrieux to prevent him from showing up empty-handed to the *half italians*. "Trust me! They care about good manners!" – Madame Dutrieux had reminded him before he left the Manor. Indeed, Aleister realised that it was the truth. Even if Marta had accustomed to the English manners and culture, she was still deeply attached to her Italian roots. Indeed, Aleister's gift surprised Marta, as her green eyes widen in amazement and a genuine smile appeared on her face.

Alice peeked at their introductions from the entrance. Her mother seemed to her chatty as usual and - since they started talking about Italy - Alice knew that she was unstoppable. Every time she talked about her country, she ended up feeling nostalgic and - if the interlocutor was interested - she used some Florentine filler words. After having introduced himself, Philip went to the living room, and so did Alice, while the others were helping to cook.

Alice noticed that her brother was more taciturn than usual, and - looking better at him - he seemed to be worried. At first, she didn't say anything to him, but the more she observed him, the more she noticed that something was making him worry.

"Is everything okay?" – Alice asked him.

---

[10] Wine produced in the Chianti region of central Tuscany, Italy.

"Coming back from the Hades made me realise that Cerberus is running low new readings. I think he's been reading the same book for over a month."

"Hmm... apart from that, what was like going to visit dad?" Philip didn't answer immediately. He changed his position on the chair, shook his head, and clear his throat.

"What do you expect me to say? The grief is always the same and I really don't understand how mum can talk to a flowery concrete."

Philip looked away restlessly, as the memories of his father's death had aroused numerous thoughts in him. It was in that moment that Philip decided to stop his bad thoughts and enjoy that night with his family. Thus, he asked Alice to told Aleister to stop cooking and join them in the living room for a chat.

"Promise me you won't embarrass him" – She begged her brother.

"Who do you think I am? Do you think I can do this to a guest?"

"Although you're unpredictable, you are predictable. Swear you won't be an asshole!"

"Yeah, cross my heart!" – He replied.

Thus, Alice asked Uriclle and Aleister to join them in the living room, while Philip began to observe Aleister carefully. He had to change his mind, and this upset him. Not only Aleister was particularly handsome, but he was also good-mannered, that kind of manners that women usually like and made them melt. However, he considered him a genuine and well-intentioned person, not just a handsome boy. Probably, he had judged him too thoroughly *"Maybe one day I'll tell him"* – He thought, *"One day..."*

Alice couldn't help noticing the way Philip was staring at Aleister, as if she could hear his thoughts. Philip looked different that night, but the reason was unknown. She thought that it could be due to his visit to the cemetery, or even the fact that he missed Brunhilde, who - by the way - had decided to spend her Christmas holydays in Switzerland. Suddenly she thought *"Oh, maybe it's the wedding"* and snorted. They hadn't talked about it yet, although she would have preferred not to talk about that.

Urielle was sitting quietly in front of the fireplace and - from time to time - she intercepted part of the conversation the others were having. They were talking about Slohan Oak, a village where - until recently - even a chicken theft would made headlines. She couldn't believe that the situation had changed in a couple of months. In addition, she was shocked by the melody played on the piano, while the presence of Philip made her feel uncomfortable. She had tried to take part in their conversation, but she was overthinking. Unlike Alice, Urielle hadn't noticed any changes in Philip, he was the same as always, except that he would soon find himself married. The idea of his marriage aroused more resentment in Urielle and - after having listened to their conversation on Wiltshire - she left the living room to help Marta cooking.

It was a typical Italian Christmas Eve dinner. The rich menu had been cooked in short time to respect the English dinner time. The table was meticulously set for five people with countless silver cutlery and *Wedgwood* porcelain plated. However, those decorations - if not accurately set - could have led to conceited adornments.

As soon as Marta took out of the oven the fragrant breads with olive oil and covered with sesame, she invited everyone to take their seats since dinner was ready. During the dinner, they drank good wine and chatters on different topics. Philip and Urielle sat next to each other. However, Urielle - although she took part in boring conversations about concessions of land redevelopment and the demonstration that took place in Maddox Street - she couldn't look at Philip right in his eyes. Then, he suddenly started talking about the latest news in Slohan Oak, coughing everyone's attention, including Urielle's.

"Did you know that after her father's death Elizabeth Harvey decided to leave the County?" – Philip said continuing to eat despite the silence had fell.

"Who told you that?" – Alice asked him.

"Lizzie, this afternoon. We met at the entrance of the cemetery."

"Did she also tell you where she will go?"

"Tuscany, I think… Alice, I think you are the last person to be really interested in Lizzie" – He said.

"That's unfair… however, don't talk about her departure to anyone" – Then she looked at Urielle and Aleister and added "No one will miss her."

Alice was lying, she was aware of it. She just wanted to prevent Elizabeth Harvey from having the same fate as her father. The conversation ended, and Marta went in the kitchen to take a pan of asparagus lasagne. Silent fell, as everyone was savouring that dish.

It was Aleister that - as usual - broke the silence to compliment Marta for the dinner. However, as soon as he started talking, everyone's attention was on him, and Philip took advantage of that and resume chatting. He asked Aleister about his job and his stay in Slohan Oak, that kind of questions that end up making the interlocutor feeling under questioning.

Then, he asked about his age, typical questions of circumstance. Aleister said to be twenty-three, even if that answer
aroused doubts in him. Not because of Philip's question. He
began wondering how old he actually was.

*"Is there an answer close to the truth? How old am I? My
body is so young; I've been existing for only one year! On the
other hand, my awareness is so old to the point that it could be
made of dust."*

He started thinking about his spiritual and physical age, and-
when he realised how little of life he had lived - he realised that
he couldn't answer differently. He was twenty-three. Although
he felt relieved as the answer hadn't aroused suspicious, he had
started thinking that in the future youth would have gradually
faded. It wasn't a matter of vanity, as he only knew the name,
not the appearance. However, he realised that - according to
the natural course of life - he would spend his day remembering
of the past, until becoming himself a memory.

Marta - sat at the head of the table - after having drank the
third glass of wine, which ended up spilled on the roasted fish-
and with her red cheeks, began to talk happily. She placed the
bottle of wine inside the bottle cooler and joyful began to talk
about how carefree she was at twenty-three years old. She
talked about their family job, the restoration, about her studies
at the Academy of Fine Arts, about the summer parties in Fie-
sole. The conversation ended with her meeting with Arthur
Murray, at the end of the 1980s.

"Ah, we were so young!" – She said. "Naïve enough to think
that the world was ours!" – Then she drank the fourth glass of
wine in one gulp.

Philip was as fascinated as ever in listening to her mother's
youth. It was a story that both he and her sister knew by heart,

but they were never tired of hearing. They had lived for a short time in Florence, a city that made them fall in love, although not enough to decide to live there forever. Suddenly, Philip's phone rang, and she had to leave the dining room for a while.

Urielle frowned at that gesture, and - when Philip came back in the room - toasted.

"A toast to love!" – She exclaimed.

Everyone's voices echoed inside the room, while the glasses clinked. However, Urielle's friends knew that she didn't like toasting. To be honest, she wasn't even that kind of person who gets excited about drinks. Thus, Philip couldn't help staying silent and meditating on that improvisation until the end of the dessert: a delicious mascarpone cream served with chocolate cake. However, he only tasted a bite of it. He took advantage of a moment in which Urielle and him where alone to talk to her. However, as soon as he approached her, she went to the next room, reminding everyone that midnight had arrived and that it was time to open the presents.

They gathered near the fireplace, around the Christmas tree, where there were wrapped boxes. Exclamations like "Ooh..." and "You didn't have to buy me a present!" echoed in the room.

Aleister had observed from the other dimension that it was natural for most of the humans to give presents and take care of the loved ones. He hadn't understood yet the meaning of sharing. However, what he had noticed was that many humans loved the act of giving presents, which was like a few seconds of ecstasy, which ended once the gift had been opened. Everyone had started unwrapping their presents, finding a numerous variety of objects inside. There were wooled socks, scarves and caps, biscuits, candles, sweaters, and even dark chocolate and then more socks.

Aleister began to imitate them and finally managed to feel a new emotion: that unmistakable thrill that precedes the unwrapping of a gift. It seemed to him the closest thing to a slight shock of adrenaline running down the back. He opened Alice's present, "Oh!" – He exclaimed. It was the VHS of *To kill a mockingbird*, which had become a collector's item. It felt like an invitation to watch it together. Indeed, it definitely was.

Aleister, took off a small dark velvet bag with a golden lace from the pocket of his trousers and gave it to Alice. He had kept it in his pocket for all that time, to the point that the bag had become warm to the touch. Alice loosened the lace. Inside the bag she found a small oval pendant made of white stone. Her heart was beating very fast.

"Does this stone have any particular meaning?" – Alice asked him.

"It's *Selenite*, and it's known as Moonstone. The colour you see is due to a phenomenon called adularescence, derived from the Adularia, the variety of stone typical of the Alps. In Greek mythology, *Selene* was the goddess of the Moon. Over the centuries, she had become one of the main symbols of the ancient civilizations. According to the Sioux people, the goddess was named *Hanwi*, meaning *sun even at night*."

"*...Be the very essence of the flare, be the moon, be light.*"

Alice suddenly thought of the dream she had and stiffened, certain that she had already lived those moments and already heard those words. Then, she looked at Aleister and hugged him to thank him for that gift. Nevertheless, he seemed to stiffen at that gesture.

Philip - who was very excited to talk to Urielle after that conversation about "culture" - thought that he would have stopped her sister's cultured conversation to start a less cultured one. He grumbled and went into his father's studio - adjacent to the dining room - carrying a bottle of wine. It seemed that wine was the only relief for that draining waiting. He sat in the dark, staring at the bottle and at the entrance, hoping that Urielle would come into that room at any moment.

Time passed and Philip - glass after glass - had almost guzzled the whole bottle of wine. However, right when he was about to lose hope, Urielle appeared, accompanied by the sound of the pouring rain. She headed to the window and opened it, holding a ciggie in her hand. The lighter - once lit up - illuminated her face. She wanted to smoke in silence, waiting for that night to come to an end. She was still shaken and overthinking to that symphony to the point that she couldn't enjoy that dinner at all. It was only in a second moment that she realised that she wasn't alone in that room, when Philip pinched the shoulder pan of her dress.

"I'll keep you company. Do you mind give me a ciggie?" – Philip asked as he walked closer to her.

Urielle - bringing her cigarette to her mouth - merely nodded and handed him the packet.

"When did you start smoking again?" – She asked him.

"I've never started again. And you? Since when have you been smoking?"

She shrugged her shoulders and told him that she had just borrowed Alice's package. Philip could see the red ember igniting every time she inhaled although he had noticed that Urielle's look was sad. Only when silence fell and become unbearable, Philip decided to finally talk to her.

"I'd like to know why you're avoiding me" – He asked.

"I came here to smoke a cigarette, nothing more" – Urielle paused to inhale again "But *prince* Philip Murray cannot be contradicted!" – She mocked him without even looking at him.

"What's wrong with you? Are you ok?" – Urielle began to stare at the garden as her heart was pounding. She would have liked to express her resentment, as it was what she felt towards Philip.

There were many unspoken words and she realised that her attraction for him had turned into jealousy. The idea that he was happily married to Brunhilde had made her livid.

"Have a good night, guys. Ah, close the windows!" – Marta suddenly went to the studio to greet them and make them the usual recommendations as a storm was coming.

Urielle was exhausted and at the mercy of the wine she had drunk that night. Thus, she decided to go to sleep. Then, Philip looked at Urielle.

"Please, say something. Talk to me."

The girl didn't say a word, took the last puff of cigarette and put it on the ashtray, ready to leave the room. Nevertheless, as soon as she turned, Philip grabbed her wrist.

"Wait!" – He begged her. "It's because of the marriage, isn't it?"

"Why do you think that?"

"You don't even look at me, Riri. You've been acting different since Alice told you about it... you're acting differently with me!" – He paused and gripped her wrist firmer. "I want to talk to you because so many things have changed...Ah, Brunhilde, she made me struggle a lot! If only I had known before!"

As soon as he tried to grab her hands, Urielle immediately stepped back. She left the studio livid, even though Philip followed her to the stairs.

"I'm not finished talking to you!" – He yelled at her from the first step of the staircase. At that point, Urielle hushed him with her back to the wall and kissed him. then, she ran to the bedroom and locked herself inside. In that moment, her anxiety transformed into a liberating cry.

Philip - on the other hand - couldn't believe what had just happened, although he was aware he had bad timing.

XV

Monday, 25th of December 2017

The following morning, Philip woke up with a severe headache. It took a while before he realised that he was in his old bedroom, and that nothing in that room hadn't changed at all. On the shelves and on the desk, there were still the books for the college admission tests, tennis trophies he won at school, old stuffed animals and photographs that portrayed him and his family. The smell of alcohol on the pillows caused him a retching. However, he quickly repressed it.

"Get up, you idiot!" – Philip exhorted himself after he had another stabbing pain on his temples. He looked at the alarm; it was half past seven. Thus, he stretched his legs, forcing himself to get up to face that day. He knew that lying in the bed wouldn't be a good idea; first because he was used to getting up at five o'clock to go to work and thus, he would end up staring at the ceiling for all day. Secondly, the memory of Urielle kissing him the night before, wasn't giving him peace. He wondered if ignoring that matter and letting things take their course would be the best choice to take. Nevertheless, he decided to go to Urielle's room and - when he was about to knock at the door - he changed his mind.

"No, this is not a good time" – He told himself. It was his pride that spoke for him, but also the clarity of his mind, given the fact that was early morning. If only Alice had been awake, he would probably have asked her for advice. However, he shook his head and thought that no one in that house would have got up before nine on Christmas Day. Not to hear him complaining. Thus, he decided to keep himself physically engaged, to go jogging outside to face that situation and to avoid drowning in his own thoughts. He would run through the path he loved. He would have gone to the Gladi fountain, then to the plant nursery until the municipal park, avoiding running through the wood, as it was too snowy. He took his phone and - when he was ready - he took a deep breath and left Shelley House.

Going out to run after the hangover wasn't the best choice. Indeed, at the end of his training, he felt unusually exhausted. He was breathless, and he had to interchange moments of running and walking, until he decided to stop. He stopped several times before reaching the plant nursery and - once he arrived there - he noticed that the streets were completely empty.

"If anything ever happen to me" – He thought *"I'll die all alone."* After he had tried to stand on his weary legs, he decided to stop to recover near the Ginkgo Biloba of Robins Garden. He began to overthink again. He was thinking of Brunhilde, who had split up with him over two weeks before. Then, he thought that he hadn't told his family that the marriage was called off. "At this point, it was good breaking up" – He thought aloud, even if he didn't know the reasons that had led

Brunhilde to break up their relationship. Then, Philip looked at the unusual clear sky which - after the storm that hit the town during the night - seemed that the clouds had been washed off from Slohan Oak.

He got up and started walking with a firm step through muddy paths, as well as some icy areas. He was overthinking to the point that he found himself to the wood. Thus, he realised that it was better going back home rather than heading to the municipal park. However, exactly when he was on his way to go back home, he heard the sound of broken branches coming from behind him. It suddenly pulled him back to reality. He stopped and heard someone whispering his name.

"Philip, come with me" – a female voice whispered. That persuasive voice was asking Philip to join her. This caused shivers on his lower abdomen, similar to an erection, which he tried to hide in embarrassment.

"Is that a joke?" – He told himself, convinced that he was hallucinating because of the hangover. However, that whisper was unexpectedly followed by shots. The most shocking thing was realising that he was the target of those shots, as the bark of the tree exploded in his face.

Urielle had just woken up and sat on the bed thinking about what happened the night before. If on the one hand she wanted to resume that conversation, on the other hand she wished it had never happened. After a quick shower, she brushed her hair and wear nice clothes. She went out into the corridor to join the other at the ground floor. She gave a look to Philip room and noticed that the door was still closed. She thought her reaction was too exaggerated but - as soon as the image of the wedding came back to her mind - she shook her head. She was angry with herself and reproached herself for having kissed Philip, her closest friend, the one who was engaged with another woman.

The atmosphere in the kitchen was festive, worthy of Christmas. Marta was busy in cooking the lunch, while Alice was trying to help her mother, although she wasn't familiar with cooking. They chatted cheerfully as they kept cooking. "Is there any coffee left?" – Urielle asked sitting down at the peninsula. "I would really need it… that bitter, strong Italian one, which would wake up even a dead person" – She added.

Alice poured her some coffee in a coffee cup. Then, she looked at her friend, noticing that she was absent.

"Is everything fine? You look lost this morning" – Alice told to her.

Urielle wrapped her hand around the hot cup sighed and hinted at a smile. "I'm okay. What about Aleister?"

"He will celebrate Christmas at the Manor with his family. I think it's right! Anyway, he will come here later to have coffee with us" – Marta replied, who interrupted the conversation to cheerfully talk about the lunch menu. "We have cooked this and that" but she stopped exactly when she was about to talk about the dessert. She had noticed that it was past ten.

"Someone wakes Philip up. He's such a sleepyhead!" – She exclaimed looking at her daughter. "Alice, can you do it? Your brother is always slow. If he wants to take a shower… we won't have lunch anymore!" – Then, she kept cooking. From time to time, she complained that her husband wasn't there to enjoy his time with his family. Unlike what many have believed, Marta had felt Mr. Murray's absence for years before he died. There wasn't intimacy anymore, and they shared they bed only because it was a habit. Only her children's love had been able to distract her from conjugal problems, allowing her to on without thinking too much about her marriage.

They soon realised that Philip wasn't at home. Marta burst out some Tuscan words, to the point that no one, except her, understood. Then, she looked incredulous at her daughter.

"How is it possible that your brother isn't at home? Did he go out without telling me? It's Christmas!" – Marta was unpleasantly surprised, and she began to not feel like preparing the lunch anymore. She tried to call him, but the only voice she could hear was that of the answering machine.

Philip returned home after a couple of hours, and his facial expression aroused concern in everyone. "Someone shot me while I was doing *fartlek*[11] in the wood" – He said slopping on the peninsula counter in front of Urielle, who gave him a glass of water. Philip took it and drank in one gulp with shaking hands.

"Who could it have been?" – Marta asked him. "A clumsy hunter? But is this hunting season? However, people can't hunt in this area! So, did you see his face? Was he a local? Phil, you have to go to the police!"

Philip - flooded by her mother's questions - said nothing, as he was unable to give any kind of explanations.

"Did you hurt yourself when you fell?" – Urielle asked, noticing mud stains on his clothes. Philip nodded, aware that he had escaped from a fatal event. Eventually, he was able to speak. He didn't tell them about that persuasive voice, as he thought it was due to his hangover and to his thoughts about Urielle and Brunhilde.

---

[11] A system of training for distance runners in which the terrain and pace are continually varied.

Urielle was right, he had fallen while escaping from what they considered a killer rather than a hunter. He must have been a killer because he had followed him. Luckily, he had manged to find shelter in an old refuge in the woods: a hatch which he and Alice had found when they were younger. Inside that hiding place, they had found a few pieces of furniture, a couple of old books and a lantern. When they had told Mr. Murray about that, they learned that it was a hideout used to escape the Nazis. The story of the hatch could have aroused concern in Marta, and for that reason it had remained a secret among Mr. Murray and his children. However, Mr. Murray had warned them, "Whenever you want to go to the hatch, you'll have to tell me."

That day, while Philip was running desperately to the hiding place, he had recalled his father's face to inform him *"I'm going to the hatch, dad."*

XVI

The Christmas lunch celebrations were put aside, as Philip decided to listen to his mother's advice, which was to go to the Police Station. It seemed to him the best thing to do. He knew that he could have relied on the police. However, Urielle and Alice's attitude was strange to him, as they had tried to persuade him not to report what had happened that same day, instead they had suggested to go to the police the following day. Alice - in particular - feared that if the matter of the music box ever came up, there would be inevitable consequences, as she had hided Dorothy's visit. She didn't want that such matter affected anyone, although she was aware that sooner or later each of them would be involved in what was happening in Slohan Oak. The more she thought about it, the more she hoped that day would never come.

"Alice, can you tell me what's wrong with you?" – Philip asked. However, she didn't know what to answer, as any possible explanation could have led her to talk about the Divum Deus. Thus, she just looked at her brother's eyes with a distant look.

"Exactly as I thought… you don't have to tell me anything. You made me wasting time, and I have to deal with important things!" – He replied annoyed. Then, Philip wore his coat and grabbed the keys of the car parked in the garage. It was one of the latest Mercedes models of which he was particularly jealous and for which he had a sort of obsession, "My baby" he had begun to call it. However, that day he didn't mind get the car dirty with his muddy clothes. He just wanted to get to the Police Station as soon as possible. However, as Alice saw him overstepping the threshold of the front door, she suddenly felt the need to go with him.

The building of the Station looks like a low brick building raised on one floor and equipped with few windows, making it seem a claustrophobic and poorly illuminates building. Exactly like many other places in Slohan Oak, that building had to face World War II's attacks, and only after the mid-21st century the local administration could restore it. Starting from the new millennium, the building was expanded during one of Mayor Brickenden's terms, during which he had dedicated himself to finish the fundraising campaign for *Fawcett Hospital* started years before. The hospital was inaugurated to allow pregnant women to no longer attend the *Melksham Community Hospital*, the closest hospital to Slohan Oak. Brinckenden's last term was the most edifying, as there was more liquidity available - twice the ones of the previous year. Thus - following the footsteps of the neighbour towns of Wiltshire - there was a desire to complete interventions of redevelopment. A wide part of the rural areas - located in the south-west - had been involved for the restoration of the water networks, as well as for the restoration of the roads and the streetlight. Furthermore, some check had been carried out on the plane trees to preserve the green areas, as some trees were potentially dangerous for passers-by. Thus, those centennial trees had torn down and replaced with new plants.

That morning there was no car parked at the Police Station parking lot, except three Police cars parked next to each other.

"Where is everyone?" – Philp asked in amazement, seeking for Alice's look.

"I told you to come here tomorrow."

"Well, I'll go in anyway. It won't take long. Would you prefer to keep watch and wait for me in the car?"

"To keep watch. Me? Since when I've been your guard?" – She asked frowning and, after having snorted she added "Okay, I'll wait for you here."

Philip got out of the car and headed to the Police Station. The automatic door opened with a long hum and - before going in - he turned to her sister and waved at her, chickling to himself thinking of the request he had made her.

Keep watch what? The Mercedes? Probably, even if Alice could arouse fear like a Cavalier King[12]. On the other hand, Philip hoped that the Station would be full of expert policemen who would have helped him. *The mastiffs* as many used to called them. Nevertheless, inside there was no mastiff waiting for him, except for a pretty *mermaid* in her thirties, looking at him from the guardhouse. The badge prominently displayed, as the embroidery under the pocket, which revealed her name, Tanisha Lewis.

"Good morning! I need to talk to Inspector Cole" – He said.

"Do you have an appointment?"

---

[12] Small breed of dog.

"Do I have to have it to talk to Cole?"

"Well, I'd say so" – the Officer replied annoyed. "If you tell me what you need, I can tell him myself."

"Look, Officer. I don't want to be rude, I'm not doubting of your expertise, but if Cole is here, I really need to talk to him."

"At least tell me why you came here on Christmas Day."

"I have to report... an attempted murder" – Philip almost hesitated before saying it, but as soon as he did, Tanisha Lewis' attention was entirely on him. At that point, the Officer said that she would have done everything possible to quicken the procedures. She asked him for his name and the detailed report of the events. Tanisha hadn't worked at the Slohan Oak Police Station for a long time. Indeed, she ignored the balanced that ruled the town - based on social class - the influence of certain people, as well as that of some political implications. The Murrays were completely strangers to her.

"When can I talk to him?" – Philip asked again.

"You can come tomorrow morning. In the meantime, I'll write the report" – The Officer replied.

"Everyone is telling me to come here tomorrow..."

"Excuse me Mr. Murray, everyone who?"

"Never mind."

Philip resigned himself. The thought that the Police Station had scheduled the work shift as if the criminals had observed their day of rest, terrified him. If until then he had thought of relying on the police, he suddenly realised that no one could ever help him. Not even the Officer Lewis.

There was a moment of silence where neither of them said a word. Philip waited hunched over the desk, looking to the clock hung on the wall to check the time. He also observed the temperature on the thermometer, which displayed more a higher temperature than the usual. *"Is it always so hot here?"* He thought to himself, tugging at the collar of his sweater.

Shortly thereafter, Officer Lewis received and internal call, making her leave the guardhouse. She moved away from the desk and began to observe the boy, analysing his tall and skinny body. Then, she reappeared, adjusted the collar of her uniform with her manicured tiny ebony hands. She told Philip that it was his lucky day. It seemed that the Inspector was ready to meet Philip in his office, even if no one had seen him in the building.

"McCarthy, can you walk him to the Inspector?" – The Officer Lewis asked to the younger policeman seated at his desk adjacent to the guardhouse, who until then had sipped hot coffee. His clumsy attitude marked his narrow shoulders, his face was gaunt, and his barycentre was higher, to the point that he didn't look very shapely.

Cole's office was well furnished, probably by Mr. Murray's fine tastes, a great friend of the Inspector. The scent of tobacco stirred in the room, as he held a cigar through his fingers. The Inspector was seated on his armchair with a businessman look rather than of a police officer. He had a well-groomed appearance, recently shaved and flawless blonde hair. The same could be said for his noble bearing, as well as for his well-defined jaws and his short, straight neck. His eyes were icy blue, capable of making the interlocutor forget of the tic he had to his eye. "Risks of the trade" – He would have said if anyone had ever noticed those tics. Even so, no one would ever think that he was almost sixty. Indeed, his athletic silhouette, his broad and well-defined chest and his convivial manners would have easily misled even his colleagues.

160

"Philip Murray, Merry Christmas! Please, take a seat and tell me what happened from the beginning" – He had welcomed Philip, who had found in him an almost fatherly attitude.

Donovan Cole enjoyed great success in the town and - having been always unmarried - many married and unmarried women would have liked to spend their time with him. However, there were many rumours about him and some of them had involved even Marta. Indeed, their friendly relationship had led many annoyed women to spread rumours that the two were involved in a love story which had begun long before her husband death.

Alice had stayed inside Philip's car waiting for her brother to finish the meeting. However, as she was tired of waiting for so long, she looked at the clock on the dashboard, wondering when that agony would end. She began to touch the Selenite pendant that she had worn around her neck, thinking how odd it was that her dreams had found a way to materialise themselves in real life. They had a "predictive" power and she sensed that something wasn't quite right. She thought that perhaps she just had to go to be visited by some good doctors relying on their care and wait for time to heal her mind. Since the night of her accident, the amnesia caused her disjointed thoughts.

As expected, Philip had stayed inside the Police Station for a long time, as he left the building after a long hour. Alice thought that her brother had successfully talked to the Inspector as Philip looked calm and relaxed.

"How did it go?" – She asked him.

"Oh, Alice! Talking to the Inspector turned out to be the best choice."

Thus, he told her about his meeting with Cole, who had recalled old memories of his youth with his great friend Murray. To celebrate that moment, they had even smoked a cigar together, and the Inspector had also given him a shot of *Scotch*, although Philip hadn't drunk it. Then, Philip told Alice that their mother had managed to get in touch with Cole, and it was for that reason that Cole had received him. Indeed, if it had been for Officer Lewis, he wouldn't managed to talk to him. Cole had listened to Philip's story smoking his cigar and drinking his Scotch, and - in the meantime - he had also checked the time on his inlaid pocket watch. He had immediately tried to warn Philip, and - as he said - there had been some thugs who had enjoyed scaring people and even killing wild animals. According to Inspector Cole, even the massacre happened in the dog shelter was due to a "probable religious person belonging to the black masses".

During that long narration - of which Philip seemed to be satisfied - a sudden need to smoke aroused in Alice. She realised that she had never been addicted to nicotine, as she had always considered herself as an occasional smoker. She knew that she could live without smoking for weeks, and so she allowed her a cigarette when she felt overwhelmed or simply to escape boredom. Alice had silently listened to her brother's speech on his meeting with Cole, nodding her head and showing little interest on that matter. She started rummaging in her pocket to look for her ciggies, of which only two had left.

"He told me to have some rest and to forget about this story. I fear that this little inconvenience has upset all of you. I'm

sorry you had to spend a horrible Christmas because of me" –
He told Alice.

Alice shook her head as she really cared about her brother's
serenity. Thus, if having gone to the Police Station made him
feeling better, then it was worth it. They both looked at the sky,
which had become dark and lead. Suddenly, Philip looked at
her anxiously.

"It's going to rain. I'll get in the car. Mum has already call
me several times, hurry up."
At the end of that break, Alice placed the remaining ciggie and
the lighter in her pocket, brushing her fingertips against an object that until then she had forgotten about. The group photo -
taken by her father in 1983 - was still inside the pocket of her
coat. As soon as she saw it, she shivered, her legs felt like jelly
and her face became paler. Although the photo was the same,
she realised that it looked different.

Indeed, other faces had appeared in the snapshot.

She bent over and vomited.

"You'd better stop with that crap, Alice" – Philip scolded
her as soon as they got inside the car. He had worried when he
had saw her going from healthy to feeble, and so he had
promptly got out the car to help her.

"I think it's gastritis" – She told him curled up on one side
on the seat. Then, she added "You're right, I'd better stop
smoking."

Alice preferred not to talk about what she had just seen,
about what her mind was trying to forget. She started staring
outside through the window, drawing small rings on the condensation, while the snow on the road - melted in the pouring
rain - had turned into mud.

"Just out of curious…" – Philip told her, catching her attention.

"Tell me" – She muttered.

Philip looked at her deep in thought, and - before he pronounced anything - Alice began searching for the musical review of the choir of Westminster Abbey in London. She hoped that children's voices could have appease that situation, which could have become thorny at any moment.

Then, Philip resumed talking.

"What's going on between you and Aleister?"

"We're just friends, I'd say."

"Are you sure?"

"Yes, that's how I can define us. Now, can you tell me what really worries you?"

Philip couldn't really understand how his sister could be so blind to the point that she couldn't catch any signs of love. However, when he turned his head to look at her, he could notice a familiar gaze in her eyes, typical of people involved in a feeling.

"Don't get me wrong, but the fact is that you haven't known him for very long. Be careful, Alice."

Alice thought about what her brother said, even though she didn't say a word. She knew that Philip felt responsible for her, and that by warning her he had fulfilled his big brother duties. Nevertheless, the more she looked at him, the more she sensed that he was hiding something from her. It could be said that Alice knew him as the back of her hand. Thus, the fact that he had been particularly thoughtful since he had come back from Switzerland was the proof that something worried him.

Suddenly, she thought again of the group photo, reproaching herself for always getting wrong ideas on things.

"Do you have to tell me something, Philip?"

Philip shook his head and tried to stay focused on the road.

"Maybe something about Brunhilde?" – She added.

"The situation is more complicated than it seems" – He replied.

"Oh, don't be mysterious and tell me about it."

"What I can tell you is that I've always thought that the marriage was a gamble."

"What do you mean? Don't you love Brunhilde anymore, or she isn't sure of what she feels for you?"

"Why do you say that?"

"Do you think I haven't noticed anything about you two?" – She told him.

"Of us two?"

"I'm talking about you and Urielle."

"She's involved, but only partially."

"Have you told Brunhilde about it?"

"Not what you think. As I told you before, it is more complicated than it seems."

"I think that if you get married, you'd make a big mistake. After all, you and Brunhilde barely know each other."

"I'm glad that the whole Murray's family thought that. What if I told you, that also dad thought that? Before he died, he used to tell me that Hilde was a complete stranger. Eventually, I ended up believing it too."

"Something must have happened to make you realise that. Your opinion on that was completely different few weeks ago."

"Brunhilde broke up with me few weeks ago, and the only explanation she gave me was that it was beyond her control. Now you know it."

"Exactly like the film *Dangerous Liaisons*?"

"Yes, exactly. She's very original, as you can notice. But please, don't talk about that to anyone. Not even to Urielle and to mum. God knows how she could react to such news."

Philip's focus was only on the road. He had turned up the radio to avoid any other question on that matter. Alice would have liked to know more about it, but she didn't want to bother him, telling herself that they would have talked about the matter later. Nevertheless, she was keeping secrets too, which were even more frightening than those of her brother. She was keeping telling herself that hiding such horrors to her family was the wisest choice so far.

Philip kept driving to Shelley House, as they were both humming Christmas songs.

XVII

Cole had reassured Marta about the events in Slohan Oak, and she had believed that the matter of Philip's report would be solved in short time. It was for that reason that Aleister hadn't been informed of that change of plan. Indeed, he had shown up at Shelley House for *coffee* time. After being informed of what had happened to Philip, he begun to feel nervous, as the same thing had happened to him. He walked along the hallway, looking at the driveway in the hope to see Philip's car. He couldn't understand why Marta and Urielle were so calm. It was under that circumstance that he rediscovered the bitter aftertaste of time that stops.

Although Marta thought she was apprehensive, she realised Aleister was even more nervous than her.

The phone rang and Marta picked it up.

"Any news?" – Aleister asked Marta, who waved her hand in a negative reply, while she was exchanging good wishes with her brother - Uncle Lory - who would have soon become father for the third time. As soon as she finished talking at the phone, Marta tried to reassure Aleister, then she headed to the kitchen. She tidied up trays and washed dishes and cleaned again the surface - which was already clean - with a wet mop. She used to engage herself in some domestic activities when she needed to think.

Urielle - on the other hand - had observed Aleister's worry, thus she decided to calm him down.

"Aleister, don't worry. You'll see they will come home soon." – She said whispering and avoiding touching him to not face any ultra-dimensional issues.

"Why are they taking so long there?"

"They both have phone. They'd have called if there had any trouble. Bureaucracy must have detained them."

"I know, she'll be back."

"Can you... sense it?"

"What?"

"Her arrival. Can you sense when she'll be back?"

"No, this isn't possible. I suppose they're coming back, or at least, that's what I hope. I sense only a call, her needs."

"Can you feel it now?"

Their voices were a little louder than a whisper.

"No, not now. It seems like there's interference. I fear that things will get more difficult over time" – Aleister replied, without adding anything else. His face and his gaze transpired great concern.

"If you feel healthy, then there's no reason why you should be so worried about her" – Urielle told him.

"I'm fine, but I can't calm myself down. I feel overwhelmed by so many thoughts. Urielle, tell me, how do you keep calm?"

"It's a natural human inclination. Sometimes thoughts comfort us, sometimes they arise concerns. Try to distract yourself, you'll see you'll feel better."

Aleister followed Urielle's advice. Thinking on things had become like dreaming; at times it made him feel good, but other times thoughts became like a prison. He tried to distract himself, and thus he went to the living room and sat at the piano. He slowly began to play the white keys, then - as the sound was relieving him - he began to play more fluently until composing a melody. As soon as the music spread within the house, Urielle - who was about to help Marta in the kitchen - stopped and amazed by the melody, she leaned dreamily against the door jamb.

"*Promenade no. 2*" – She said in hushed tones. Shortly after, Marta joined them, as she was in ecstasy by that melody.

The boy - who had never shown such skill - had proved to be a master in playing the piano without even the aid of the musical score.

Promenade no. 2 by *Musorgskij* aroused childhood memories in Urielle. Thus, she told it to Marta.

"*Maman* played it to me when I was little."

Aleister had continued to play, and - from time to time - he looked at her and then returned to observe the keyboard. As soon as he finished, Urielle asked him where he had learned to play, while Marta was amazed by that question which considered banal.

"Where do you think he have learned it? He must have taken piano lessons. It must be said that he plays it very well" – Marta told Urielle.

Aleister told them that he had learned playing the piano without taking any lesson. It wasn't totally a lie.

Urielle bit her lip for having embarrassed her friend with such a stupid question.

The sound of Philip's car engine made Aleister suddenly stopping playing the piano, and the sweet melody was immediately replaced by the sound of a low note accidentally played while he closed the keyboard cover. Thus, Aleister rushed to the front door. As soon as he tried to get closer to Alice, she walked away, aware of her breath with the aftertaste of vomit. She apologised and run to the bathroom.

"What happened to your sister?" – Marta asked Philip.

"Nothing worth worrying" – He replied unclearly. "She just threw up."

When Alice returned, she felt relieved at the idea that Philip had already begun to talk about his meeting with the Inspector, especially because everyone was focused on him. She took advantage of that moment to talk to Aleister, the only person - according to her - capable of explaining her what had happened. They went to the living room and sat down on the sofa. Alice noticed that he was particularly relaxed despite the circumstances, while she was worried, as usual. She continued to keep distances from Aleister, although she had brushed her tooth. Then, she cleared her throat.

"You looked worried" – He said.

"Aleister, I need to ask you a question. Do you believe in the paranormal?"

"I can tell you that it's like an airbag for humans, useful when something that can't be proved become intelligible. So yes, I believe in it. Why are you asking this?"

At that point, Alice gave him the photo, although he could only see a group of well-dressed young people.

"Who are these people? What does this photo have to do with the question you've just asked me?" – He asked confused.

"This photo was taken in Oxford and dates to 1983. I found it among some photo albums shortly after my dad's funeral. Until then, only my father and the silhouette of that young woman in the pink dress were recognisable. Now, I don't know how, Mayor Brickenden and James Harvey have also appeared" – Alice said, pointing out on their clear faces. "If you believe in paranormal, Aleister, it could be easier for you to accept all this. But I don't believe in anything related to the paranormal, so it's hard for me to understand."

Aleister was surprised. There could be the possibility that Alice's father had found himself - even accidentally - involved in the matter related to the Divum Deus. He began to run his hand on his chin and then up to his cheeks. Then, he finally spoke.

"I think that the Divum Deus is the common thread of all these deaths. I'm sorry to tell you that, but I think that also your father's death has something to do with this."

"The Divum Deus? Do you think that this could be an esoteric coven?"

"I fear so. We need to talk to Urielle about it."

Alice became paler. In the bottom of her heart, she had hoped that such affair wasn't related to any supposition. After all, in her clear consideration of life - where the world could be perceived only black or white - all other shadows were unacceptable for her. Until then, she shied away from any possibility that it could be part of the esoterism, just as she considered unacceptable that her father had lived a secret life.

"All my beliefs are now falling apart, one after the other. I can't imagine my father living in such a decayed context. There must have been a mistake" – She said agitated.

The verdict had considered Arthur Murray acquitted of all possible accusations. Nevertheless, they were aware that those words would have only anaesthetised the grief and avoided any bad thoughts on him. Therefore, Aleister tried to reassure her rather than to dissuade her.

He began to believe that Alice knew the answer to those questions. He realised that was really frightened her was to deal with the truth that would end up tearing down all the certainties she had.

XVIII

Sunday, 31st of December 2017

The following days slowly passed up to New Year's Eve. Aleister took the opportunity to reconfirmed Orpeco's invitation to Alice to celebrate together at Manor Falkenberg. Indeed, Aleister extended the invitation also to her family, who had except, other than Philip, who had to leave for Bern, although it seemed that he had planned the travel only the night before. He had informed his family less that twenty-four hours before, saying that there were some urgent matters to attend at work. When Marta was informed about it, she worried, as none of them was aware of how long he would be away from home. No one except for his siter, who could imagine the reason behind that sudden departure. She knew that it had something to do with Brunhilde and thus - aware of what her brother had told her - she didn't ask for further explanations.

Alice had something else to focus on than her mother's discontent. The matter of that photo had led her to focus on exonerating her father from the serious accusation regarding him and the Divum Deus. All that she needed was to be dynamic to prof to everybody that her father wasn't involved in such a matter. Thus, she took advantages of those quiet days to prove Mr. Murray's innocence.

She began her research soon after Christmas, as she could rely on Aleister's help, but not on Urielle's, who wasn't much enthusiast about that treasure hunt. Following the lead of the music box and the diary, they thought that if there have been a third stone, it could have been hidden in a valuable object or in something related to her father's childhood. Thus, they first went to Mr. Murray office located in Maddox Street, where they found only paperwork and deed of purchase and sale related to auction houses.

They spent the whole day sifting through the basement at Shelley House, where they had found only Alice's junk of which they had got rid of. Among the numerous binders there were Polaroids and snapshots dated to different years. However, nothing in there was dated to the same year of the group photo. They checked everywhere; at the back of the frames of every single pictures hang on the walls, among the ornaments scattered inside and outside the house, certain that their behaviour hadn't aroused any suspicious among the family members. During that last day of December, Alice had even checked through the closets of the house, and inside the drawers in the studio, until her mother interrupted her.

"Is Aleister here?" – Marta said while opening the door slowly. It seemed to her that she had to cross a barber wire, as Mabon was lying on the floor and seemed not to like anyone's presence, not even hers.

She went into the room cautiously.

"No, he's in the basement now. He's putting away the boxes to throw away. Did you need to talk to him?"

At that point, Marta closed the door and then added "Good", which conveyed her disappointment. "May I know what you two have been up to for days?" – Burst out Marta.

"Nothing, we're just tiding up."

"Alice, I'll tell it now as he isn't here: it's inappropriate to involve him in such affairs."

"Why?"

"Don't you know I don't like you to rummaging through the house? Especially in your father's studio. Philip had found it very hard to gather the files of the bequest."

However, Alice seemed to haven't grasp the message and - even more stubborn and after having stared at the desk - she turned her gaze to her mother. She asked her about the binders and the Oxford yearbooks, of which Marta seemed to have forgotten about.

"You should ask your brother" – She said with a biting tone. "Oh, no, you rather don't bother the *prince*. He's still in his room packing his suitcases."

Although Marta was looking for Alice's support to protest the sudden departure of her son, Alice didn't give her mother the opportunity to keep complaining. She would end up lying to her mother again if it wasn't that in that moment Aleister knocked at the studio door. Marta opened it and looked at him in dismay, thinking about what her daughter would have in store for him.

Aleister and Alice thought that - as they were running out of time - what they were looking for could be found at the house on the lake. If they hadn't made it in time that same day, they would have gone there the next day.

Philip finished his preparations. After having packed and put his shirts in the dustproof bags, he stored his already ironed clothes. He looked at his watch, realising that he still had time. However, he decided not to go downstairs to attend to her sister's staged moving. *"No way!"* – He thought. Thus, he took the opportunity to shave off the short beard that had appeared on his face in those days, and which he hated as he considered it a form of carelessness. In the meantime, he thought several times about what had happened to him in the woods and the annulment of his marriage, as well as to Urielle's kiss. Philip regretted having spent the holidays in Slohan Oak, as he had never felt as helpless as he did during the last few days at Shelley House. He could have clarified that matter by simply talk to Urielle and - although he considered her as the only person free of prejudice - he knew that telling her about the call he had received on Christmas Eve would have only confused her.

He preferred not to talk to anyone about that, as the situation was dangerous. He didn't talk either to his siter, who was partly aware of the situation.

Urielle was reading lying on her bed - or at least - she was trying to read, as she had been read the same paragraph countless times. In those days, she hadn't really felt like helping Alice and Aleister searching for clues related to Mr. Murray's photo. There was only a Murray haunting her mind.

After that kiss - better saying *the* kiss - she wondered if their relationship was only of pure friendship. She couldn't recognise if it was resentment of sadness prevailing over her reason. What she knew for sure was that their relationship would never be the same.

She tried to change her position on the bed, thinking that she could focus on her reading. Then, she set the pillows and started the chapter of the book over again. Even so, she lost her focus again after a few pages. Thus, she decided to close the book and place it on the side of her legs and started staring at the closed door. Suddenly, she had the feeling that there was someone behind the door. She got up and, on her tiptoe, reached the door, opening it slowly. Surprisingly, Philip was there.

"Were you spying on me?!" – She asked surprised.

"Don't be a fool. I was about to knock. I came here to say goodbye before leaving."

Initially, Urielle didn't tell him to get inside the room. However, as she was leaning behind the ajar door, she decided to open the door and ask him to join her in the room. Her heart begun to beat faster and sudden she felt unable to look at Philip's eyes.

"Do you have any idea what Aleister and Alice are up to?" – Philip asked.

"They're tiding up, or something like that" – She replied hastily.

"My sister always impresses me. Aren't you joining them?"

"No, not today."

"Good choice. What are you reading?" – Philip asked her while looking at the book on the bed. Then he took it to leaf it through.

"It's a book by *Le Whytes*. I've been stuck at the same chapter for a while. I think I'll give up for today."

"Is it interesting at least?"

"A lot, if you like this genre, of course."

"Do you think it's worth to be read?"

"Before today, I had no reason to think otherwise."

Philip didn't care at all about that book, they both knew it. Nevertheless, none of them had the courage to talk about what happened on Christmas Eve. Thus, they kept talking about that book with allusive words, until when Urielle couldn't take it anymore.

"Phil, we should talk about what happened the other night. It has been hard for me to ignore you for all these days."

The guy closed the book, causing a suspenseful pause. Now, Urielle had gotten his attention.

"Do you want to start?" – He asked her.

"Maybe we should ignore it."

"As you prefer."

Although Philip played it cool, Urielle forced herself to look at him, and recognised in his expression her own sadness.

Philip looked at her in the same way as one's attending the end of something that had never began with regret. All he could do was saying goodbye, but just like her, he wasn't ready for a goodbye.

"Take care Riri."

As soon as he stepped outside her room, common sense overwhelmed Urielle. Literally. She realised that letting him go would be such a huge mistake, which would haunt her for the rest of her life. Urielle couldn't be wrong once again.

She chased after him and grabbed the sleeve of his sweater.

"Phil, please stay."

That was enough to lead them from the corridor to the bedroom, stripped of their clothes but not of their fears.

XIX

Marta - as she did every year on the 31st of December - went from shop to shop. She bought homemade panettone from a bakery run by two Italians, the Clemente brothers. Then, she went to the flower shop and wished Mrs. Beans a happy new year, who had detained Marta more than necessary to talk about her old husband. Then, she gave Marta a small bag full of potpourri with the word *Greetings* embroidered on it, which Marta appreciated. They were small yet meaningful gestures that only old acquaintances could appreciate.

She went to other shops in Maddox Street, glancing at several shop windows decorated with shimmering colours. Then, she stopped at *Rose & Other Stories* to buy tiny box of butter biscuits. At Mrs. Danton's store she bought the blend of Italian coffee to be prepared with mocha, as well as candied fruit and spices. After the owner - a friend of Marta - had invited her to go to her house in Blagdon Lake in the Somerset, she left the shop. If Arthur Murray had still been alive, that afternoon would have been full off chaotic preparations. Indeed, they would have organised countless dinners with people of note in

Slohan Oak, such as the Brickenden, Donovan Cole and his girlfriend of the period, maybe the Harveys and the Prosecutor General Prestcote-Hill who - despite being widower - had always celebrated the New Year's Eve at his luxurious mansion.

The thought that some of them were passed away in the last months grieved Marta to the point that she didn't feel like going shopping anymore. However, she decided to go to Poppy Field Refuge. Months had passed since the last time she went there in July, and she felt a little ashamed of it.

The Poppy Field Refuge - which once was known as *Slohan Oak Community Home* - is located far from the centre. More precisely, it is located nearby the cemetery and close to Manor Falkenberg. The name was changed when Mr. Murray came to the presidency. Since 2008 - after having been shuttered for years - the refugee had had enough funds to restart the non-profit activity of the educational community. Arthur Murray had given it a name that could symbolised hope and - at the same time - the awareness of the difficulties of life, to which every human being has always been at the mercy of. Even so, the Council had revealed its disappointment. "Poppy Field? People will think of those who had died during the war!" the member had said, even if Arthur Murray had managed to obtain enough consents. He had often repeated that each of the kids at the shelter had fought a battle in their own way, and he didn't give in on this! Marta considered the shelter as her husband's one of the most significant charitable actions, while - on the other hand - the Council had always encouraged him to exert power over the Slohan Oak community. However, Marta had never had a say in that project, she was only appointed to take care of the garden around the building. Thanks to the gardener Gavin Amilia, that garden had become a jewel.

Gavin was a few years older than Alice and - exactly like her - he had both Italian and English origins. He was a smiling boy, and everyone could see that he was devoted to his work, even if it can't be said he was as lucky as Alice. His past was - indeed - troubled. Both his parents had passed away shortly after his eighteenth birthday, and since then, he had changed different jobs to live a better life.

Mrs. Murray had always appreciated his devotion to the gardening and his unconditional help towards Marta, but there was something about him that made her blush. She had the feeling of always having his eyes on her. On one hand, her tendency was to become more distant because of the embarrassment, but on the other hand, she felt flattered.

That afternoon they say goodbye to each other as always, and she smiled at him from distance. *"Oh Gavin, you could be my son"* she thought, then headed to the front door of the shelter.

The building is made up of two floors and is characterised by wide areas that serves as a dining hall and common rooms. The old dark furnishing had been replaced by light and colourful furniture in contrast with the imposing building. The bell rang to mark the start of the break. The children walked out of their classrooms, at first chaotically and then forming a single file. They were being accompanied to the canteen by four educators. The oldest kid was twelve years old, while the youngest - as required by the regulation - must have necessary turned three. There were thirteen children in total, coming from different places of the County. Although their life had been bitter, they looked as carefree, as if they were attended a normal school rather than a shelter. They welcomed Mrs. Murray by going to meet her joyfully, as their childish laughter echoed in the corridor. Then, Marta was noticed by one of the educators who joined her. It was Lauraine Ratcliffe.

She was the most loved volunteer among the ones of the refugee. This was probably due to her infectious smile and her relaxed expression which reassured the children. Walking towards Marta, the educator thought that Marta's visit was at the right time.

"Miss Ratcliffe, I don't want you to waste your time. I came only to say hello and to apologise of not having given the gifts in person this year."

"Oh Mrs. Murray! I'm so happy to see you. You don't have to be sorry for that" – She said, placing her hand on Marta's shoulder. "I would have called you in the next few days. Now, let's go to my office."

The woman had long dark hair tied in a ponytail that run down her back, and which swung as she walked to her office.

At first, they talked about general issues, then, they had to deal with more serious issues: lack of funds and the risk of shutting down.

"How is it possible?" – Marta asked.

"We no longer receive donations like we used to. It seems that people have forgotten what this shelter means for these kids. We thought that things would have changed during the Christmas period, but that didn't happen."

"We must find a way to sort it out. The shelter can't be closed."

Miss Ratcliffe went to the desk and took a brochure.

"There would be a solution. This year we should celebrate the tenth anniversary of the shelter, but it would be in May. However, we don't have enough funds to make it until May."

Marta hesitated, then she replied, "My husband, Arthur, has always made sure that I don't get involved in the management... nevertheless, this belongs to the past, and I think that now it's time for a change. If you don't mind, I can apply for the Council."

"I wish I could support you, but it's not easy to make those people change their mind. You'll probably clash with the current President, as well as your husband's deputy, Ronald..."

"Ronald Carmichael, I know him. However, if I put pressure on the issue of my husband's death, maybe I can obtain something. You could put me in a good word!"

Suddenly, a tiny blond little girl appeared. She didn't reach the door handle since she was very little, and she had started eavesdropping behind the door instead of having her snack with the other kids.

"Come in Wendy. I want to introduce you to someone" – Said Miss. Ratcliffe, encouraging the little girl not to be shy.

"Tell me Wendy, how old are you? – Marta asked her. However, Wendy didn't answer, she rather made a sign that she was four. She tended to cover half of her face as she was suffering from a reddish angina. This, along with her inability to speak made her shy and unwilling to play with the other children. Then, the little girl began to observe Marta with suspicious, grabbing to the educator's arm whom she considered the only lifeline. At that point, Miss Ratcliffe made her sit on her lap. "You should join your friend to have your snack, little girl."

Wendy continued to hide her face on the educator's chest.

"Come on, let's go!"

Before the little girl was taken to the door, Marta rummaged through her bag and gave her a box bought at the pastry shop.

"Take it" – She said. "Go share them with your friends."

Then, the little girl left the office.

"Wendy Boyton is one of the rare cases. She was born with a malformation of the larynx that doesn't allow her to speak. However, she's able to breath and feed normally. She struggles to integrate with the other kids; she's learning sign language. The only person she's comfortable with is the gardener, Gavin. Perhaps he reminds her of her brother killed by her father."

"What about her mother?" – Marta asked, while Miss Ratcliffe sighed.

"He's a monster. One day he came home in withdrawal and killed both his wife and his son."

Marta shaken.

There have been some horrific events in Slohan Oak of which she couldn't get over. Until her husband's death, she had thought that the microcosm of Shelley House could her family safe from real life atrocities.

On her way back home, she was certain that the town was no longer as safe as she had thought. She had the feeling that something evil was creeping exactly like water flows into crack, digging up until becoming a flood.

XX

Eight o'clock came in a flash, and so were the celebrations at the Manor. The Murrays were greeted by Madame Dutrieux and Mr. Orpeco, who unexpectedly smiled, and wore an orange silk waistcoat. He looked at the guests as one looks at a successfully made work. There was no hint of annoyance on his face, nor a hint of regret in having invited Alice's family.

Dinner was the fateful moment. While seated around the table, they talked about different topics, interchanging with few moments of embarrassing silence. However, there were much empty moments, as Orpeco led the conversation to different topics, for each of which he seemed to know a lot.

Aleister had the feeling that both Orpeco and Madame Dutrieux were following a script.

"It's strange that before I met Aleister I had never known about you. I've heard a lot about the property" – Marta said.

"This place has withstood the war; we are only transitory beings. but I'm pleased to finally thank you in person. Your husband's help for the Falkenberg's property meant a lot."

"Arthur only acted for a good cause. He has always been altruistic, and I'm sure he would have appreciated these words."

"Behind the action of every great man, there's always the virtue of a great woman. For this reason, I chose to pay homage to you husband's kindness by making build the samurai statue. I don't think there's a stronger symbolism capable of enclosing the very essence of a man of values."

Marta just smiled at Orpeco, thinking that she had avoid thinking to her deceased husband. There were no reasons, not in that context. *Behind the action of every great man, etc., etc.* seemed to her a mere phrase of circumstance. For an instant, she realised that every single person she had bumped into had always found a way to talk about Arthur Murray.

"What statue are you talking about?" – Alice suddenly asked.

"The statue of the samurai portrayed with his fox, the *Kitsune*" – Orpeco replied, almost astonished that the girl didn't know about it.

"Come on Alice, the samurai statue…"

Marta - who was seated next to her - touched Alice's leg with her foot as a sign to stop asking questions. It was clear that Alice had never known of that statue, as her mother had always considered it inappropriate for Shelley House. Indeed, Marta had arranged the statue elsewhere, more precisely at the house on Lake Hoarmere. Away from everything, especially from her gaze.

"Oh, now I remember."

Alice was clearly embarrassed, and Orpeco had noticed it too. It could be seen on her face that she was lying. It would have been impossible not to remember the life-size bronze statue, so, how can it not be noticed inside the house? The man tried to ignore it, hiding his disappointment. He couldn't believe that Mr. Murray had hidden that priceless gift from his family.

When Aleister was asked if he liked the statue, he lied exactly like Alice, saying that he was amazed by such beauty. Orpeco didn't believe a single word, and his disappointment became more and more evident. Only after telling oriental legends, he became more relaxed.

They had told stories until dessert, as Orpeco had tried to focus on the whole conversation not to find a possible contradiction in anyone. He talked incessantly about traditions, about the founding fathers and finally about the Japanese emperors. Although he knew a lot about the topic, he ended up boring everyone.

"Do you have any brothers or sisters, Wallace?" – Marta asked, interrupting his tales. Then, she began to look at the man. According to her, Orpeco embodied the typical refined man, both in appearance and manners, although she couldn't understand why he wore a huge napkin around his neck.

"A sister."

"Does she live in Wiltshire?"

"Not anymore. Aleister's parents died many years ago."

As soon as Orpeco pronounced those words, he looked at the dessert avoiding Urielle and Aleister's gazes.

Aleister puzzled as Orpeco had tried to come up with that story. He turned his gaze to Madame Dutrieux, who - contrary to what he expected - showed no hesitation. Marta apologised for having asked such a personal matter. Thus, her attempt to shift from the tales about the samurai ended up saddening her.

That evening ended with the traditional countdown, and, after the midnight, the sky was lit up and coloured with fireworks. A succession of colourful explosions, spheres of whitish stars of *chrysanthemum* and combinations of bright *planets* appeared in the sky.

As expected, it began to snow again, first weakly, then a storm hit the town. That inconvenient anticipated the guests' leaving. Marta took a taxi with Urielle, while Alice and Aleister chatted in the ballroom. They laughed at Orpeco talkative behaviour and at the tales about the samurai. None of them mentioned Aleister's childhood.

"Tell me" – Aleister said. "How is this *Kitsune*? I would have noticed it if he had been at Shelley House."

"If I tell you something, do you promise you won't tell it to your uncle?"

Aleister nodded, ready to hear her confession. Alice told him that the statue was elsewhere, along with other valuable antiques. They both grasped the irony behind the word "valuable".

"You'll show it to me tomorrow" – He said.

Alice began to hint to uncoordinated, yet graceful, dance moves on the notes of an absent music. Aleister observed her refined body moving and forming wheels with the hem of the fluttering dress. Then, he went to the piano to play her a sweet melody which could allow her to dance.

"What are you playing?" – She asked.

"It's called *Borealis*."

"The name is familiar, although I think I've never heard it."
Alice continued to dance like a butterfly close to the piano.

"Who's the composer?"

"I'm composing it right now, just by looking at you."

Alice stopped dancing after that answer. Then, she walked to the piano. That feeling was growing in her chest, her stomach was like a tangle of dancing moths. But she was scared to indulge that instinct.

"It's late, Aleister. I'd better go home" – She told him.

XXI

Monday, 1ˢᵗ of January 2018

The fateful day of the year, January 1ˢᵗ, came, and bringing a leaden sky that suddenly turned into a bright blue one. As usual, there were those who had drawn up their own balance sheet of their past year. You could see people smiling everywhere: on the porch of their houses, along the streets and even in their beds.

Once again, good intentions had influenced everyone's way of thinking and buried the old intentions, while hope spread among the people, still sleepy from the celebrations of the previous evening.

Aleister got up in the early morning. Although the atmosphere of the new year could have influenced him too, he thought that any good intentions would be a vain attempt to interfere with fate, as mad had always tried to list their good intentions and then destroy them. He had heard of good intentions from anyone but himself. He couldn't promise to behave differently as he thought he had always acted in the name of good, solving any possible situation without telling lies. Nevertheless, the more he thought about his morality, the more he realised that if there was anyone in the world who had to promise himself to improve his behaviour, it would have been Orpeco. Indeed, Aleister hadn't been able to rest that previous night as the man - who Aleister called uncle - had unexpectedly told him his false secrets. The boy couldn't understand why he came up with such a lie on his presumed deceased sister. To be honest, Aleister hadn't even tolerated that Madame Dutrieux covered Orpeco's back.

He couldn't indulge Orpeco's lies anymore; he got nervous at the idea of having to listened to other lies without any right to reply. Thus, he would have changed his mind and take into consideration the idea of drawing up a list of good intentions. Aleister realised that he couldn't pretend anymore, thus, he decided that it was time to talk about that to those who were involved.

Orpeco was in his studio, sitting at his desk, next to a pile of books that he would take with him to the bookshop. He was sipping a cup of coffee, the first one after a long time as he suffered from tachycardias. He was having breakfast while reading some boring bills and - from time to time - he adjusted his glasses. He was surprisingly relaxed and - as soon as Aleister made his entrance in the studio by slamming the door he knew that quiet would be broken.

"Orpeco, I need to talk to you. Where is Madame Dutrieux?"

"Good morning, son, and happy new year. Today is her day off. Tell me, what troubles you?"

"Please, tell me you're joking!"

"Oh, are you referring to this?" – The man pointed to the cup of coffee. "Sometimes I allow myself to have a cup of coffee, even if Madame Dutrieux doesn't want me to overdo. Let me pour you some, you look tired."

"Stop it! You know what I'm talking about. You're going too far."

Although Orpeco had a lot to say, at first, he didn't answer. Then, he put his bills aside, placed his glasses in their case, sipped his coffee, and folded his arms.

"Well, this situation has worsened for a long time" – Replied the man – "I'm sorry to have to tell it to you and hurt your pride. If there's someone to blame, that's you. If we've come this far, it only because of you" – Orpeco scolded him.

"And so, I would be the cause of your deceptions. Is this the truth?"

"I don't expect any kind of gratitude from you, our agreements were clear. You would have stayed here to watch over the girl, without inviting her family and other things like that. What do you think? Do you think that you came here to write your story on earth? I suggest you consider the idea of lying when the situation requires it. That's what humans do!"

Orpeco stretched out his arm to take a key from a small box to unlock the drawer, from which he took various photos.

"Humans? You don't know anything about them! You've been locked up within these walls thinking that you could forget; thinking that your regrets would have disappeared. Orpeco, you're just a coward!"

Orpeco suddenly stopped rummaging through the drawers, as he had found what he was looking for: a mint green coloured folder. Inside it there were numerous documents, including pages of an old newspaper.

"I really had a sister" – He said – "Her name was *Cecile*, and she was adopted too. She died in a tragic car crash with her husband. That they weren't your parents, that's another matter. Anyway, once you've finished reading, put the file into the drawer and lock it. Ah, don't mention it to anyone. Remember, *no one*" – He sighed sadly. "Only over time you'll understand what humans are capable of. I fear that your appearance has only speed up the process..."

XXII

Marta was standing on the threshold of Shelley House's front door, wearing a warm jacket, and overwhelmed by her thoughts. She seemed absent, and - as her gaze was lost in space - she cuddled in that jacket which once belonged to her husband. She had the strange habit of relieving her sorrow by wearing one of the clothes belonged to those she loved to inhale their smell. Indeed, she often wore Alice's t-shirt, as well as Philip's sweaters, especially when he attended the college. She used to do it when melancholy or anguish knocked on her door.

On that festive day, full of expectation, Alice kept company to her mother. She went downstairs to catch up with her mother and noticed her exhausted expression.

"Mum, what's up? You look so sad. You miss him, right?" – Alice said, pointing out to her father's jacket.

Marta sadly told Alice that one of the girls of the shelter had disappeared during that same night. Indeed, little Wendy Boyton couldn't be found since the previous evening. For this reason, Marta had talked on the phone with Lauraine Ratcliffe for the whole morning, and she couldn't understand how it could have happened. Not sure whether to go to the Danton's house on the lake, Marta feared that little Wendy was victim of a criminal and that she would probably never return. She thought about how the educators could have felt, especially Miss. Ratcliffe who - as she couldn't have children - took care of other's kids as if they were hers. Marta couldn't believe that something like that could ever happen to her children, and - the idea that Philip was away from home - made her even more scared. Although she was aware that her staying in Slohan Oak wouldn't help find Wendy, she was also aware that staying was the right thing to do. She was looking for her daughter's gaze, as if she had the answer for all her doubts. However, Alice just hugged her.

Alice could smell her father's scent on the collar of the jacket and - for few seconds - the memories of the rare moments of tenderness shared with her father came to her mind. Suddenly, she felt nostalgic, she missed his hugs, then swallowed, trying to repress every emotion.

Eventually, Marta decided to accept the invitation and thus go to the Danton's home. She packed everything she needed inside a huge suitcase that she put into the boot. Then, she asked Alice if she wanted to go with her to Somerset. Alice refused, reminding her mother that she was going to the house on Lake Hoarmere with Aleister.

Later in the morning, Alice put all the boxes - full of trinkets that had encumbered the basement - into the boot of her car. She realised that there were a lot of boxes to get rid of, and that - if she had kept wasting time - she would have never made it in time. Thus, she made her way to the Manor to pick up Aleister.

The journey to Hoarmere took longer than expected, aided by the fact that the story Alice told Aleister about little Wendy had left the boy speechless. Although they tried to convince themselves that the affair wasn't related to the recent events and to the Divum Deus, they had concluded that everything was actually connected. By thinking so much of that matter, Aleister fell asleep. His ability to have dream had developed over the last weeks, although lately he was only able to experience nightmares. He dreamt of shots, followed by female screams and the sound of shattered glass underfoot. He couldn't find peace even when he slept. His body unconsciously startled a few times, until when he opened his eyes and woke up with a jolt. Then, he saw Alice approaching to the house.

"Are we still on the way to the lake?" – He asked.

"The highway was detour. The police halted some areas as investigations are underway. It took us a little longer, but we have just arrived. By the way, what were you dreaming of? You said, '*Watch out!*'"

They both tried to turn on the heating, but when their hands touched, Alice noticed that his skin seemed to be on fire.

"I don't remember" – He replied.

"I still don't understand why your skin is so hot, but you always feel cold. Are you sure you don't have any kind of flue?"

"Don't worry, I'm fine" – He said sharply.

Once she parked the car in the garage, he gave her no reason to talk again about that matter, and - although he was freezing - he unbuttoned his coat.

Alice ruminated on what happened. Every time it came to talk about him, he was unable to open up with her. In the last few weeks, everyone's life had been hard, and this should have inevitably brought them closer. They had become the protagonists of horrific and unknown events, whose end was still undefined. Could she really consider her father's death the cause of her family's daily life deterioration? Or it was due to something else, like Aleister's arrival? Besides that, he hid secrets that - if put together - would form a chasm. Alice was aware of that. She thought of the first time she met him and - since then - she hadn't been able to figure out where he came from. Nevertheless, she hadn't lost her nerve, as – otherwise - she would have also been wary of Urielle, who had behaved strangely on that situation.

Inside the garage, there was a small boat - the *Amor* - with outboard motor, belonged to her father. It was old-fashioned and decorated with white and blue friezes resembling the tail of a mermaid. That boat was mostly used when they spent Sundays on the lake. It occupied enough space in the garage, and indeed Alice's car was half parked under the porch. When Alice got out of the car, she hesitated a few seconds to look at that boat, without saying anything. It had been a long time since the last time she had seen the *Amor*, and this saddened her. Even when the police had informed her family of the incident, she hadn't' rushed there that same day. Indeed, she had left her job to join her mother in the hospital, preferring not to ruin all the good memories she had of that house.

Aleister got out of the car, admiring the winter shades of that place. Lake Hoarmere was frozen, the trees were partly covered with snow, while the sunlight warmed up their faces. All those details turned the coldest season of the year into an intimate one, although they hadn't the chance to grasp those details when they went to Brinckendens' house. Now, Aleister could enjoy the peace of that place.

The wooden building - which overlooks the lake - is set next to the parking slot, while a footbridge connects the house to the lake. Alice headed to the porch, covered with leaves and branches, noticing a wet plastic enveloping the swing, thus she decides to remove it.

Anyone who saw the house would have noticed that it was uninhabited. The phone line was out of order, while the white phone had become an ornament. The furniture was covered with sheets to protect it from dust. The house was animated only by the small entrance hall full of fishing equipment.

"It's beautiful here" – Aleister said, taking a box with him.

"Yes, a lot. We used to come here in the summer. It was fun."

"When was the last summer you came here?"

"A few years ago. Shortly after my brother moved to Brunhilde's house. She came her too, only once."

"What happened afterwards?"

"Things have changed over time. Since my brother had left, my family split. My parent's marriage was the first to be affected by his departure. Thus, my father had started to come here alone."

Alice put down the last pile of boxes, then sighed. At that point, they only had to place everything inside the outside cabin. She began to look around herself, observing the number of everyday objects scattered around the room. Everything seemed new to her, including some copies of white marble totem animals. She had the feeling that she couldn't consider that place like home, not anymore. She walked to the fireplace and took an old family photo. Alice thought that she hadn't seen none of her family smiling in such a way in a long time. The way she talked about her family made him notice that she was worried especially for Philip. Indeed, Alice was sure that behind her brother's carefreeness there was only a strong need of approval. He hadn't been able to say *no* at the right time, and that life that his father had bequeathed him had only made him hostile towards the father.

They got back to their business. The dust had covered all those antiques, as well as the old furniture, once considered refined. The samurai statue had disappeared, but Alice was not surprised with that. Even though they only had to tidy up *a few things*, they would have time to enjoy their day on the lake.

Aleister did exactly what Alice was doing.

He was placing the boxes when he was suddenly distracted by some old sheets of paper on the ground. He bent down and pick them up. They were poems written in Italian belonged to Marta, as there was her signature at the bottom of the page.

Intrigued, he read one.

Boreal

Hypno in oblivion,
which motionless satisfies us,
summoning minds in a deceptive death.
One day it left poppies
and reached the eternal light.

Marta Brunori

As soon as he looked up to ask Alice how it came that those poems had ended up there, the glint of a metal object - hidden among other trinkets - caught his attention. It was the glare of a katana held by the samurai and placed next to the *kitsune*. He had managed to find the statue Orpeco had talked about. Then, he told it to Alice. Inside the intertwined handle of the weapon, there was a stone, which was identical to those found in Timothy Brickenden and James Harvey's relics.

Aleister frozen.

He couldn't believe that their suppositions on Alice's father were turning out to be true. Mr. Orpeco's thoughts on the human nastiness were true. At this point, they had to find the responsible who had started all those atrocity in Slohan Oak.

"Alice, we are in danger" – He whispered.

XXIII

Urielle was sitting on the windowsill of the kitchen window in her tiny apartment, while her eyes were turned to the sky. She was trying to absorb as much as possible the positivity and the heat released by the sun. A thoughtful air was drawn on her face, as she couldn't find the answers to all her doubts. That morning, she had tried to get in touch with her parents, but they didn't reveal themselves. It had never happened before that day that her parents didn't respond to her request. It seemed that they were fading away as quickly as a cheap and volatile perfume evaporates from the collar of a dress. Urielle couldn't bear it. She decided to talk to her grandmother Yvonne to figure out what was interfering between the earthy and the astral dimension. Nevertheless, her grandmother revealed herself only for a few moments, not enough to prove her with an answer. Probably, it was time to say goodbye to them. Maybe they had permanently ended up into the cosmos, as it often happens to the wandering souls.

As soon as the impossibility of get answers caused her nausea, Urielle began to look for something to eat that could alleviate starvation. She settled for a cup of cold milk and warmed up a packaged of chewy chocolate croissant. Bite after bite, the thought of Philip spread in her mind. The memory of their intimacy, as well as that of his skinny body, accelerated her heartbeat. She took a firm bite of that croissant, while a sense of shame rolled down her back; the fact that the guy could leave her pending, made Urielle feel embarrassed. Feelings had taken over reason, she was aware of that, but she couldn't accept such a truth.

She needed to get distracted.

Urielle finished her breakfast and then went to her room. She unpacked the duffel bag she had brought for her staying at Shelley House. After having put away some of her clothes, her eye was caught by James Harvey's diary. She thought that - focusing on the diary - she would have mitigated the sense of dismay. She took a piece of paper and then sat down on the bed. She had decided to write down the seven animals mentioned and - as soon as she tried to link the animals with the faces portrayed in the photo dates 1983 - a possible solution popped in her mind. The horned snaked mentioned was the author of those events: James Harvey himself.

She had completely forgotten of James Harvey's dental diastema that made him hiss, making him look like a snake. However, those were only Urielle's deductions, there was no certainty. Indeed, also Timothy Brinckenden's connection to the crow seemed improbable to her. The girl knew that the enigma was out of her league. In any case, what was written on the last page - before the ink faded on those pages - confused her even more.

"...*Where silence reigns forever*. Go to hell!"

Urielle threw the diary against the wall in anger. Then, she ran her hands through her head, and sank into the blankets, staring at the ceiling. That was the version of herself she hated the most: when the only solution was to give up. She was too upset to keep her focus on finding answers. She would have had all her answers in any other context, but at that moment, it seemed that her reason was obfuscated, while her feelings were all the rage. Urielle was on the verge to throw in the towel. However, she wasn't aware of what time had in store for her.

Shortly after, the door rang, making her start and interrupting her thoughts. She wasn't expecting anyone's visit and - as far as she knew - Alice and Aleister had gone to the lake. Thus, she thought it was Orpeco. She had glimpsed him from the shop windows, busy in tidying up the shelves. She hadn't considered to involve him in her research. However, his visit would have been helpful; at that thought she almost cheered up.

She tied her long brown hair into a ponytail, then rushed to unlock the door. It wasn't Orpeco standing on the threshold, but Philip.

"Why are you here? Or better, how did you get inside the building?" – She asked him.

"Hi Urielle. I'd say you're glad to see me here. By the way, it seems that you need to fix the main door, it remains open" – He replied ironically.

"I wasn't expecting you. I thought you were in Switzerland."

She invited him to join her. Philip dropped his suitcase on the floor - the same ones he was carrying the day before – except for a leather briefcase. He told Urielle he needed to talk to her. Then, he sat in the living room, opened his briefcase, and began taking a set of documents off a small gray folder. Philip seemed anxious to hand the folder over to Urielle. However, he wanted to make sure that she wouldn't tell anyone that he was back in Slohan Oak.

"By the way. I didn't go to Bern yesterday. I stayed at the Baglioni, in London" – He confessed her.

"Why did you do so?"

The guy sighed. "I had a meeting with Investigator Simon Basset. I hired him to carry out investigations."

Philip was ready to share with her what it seemed to be a state secret. He handed the documents to Urielle, who read them quickly. The first sheets were a list of bank transactions, followed by countless event reports, marked by dates and times. Among those sheets, something caught her eyes. There were some notes reporting Brunhilde sightings both at Bern and Southampton airports. Then, she read the label of the file aloud.

"*Brunhilde Richter.* Are you serious? Are you stalking your future wife? I don't understand, why did you hire a private Investigator? I don't think she would like that" – Urielle claimed, while Philip began to tell her the story.

"Shortly after Brunhilde and I decided to get married, she broke up with me for no reason…"

"Go ahead."

"Of course, this is not the reason that had led me to take a similar decision. In case you were wondering, I'm not that dumb. She had split up with me over a phone call. After we broke up, I went to the place she works to give her the keys of her apartment, it was the right thing to do. I didn't want to send

204

the keys to her apartment by post. And guess what? Brunhilde had never worked at the law firm as she had always told me."

"Why has she lied to you? If she doesn't work there, then where?"

"That's why I hired Bassett. Well, Brunhilde doesn't work for any law firm, neither in Bern nor elsewhere in Europe. According to Bassett's research, she's not qualified as a lawyer. As for the documents you have just read, an encrypted bank account pays her a fixed amount of money early in the month. Can you guess where this bank account is from?"

"I really don't know" – Urielle replied uncertainly.

"From Paris. Basset is taking care of the case. I know it's complicated, but it's my duty to safeguard my family's financial interests. I cannot act foolishly this time. It hurts me to say it, but my father was right; I had to stay away from her."

"Are you sure you're okay?" – She asked him.

That wasn't a question of circumstance; Philip's face expressed resignation and awareness. Learning about such a news would have been a blow to anyone. Nevertheless, Urielle could notice that - compared to the last few days - the boy seemed to be completely reborn.

"Yes, I'm fine" – He replied. "Now that I know the truth, I feel at peace with myself."

Urielle was even more confused. First the Divum Deus and its stones, now Brunhilde and her deceives. That period was strange and full of inexplicable and unknown events. Urielle didn't know whether to feel flattered or to be alarmed that Philip hadn't talked to anyone else about that story but her.

"Was it this story what you were trying to tell me on Christmas Eve?" – Urielle asked him.

"Yes, Riri. The Investigator had called me in the middle of dinner, before your toast. "

"If Brunhilde hadn't lied to you in such a horrible way, would you have acted in the same way?"

Philip slowly got up from his chair and sat down next to Urielle without ever stopping to look at her, just as if in that way he could anticipated her reactions. Then, he could notice fear in her gaze. He could clearly see that she feared abandonment, and that sensation was confirmed by her behaviour, as she tried to take her distance from Philip. She firmly thought that feelings would have only complicate things. She had always been enough for herself and lived with this condition and certainty: the truth was that she feared bonds and relationships.

They didn't bring the conversation to a higher level, as it wasn't necessary to add anything else that they both didn't already know. However, in the very moment that Philip took her pajama bottoms off - without ever stopping kissing her - the doorbell rang.

Ding- dong.

XXIV

"Were you expecting someone?" – Philip asked confused, while his erection was pushing against the fly of his trousers. He begun to gather all his belongings, hoping that it wasn't her sister. However, as soon as he heard a breathless female voice from the doorphone, he realised it was Alice. Thus, he had to accept that sudden meeting.

He hadn't considered that her sister's arrival would complicate the situation. She would have become suspicious of his non-departure from Wiltshire. In the best scenario, she would have sulked at him. However, Philip feared the worst, not knowing how to deal with it, unless telling her the truth.

Alice looked awfully afflicted. She didn't come alone as Philip had thought. Indeed, Aleister came with her, which would have made the situation worse. As soon as Alice crossed the threshold of the apartment, she noticed the luggage on the sidelines. The first thing she did - without explaining the reasons of her sudden arrival - was to ask if her brother was there.

Philip's voice came from the end of the corridor, which served as answer to Alice's question. When he shown himself up, Alice noticed that his hair was completely messy, and his shirt was untucked. Anyone could have understood that Alice and Aleister's arrival had interrupted them. Philip didn't hesitate, as if he were act mysteriously, he had only worsened the situation.

"It's because of Brunhilde. I have to talk to you" – Philip said, trying to calm everyone's down.

Urielle didn't say anything, she just looked at Aleister. Then, they both went to the kitchen to make some tea. Neither of them wanted to interfere in Alice and Philip's conversation, although it was almost impossible to ignore Alice's disappointment coming from the adjacent room.

"Please, tell me that's not what I think... does it have to do with Mr. Murray?" – Urielle asked Aleister.

"Yes, it's exactly that. Arthur Murray was involved in the Divum Deus affair."

Their conversation quickly moved to another level. Exactly as it had happened some time ago, she could grasp that Alice and Aleister's arrival was always a presage of unpleasant news. A split second was enough for Urielle to grasp it. The girl put a hand on her forehead and stared at the floor. She was aware that detail would make a difference and overturn the situation. Such a news not only would have upset Alice, but also Philip. Moreover, involving him in their investigation would have only increased the bad consideration Philip had about his father.

"I don't think it's a good idea to tell Philip about that" – Urielle thought aloud.

"It's hard for me to hide my real nature, but you can be honest with each other, so I think you should stop lying. Lies are like an addiction" – Aleister claimed.

When the tea was ready, the two brothers made their entrance into the kitchen and, as Urielle noticed their facial expressions, she realised that Philip's fears turned out to be unfounded.

Besides some misunderstanding and Philip's decision to keep Alice in the dark about Bassett's investigations, everything seemed to be sorted out. Philip felt relieved, even if - sooner or later - he had to inform his mother.

That moment of lightheartedness didn't last long. Indeed, Alice took the photo dated 1983 out of her jacket and placed it on the table. Then, she placed the milky stone that belonged to her father next to the photo. Her decision to disclose all those events to her brother was due to an impulsive behaviour, as she hadn't asked anyone's opinion on that.

"What's that?" – Philip asked.

"We need to talk" – Alice said.

"Oh! Amazing."

"Philip, the less you know, the less you'll be disappointed. You can leave the room if you want. It's up to you. Alice don't involve him in this affair" – Urielle interrupted them.

Philip laughed, as he didn't really gather the meaning of Urielle's words. He thought that his sister had become obsessed with some old stuff she had found in the basement at Shelley House, and that she considered that moment suitable to recall the good old days. Then, he looked at Urielle and Aleister, realising that they were both unperturbed, exactly like Alice, who hadn't replied to Urielle's petitions.

"It will upset you to know what I'm about to say, but it's necessary" – Alice told her brother, before telling him the story since the beginning.

"That's not good at all" - He thought.

When Alice had finished to informed him about those latest events, Philip's reaction was predictable. As Urielle had thought, he felt subdue by a crescendo of feelings: scepticism, amazement and even disappointment, in that exact order. He didn't answer, yet it was Alice who incited him, as she had said "Please, say something". Then, she had sipped her tea, as her mouth had become dry for having talked too much. The situation suddenly worsened, as Philip's lost, yet accusing eyes was focused on the three of them. Only after he had poured out, he ran his hand through his soft brown hair while observing the artifacts placed on the table. He had never seen anything quite like it.

He could never have imagined that his father - as well as many other familiar names - could have been part of such a strange coven for all those years. Thus, he asked for more explanations.

Aleister tried not to betray himself by saying something wrong as he had decided to provide Philip with more explanations. The *explanation*. He stopped talking only to look at their faces, especially Philip's. Aleister was about to reveal his identity and - after that speech - he thought he had aroused doubts about his real nature. The Murrays would have lost faith in him if they found out about him, Orpeco, and the Altors. Although he had chosen to be part of the earth only to keep Alice away from danger, Aleister had realised that the real danger was the humanity itself.

"When people make fortune, they do everything they can to preserve it. It has always been like this. On the other hand, dealing only with human beings is not enough. It is at this point that the occult world come into play. Greed is a disease, and it has infected people for centuries. Individuals increase their power, creating favorable alliances and treaties. The seven people portrayed in that picture are - and were - authoritative and influential personalities. Something that goes beyond the human knowledge must have given them the esteem they had sought in the past. The real question is: what is the reason that led them to death? In my opinion, this aren't ordinary stones, but runes. They might reveal their belonging to the Divum Deus, of which they were provided with during their rite of passage. Clearly, I'm just supposing. What is certain is that the other people portrayed in the photo are still alive."

Philip - shaken by that *explanation* - didn't reply immediately. As he was a pragmatic person, he now had to make an enormous effort to open up to the reality, which he had always denied. His world lied only on dogmas, calculations, and scientific proofs. He was able to believe only in rational solutions. He didn't accept any other shade, and indeed, he found it difficult to believe to a single word Aleister had said.

Urielle went to her room and took Mr. Harvey's notes and diary as a support of Aleister's speech. Thus, she handed them over to Philip, so that he could see for himself and then share his own thoughts.

Finally, Philip leafed through the diary.

After having quickly scrolled through the pages, he pointed at the last pages, the one that had kept Urielle busy in the past hours. He analysed the writings several times, then he decided to read it aloud.

"The owl, the one who works by double standards, has lost his time where silence reigns forever."

He ruminated in silent for a few seconds, then he begun in his usual biting tone "Harvey was really disturbed".

Then, as if he had been enlightened by a sudden thought, he realised he might have found the solution of that statement. "I think the rune in the Hades... I mean, in the cemetery!"

Philip's conclusions aroused some confusion, as everyone had thought that - if the stone was in the cemetery - it would have been within everyone's easy reach. On the other hand - according to everyone's reasoning but Philip's - the cemetery was a perfect place to hide it, as there was no living being there.

XXV

Ashley Danton had made sure that Marta's reception at the lake house was the best. Indeed, she had spent the whole morning walking the sleeping area corridor to arrange the guest room, counting her steps "One, two, three ...". The heel of her boots cracked on the wooden planks of the upper floor, as she walked back and forth from the rooms to check that everything was perfectly in order. Then, she repeated those actions over again. She had often changed Marta's bed sheets, thinking that a purple or black duvet could have reminded Marta of her husband's death. Yes, Ashley's paranoia had just began. If she could, she would have erased dark colours from the colour wheel. However, her dearest friend – benzos - had helped her once again. "Like a candy" – She tells herself every time looking herself at the mirror. Then she took the *lorazepam* tablet, drinking in one gulp the water from the usual glass, which was bigger than her hand. Then, she calmy resumed her housework. No one could actually say why that woman - who was only forty of a rare beauty and a model body - suffered of such anxieties. She had married the man she had always loved, and had given birth to her son - Reece, a lovely boy of nine - on the first attempt. There was nothing that made people think that her life was not in order. However, she hadn't talked to anyone about her psychotherapy sessions, not even to her husband, with whom she was deeply in love. Ashley loved Mr. Danton in the only way she knew - morbid and obsessive - but only when she was allowed to show her nature away from judgmental eyes: in the solitude of their own echoes.

It was time to put aside her manias and insecurities, as Marta would be her guest that morning. They would have spent "two days in pleasant company", after Ashley had insisted on hosting her.

"Yes! The orange and yellow duvet will be perfect. It will remind her of the Italian sunsets" – She told herself, finishing all the preparations.

No one could know that Mrs. Danton was a pathological impostor, included Marta, who would have never failed to help her. No one would have doubted Ashley, who had always looked kind and reliable. Her culinary skill was well-known in town; she could turn into a delicacy even an ordinary jar of pickles. She could also be capable of convincing anyone that the coldest season could became warm as a hug if faced with a good brew or one of her aromatic blends. She was happily married to Oliver Danton after they had met at the opening of the store. Indeed, marriage was her biggest dream. She yarned for the wedding dress and married life as she considered it an expression of the feminine being. Her life was formed by the shop, the house, the school Reece attended, and the church. Her routine - precise and accurate - repeated day after day, creating a microcosm of absolute serenity which cannot be disturbed by any variable. Mrs. Danton had met Marta shortly after the shop opened. Despite the age gab between them, the variety of coffee available at the shop had made Mrs. Murray a loyal costumer. Thus, purchase after purchase, they became friends. To be clear, when Ashley was born, Marta was already a teenager who listened to the vinyl records to sooth her impossibility to hang out with friends, as back then people feared the multiple murders of the *Monster of Florence*[13]. According to Marta, the age gab was just an illogical number, and the same could be said for Mr. Danton, who was several years older than his wife.

Mr. Danton worked at the Hampshire administrative division, and for some years - thanks to his accounting knowledge - he had been nominated treasurer of the Poppy Field Refuge.

That Monday - which hadn't started in the best way - had finally made Marta birthing in relief. Although she hated it, that morning she had only lazed. Indeed, she had promised herself not to idle anymore, not now that her husband couldn't interfere anymore with her evening meeting.

At first, doing nothing had relaxed her. During the afternoon they had sipped tea, chatted, while Mrs. Danton had reproached Reece several times, as he would have wanted to play outside, but ended up watching the tv. The more he wandered around the two women, the more Marta couldn't help looking at him. It was Reece who had spotted Arthur Murray's corpse along the banks of the Lake Hoarmere. Eventually, his parents hadn't told him that the man was dead, after all it wasn't necessary. However, Reece had understood it, and wisely pretended to believe his parents' lies. It was hilarious how Mrs.

---

[13] Is the name commonly used by the media in Italy for an unidentified serial killer who killed fourteen people between 1974 and 1985.

Danton was convinced that the dark linen would end up bothering her guest. She had ignored that the possible trigger of Marta's annoyance could be at hand: her beloved son.

What had happened to Wendy could have happened to Reece as well, or to any innocent child. The little girl had disappeared, and they were lounging comfortably in the living room of the lake house, talking about futile matters, as of the latest renovation of the Dantons' home, her son's nightmares, and his not very satisfactory school grades. Of course, they had also talked about Wendy, but not enough and not in the way Marta would have liked. Indeed, the way they shared their opinion on such a matter looked like rumors, which made Marta feel a coward. Marta decided to give herself a chance and stayed there. "*I will not go further with that conversation*" – She had thought to herself. If things hadn't changed in the short term, she would have left Mrs. Danton's house on the lake, coming up with an excuse on her malaise.

Around nine o'clock Mr. Danton came home. Marta hoped that the long and stressful wait had not been in vain. The continuation of those days she would have spent there would depend on Oliver's presence, who - she hoped - might have some more updates on Wendy. He had been at the shelter all day with a couple of officers, so that made him the closest person to the investigation. Marta could have taken advantage of those circumstances to inform him of her candidacy as a member of the institute Council, clarifying that she would be the natural successor to her husband's position. She could have said many things, but she realised it was better to not display her decision given the gloomy situation.

"Reece! It's time to turn off the television and go to sleep" – Ashley told her son. Then, she turned off the tv and handed the remote to her husband as it was a scepter.

"Mum, it's still early!"

"It isn't. Don't forget that tomorrow you must wake up early to go downtown with dad. Come on! Get right to bed!" – She said shrilly.

Reece obeyed. He propped his thick glasses on his nose and went upstairs to his bedroom, while his mother followed him.

Wendy's story had made it to the local news and had aroused everyone's concern, especially Mr. Danton's. He had changed the channel to the evening news, which seemed updated only with the news of the morning. There weren't updates on her disappearance. No one had talked about kidnapping, but only about a presumed prank among children. Assuming the refuge's imminent closure, Wendy's disappearance was the last thing they needed.

"God knows how afraid I am for Wendy" – Marta said, holding a cup of hot tea in her hands and her eyes glued to the tv. She started looking at the flame crackling in the fireplace like pop corns in a pan. Each crack caused her unbearable shivers running down her spine.

"I talked to the police officers today. Tomorrow they will keep carrying on the investigations. They'll also listen both to the educators and the collaborator" – Mr. Danton replied. Then, he turned off the tv.

"We have to intervene. We have to do something, Oliver."

"Everything we can, Marta. However, we can't help with the investigation. You'll see, they'll find her soon. That's what I repeat to myself over and over again."

Oliver stopped talking, then resumed. "I know you and Lauraine Ratcliffe met yesterday afternoon" – He began.

"She told me that most probably the shelter will be closed. Is that true?" – Marta asked.

"After what has just happened to Wendy, it will certainly be closed. No one would ever have faith in such an institution, unable to look after its children. Let's be honest, Marta! We both know that even if the girl will be found, the fate of the refuge will be the same."

"Not if the shelter gets fair financial support."

"I know of this matter too. Lauraine told me that you would like to candidacy yourself as a member of the Council."

"My husband strongly believed in Poppy Field Refuge until the day he died. We own enough assets to continue financing the shelter. I don't want my family to be act with simple donations. I want it to be an active part of it. Maybe that's what Arthur would like too. I will succeed him in what he had done in his long life: caring for others to serve the Slohan Oak community. But I'd rather not discuss it now, on the contrary, if you don't mind, I'd just avoid talking about money. "

"Marta..." Mr. Danton looked like a hangdog, while his wife interrupted that conversation after having put little Reece to bed. She sat down on one of the recliner chairs, then she shook her head and closed her eyes. "Our son is becoming more and more impertinent. if his attitude doesn't change, we'll have hard times ahead, Oly!"

"*These are the real problems!*" – Marta thought.

"At least Reece watches films with knights and dragons. I hope he can stay away from the cruelty of this world" – Ashley's husband said, referring to the 1950's style bar cabinet. After the renovation of the house, the furnishings reflected the period of the great economic recovery: lacquered kitchen cabinets, solid wood table and crystal ornaments, green wallpaper, and wooden floor polished with wax. It seemed that the Dantons had generated a recession of contemporary design as it's conceived today.

Oliver took out a bottle of gin and poured the liquid into four glasses.

"Four glasses? So, you're serious" – Marta was particularly surprised.

"Carmicheal... he's here. We had an appointment at this time. I really hope it's not a problem for you, we need to talk about the situation. Financing included" – He said.

The woman shook her head, both surprised and disappointed.

"All right, he should be here by now" – Mr. Danton got up to reach the entrance, then turned towards the living room "Marta ... I will follow your advice and we will not talk about your intentions unless it is Ronald to bring it up. Miss Ratcliffe discussed it with him too. Believe me, that matter cannot be taken lightly."

Marta didn't feel ready to meet that man. She knew his reputation. However, Marta continued thinking of why they had omitted his invitation. Carmicheal couldn't be even considerated a resident of that area as - exactly like all of them - he lived in Slohan Oak.

"*Stupid me*" – She had thought, aware that Oliver and Ronald had planned their meeting to stop her inappropriate candidacy.

The bakelite doorbell rang twice, producing a deafening and obsolete beep which reflected that of the furniture. The typical silver fox showed up at the door, grizzled and handsome, with his charming green eyes. It could be said he was handsome and detestable at the same time. Ronald was highly respected in the community for his professional authority in forensic matters.

He owned a law firm both in Slohan Oak and in London near St. Paul's. Unfortunately, his friendship with Mayor Brickenden had turned into a political rivalry, which reach its peak after Carmicheal's defeat in the last administrative elections. For this reason, he had become even more hostile towards Brickenden, and he had begun to harbour an inexplicable scorn even towards Arthur Murray. Thus, he had voted against Murray's management of the shelter.

"We were about to take some gin" – Oliver told Carmicheal after letting him in.

"I don't drink, you know it. I'll take a cup of tea. If you have tea, of course. Otherwise, a glass of water would be fine. Thank you."

Mr. Danton went to the kitchen to fulfil Carmicheal's request, while the latter walked slowly towards the living room and politely waved to both women. He tried to ice breaking by commenting on the refurbishment of the house, which was conducted by the construction company he had recommended to Oliver. However, Marta considered such statement as an attempt to strut around.

"You haven't seen this house's condition before Oliver, and I got married. After her mother died, we decided to restore it. Can you imagine? He told me that mold had also crept into the furniture" – Ashley whispered. "Marta, if I don't get wrong, this is the first time you too come here at Blagdon Lake."

"It is so. As I own a house on Lake Hoarmere, I have rarely visited Somerset. However, there's always a first time."

Marta observed the man who was staring at her, while Mrs. Danton dealt with pleasantries. It seemed that she was trying her best to let the two of them chatting.

"I remember when I visited your house on the lake Hoarmere, and how impressed I was by the amount of antique and work of art" – Ronald said.

"I haven't been there for a long time. The last time I went at the lake house was for an unpleasant situation. However, you must know what I'm talking about."

Oliver returned to the living room holding the teapot and served it to Ronald, pouring the tea into the gin glass. Marta widened her eyes, while Ashley emitted a squeak, but the host seemed to ignore his friend's gesture.

"Do you have any updates?" – Oliver asked him.

"The policemen are gathered around the shelter area. However, we all know that investigation must be extended to the area of Hoarmere Lake."

"Why?" – Marta asked.

"The clearing is cursed. You should know that."

The man took the first sip of tea, then smiled mockingly. "So to speak, of course. Although I don't think the agents should investigate only nearby the shelter."

Mr. Danton dealt with the administrative issues of Poppy Field Refuge, and the negative impact the latest event would have had on it. Marta listened in silence, although she wanted to participate. She still couldn't understand why they had decided to give up. The starting of a solid fund campaign would have prevented the shutdown of the shelter. Marta relied on Slohan Oak and Wiltshire inhabitants' goodness. She was aware that the disappearance of the child would not have made them surrender. On the contrary - without exploiting what had happened - they would have come to the conclusion that the building would need support to strengthen security and increase the personnel. The County would become the only jury capable of judging and securing an equal allocation. Marta knew that it was the right thing to do, and nothing would have stopped her.

After witnessing the umpteenth discussion about the sales and the numerous paperwork to be produced for the lawyers, Marta exploded like a pressure cooker after Mr. Danton's self-pity and some inappropriate comments on the weather.

Thus, she interrupted their conversation.

"We are all gathered here" – She said – "to drink gin or tea, to talk about lack of funds, while outside there, a little girl is missing. We do not know where she could be, nor if she will be found alive. I know for a fact that my husband would not have acted so brazenly. Maybe, I shouldn't come here" – She got up and started gesticulating as every Italian do. "Well, I'd rather say that you are wrong. I don't know how you can have the nerve to talk about it in such a way."

"We don't know anything about the disappearance, and you can't expect everything to rely on paltry decisions. Your husband no longer has a say in the matter. As regard the other children, their faith is uncertain. They will see the doors of what they considered a safe heaven close. We have to be ready for the worst scenario" – Mr. Carmicheal jumped to his feet arguing and addressing to the woman. He talked with the same verbal violence as a lawyer about to lose a case.

"Actually, there would be a solution, which is accepting me as a member of the Council. Tell me what you want? More money? I can do even better. I can open part of the properties to the public. Are you afraid of collaborating with a non-compatriot woman? You can't give up on the shelter, a place that has given hope to those who no longer had one. I'm asking it from the bottom of my heart. The institution won't be closed, even if I can grasp resignation on your faces. I'll fight for it. And I'll tell you more: if you'll close the shelter, I will reopen it, with or without you. Well, certainly without you."

The typical annoying silence that usually precedes a confession fell. Then Ronald walked closer to the woman, "Do you really think that it's about money?" – He swallowed, as if he had gulped a sharp blade down. "We are protecting you from a great disappointment. Trust me, stand back before the truth come out. Keep out of the refuge business."

"Are you threatening me? Which truth are you talking about? I've immediately understood your intentions."

"No, I don't care about your husband blood-stained money. Mrs. Murray, you don't know anything about your husband" – Carmicheal left the living room to take his coat and leave. "Excuse me, I have to go. Oliver, thanks for the tea, it was excellent."

Suddenly, before the man opened the front door, there was a thud coming from outside. Concern aroused in everyone as their gazes were focused on the entrance.

Mr. Carmicheal - who was not intimidated by the noise - opened the door, ready for anything. However, he realised that no intervention would be needed.

"Donovan?" – Marta asked, walking to the man who was sitting on the ground covered with snow. "You, here?"

"You had us scared, Inspector" – Mr. Danton added after having breath in relief.

"Oh, I apologise. These shoes aren't good to walk on the snow" – The Inspector said, pointing to a pair of expensive Italian high-laced boots. Then, he cleaned his jacket with his hands, greeted Mr. Danton and, when he was about to greet Marta, she stopped him.

"Is there any news on little Boyton's disappearance?" – She asked him.

"A while ago they called me from the Police Station. They've found a corpse. Now..." – The Inspector looked at the Dantons and Ronald with an inquisitive gaze. "Now, I can't tell you anything else, Marta. I'll keep you posted."

Every unpleasant aspect of that evening seemed to have come to an end when Mr. Carmicheal left the house. Nevertheless, the sudden scream of Reece echoed through the house. Screams of horror came from the boy's room. The two men reached the entrance of the house and rushed to staircase frightened.

Mrs. Danton run to his bedroom. "Honey! Calm down, I'm here!" – She said, "What's going on?"

"He was hungry! He always is!" – The boy was crying in terror, emitting long sighs. He pressed the lids of his eyes as if they were power bottons.

"Who?" – Mrs. Danton asked.

Reece slowly calmed down and widened his eyes, observed his palms and his wrists. Then, he looked at his mother confused. He had had a nightmare, one of the many that had made him panic in the middle of the night for over a month.

Ashley - upset and unable to keep the situation under control - had rested his son head on her bony chest. She hugged him so tight that she could smell the scent of the pajamas. Tears shone at the corner of her eyes, as the need to cry out in despair had aroused in her. She tried to comfort her son, grabbed his hand, and told him to go downstairs with her and join the chatter coming from the lower floor.

Reece took his first steps on that cracking wooden floor, then stopped abruptly as if the nightmare wasn't over yet.

"That man" – He said, pointing his finger at those standing at the entrance – "That man has as sharp teeth as a dragon."

Then, he collapsed.

Oliver was frightening. He rushed to his son who was unconsciously lying on the floor. The kid's breath was as week as a deflating balloon, while his skin, his lips and his eyes were becoming more and more paler. He had fainted, but he looked dead.

"Reece, wake up! Please wake up! Someone calls for help!" – Oliver was holding him in his arms in desperation, while his face had become purple.

Marta reached the kid to help him, while she traced in her memory the basics of first aid that her father had forced her to take *because you'll never know*.

As for Ashley, she witnessed the scene standing on the first step of the staircase. She seemed frozen, as if something was dragging her to the bottom. She begun to count within herself, "*One, two, three, four, five, six, seven.*"

XXVI

Forty-five miles from Somerset, the officers of the Police Station were awaited the Inspector's arrival. They were standing along the sloping grounds of the clearing like a group of witnesses waiting for the groom. A hundred steps divided Cole from the barking dogs and the flashing lights of his colleagues' cars. McCarthy had run to catch up with his colleagues, almost bumping into the tapes that surrounded the area. His face looked tired as he had spent the last days investigating on the disappearance of little Boyton, exactly like the other officers who had took part in that investigation. He informed his boss to be careful, as the ground was slippery due to the mixture of snow and mud. Cole thanked him. However, McCarthy's second attempt to make Cole slow his pace, had led him to a series of offenses and rhetoric questions.

"Do you think I'm an idiot?" – Cole asked.

McCarthy walked away from him.

McCarthy and Cole reached the clearing, where other officers were motionless standing, forming a squadron. Cole knew he could rely on his men, as they strongly respected the hierarchy. Without him being there, no one would have acted. Nevertheless, this couldn't be confused with laxity; it rather was a form of respect towards the Inspector.

McCarthy - who looked younger than he actually was - was Cole's trustworthy man. As a sign of proof for his unconditional esteem towards Cole, McCarthy had decided to stall with the forensic policemen. However, it could be said that Cole wouldn't have done the same for McCarthy, who - on his part - demanded that Cole was the first to find the corpse.

The Inspector pointed the torch to the ground, enlightening a skein as pale as hay, placed in the midst of branches and muddy ground. Suddenly, he spotted a lock of blonde hair. Cole bent down on the muddy ground, while his shoes drown in the slime. He tried to clear the surface of that heap of earth with a thin branch. However, he lost his patience as one of the dogs - probably a German Shepherd - kept barking annoyingly.

Barks would have distracted him from his unfinished work.

"Officer Bailey! Damn! Shut your beast up!" – He yelled, and slowly began to unveil a tiny body, pale as dawn. "Shit…"

He took a deep breath. Cole put his hand to his head and stood up, keeping his eyes on that tiny corpse.

"It corresponds to the description" – McCarthy said.

"Yes, it's her corpse. We've found Wendy Boyton" – Cole replied, pointing the torch on her reddish angioma. Then, he looked at the sky, realising that it was about to rain.

"This place will become a marshland in less than an hour, Chief. Forensic policemen will soon be here" – McCarthy said.

"McCarthy, Bailey, you already know what to do."

"Let's cover the corpse. Unfortunately, the scene has been contaminated, let's save what can be saved" – McCarthy said.

Wendy lay on the cold autopsy table, like *Mantegna's Lamentation of Christ*[14]. She was covered with a white sheet from the waist down. It looked like a desecrated holy picture. That poor girl had only been able to savor the sorrows of life.

Cole looked at her, imagining how that little girl - kidnapped from life's joys, disappointments and victories - had come to death in such a horrible way: her jugular had been torn. There was the mark of the teeth that had torn the skin, the signs of the incisors and canines of an adult man. She was bitten by a *bastard*, by *someone with a corrupt soul*. Poor Wendy was torn apart by a *child-eater*, as the press would have defined him.

Devouring her hadn't been a remedy to mislead the police from some obscene abuse. It seemed that Wendy had simply been someone's evening snack. Which monster would have been such hungry seeing the poor little girl? The policemen had found her far from the Poppy Field Refuge, wearing a blue jacket, some grains of sugar on her livid lips, and pretty rain boots on her foot. Who knows how long she had walked before being murdered. Probably a lot, as her shoes were completely covered with mud. Wendy loved the rain, like every other child. Of course, she loved it. She loved the rain because it was a good listener; it didn't ask for answers. It only listened in silence, exactly like her. Now, her tiny body wasn't no longer able to communicate. It lay helpless.

Donovan Cole - who lived in Castle Combe - went home late at night driving along the A350 route. His home - the real

---

[14] Lamentation of Christ: painting by the Italian Renaissance artist Andrea Mantegna. The work portrays the body of Christ supine on a marble slab.

one, *Barrow Cottage* - was immersed in the silence, that silence he needed to free his mind after that exhausting working day. The house was surrounded by a few windbreak trees, and it couldn't be defined neither beautiful, nor ugly. The little garden was neglected; the ancient stone statue was crumbled by an old cataclysm. The statue once depicted a cherub - now beheaded - who hold a lyre in his plump hands. A bright green patina brightened the bricks, while the roof tiles were likely to fall down like children's teeth. Nevertheless, a well-planned reasoning relied behind that choice. If Cole hadn't attracted attention, no one would have been suspicious of the luxury that he thought he deserved.

He got inside the house and took off his coat which - drenched in rain - he hung on the clothes hanger. After having washed his hands under the running water of the kitchen sink - as he always did - he went to his studio. Then, as Cole used to do, he took a glass of Scotch - a *Dalmore* - and sat down at his desk. Then, he began to pass the pocket watch between the fingers of his hand. His thoughts were consuming him, and he was still too alert to go to sleep. He opened one of the drawers and took out a silver case containing some illegally imported cigars. *"There are only three left"* – He realised looking at the box and thinking that - from that moment on - he should have made good use, as they couldn't be found easily.

Cole lit up a cigar, then he passed the watch - which struck a quarter to four - between his index finger and thumb. He smoked restlessly, inhaling with the same intensity of a vacuum cleaner.

The door of his studio opened slowly, emitting a sinister creak which divided the blue mist of the cigar into two. A *beautiful* blonde woman came in wearing a satin slip. As soon as she entered the room, Cole put the watch in his pocket, while the cigar remained nestled between his lips.

"Maggie, I thought you were sleeping. I must have woken you up" – Cole muttered. Then, he looked at her with satisfaction, perhaps because of her beauty, or probably because that almost thirty years old woman had chosen him, the aging Inspector with a twitchy eye. However, all of that was at the bottom of the list. A more sordid thought livened him up. That *beautiful* woman - Margaret Prestcote- Hill - was the daughter of the former Prosecutor General - the flagship of the man, once his friend - who was unaware of Cole's relationship with his daughter.

"Don't call me *Maggie*, I've already told you. You remind me of my father" – She snorted – "What time is it?"

"Oh, your father would pay millions to be at least half as charming as I am" – Then Cole glanced at the pendulum clock. "Almost four. I'll catch up with you once I'll be done with this" – He raised his glass and involuntary his eyelid twitched.

"Tomorrow will be a though day for us."

"Mine will be for sure tough. But on the other hand, since you have the choice, in a few hours - instead of going to the Police Station - you can return to London Road to your subordinates. Or better yet, wait here for your favorite subordinate, Maggie" – He replied with a hint of irony, grabbing the hem of his jacket to put himself together, then resumed "Why do you insist so much on going there?"

The woman walked closer to the desk, leaned one of her bare thighs against it, so much so that she lifted her slip a little and let a glimpse of the dark lingerie she was wearing. He lingered on the chair, yearning for her like Eve had craved the sinful fruit.

"You've tried" – She recomposed herself and resumed speaking naturally – "I hadn't come with you only because you hadn't told me that you were going to Slohan Oak. If we don't want to end up in the paper, you'd better include me in the second wave of interrogation tomorrow."

Margaret had received a call from Cole before he left his home in Somerset. He had tried to tell her to wait for him at home - *the real one* - the house where the phone lost its signal as the thunderstorms destroyed the repeaters of the area. Indeed, it would have been hard for Margaret to be updated by the Police Station. Cole didn't want to involve her in that affair, as he had tried to keep the matter of the disappearance of the little girl away of the headquarters. He could have been admonished for voluntary omission. Even worst, he could have been dismissed for misconduct, but Margaret had pardoned him. She had acted in such a way because she knew that under the mahogany desk at which Cole sat, she would have found his big hard penis, faithful only to her. It had always been like this: the more she raised the stakes, the more he couldn't stay away from her.

He would have bet everything just to stay with her.

She was his puppeteer.

He let her believe so.

She asked for a glass of Scotch to take part in that late night drink. She shown with her fingers the amount of alcohol he had to pour in her glass, just a little try. Indeed, she didn't want to get drunk and then wake up in the morning with the usual headache. She acted like she was a great alcohol expert. Then, she asked more details on the schedule for the next day's interrogation that she already knew. Her aim was to harass the Inspector who looked more human than ever.

"Remind me again who will be the first to testify" – She asked.

"My boozer neighbour in Blagdon Danton. He just needs to confirm the version he told this afternoon. I'd really like to slap his face, but he isn't who we are looking for."

"What about the gardener? It turns out he was the last person who has seen Wendy."

"Amilia will be the second one. The *mastiffs* had already questioned him this morning. Tomorrow he will go through hell. He didn't tell the truth; his alibi doesn't hold up."

Finally, Cole put the cigar in the ashtray, determined to cut off that unbreakable bond with the Cuban contraband. He took a sip of Scotch deposited at the bottom of the glass, then he walked towards the *beauty* and pushed his pelvis against her dressing gown. Like in a James Bond' scene. It didn't take long to make her understand that wanted to scream, "stop talking about work".

"I know what you want. You're yarning for it, otherwise you wouldn't be here" – He told her.

Margaret had clearly turned on. She had inarched her back and had run her tongue over her lip, as if it were velvet. Then, she turned her gaze elsewhere, more precisely on the pendulum clock. It was four o'clock, perhaps a little too late to take a ride on the carousel, but Cole was right. So, she pulled her thighs away and opened the doors to heaven.

While she was busy to unfasten Cole's belt, the man put his hand in his pocket to check that his pocket watch was still there. He felt that he couldn't waist any more time, as he had become aware that he no longer had enough.

XXVII

Tuesday, 2ⁿᵈ of January 2018

The following day, Gavin Amilia would rather have not shown up at the police station. In fact, it had been the *mastiffs* to escort him, playing the role of *Charon*[15], leading him towards his miserable end. As Cole had ordered, the officers had broken into Amilia's house at dawn. His sister - terrified by their noisy knocks at the door - had opened it. They had literally broken into his tiny apartment and had woken him up, almost picking him up from the sofa where he was sleeping. They had dragged him out half naked.

"Hey, wait! You cannot do that!" – Her sister had scream while the men pushed her back into the apartment – "This isn't over, you beasts!"

Then, one of the officers went back and shout to her.

"We both know who's the real beast! Now, shut up! Otherwise, I'll take you to the Police Station for obstruction."

---

[15] In Greek mythology, *Charon* is the ferryman of Hades, who carries souls of the newly deceased across the Acheron.

Then, the policemen had carried the young Amilia to the gates of hell, while his sister's scream echoed.

Gavin knew that place, he had already been there as a teenager, and he had promised himself that he would have set foot in that place never again. He had been suspected of having beat his ex-girlfriend - Molly Price - and thus he had been put behind bars. However - if the neighbours hadn't intruded - the culprit would have been only Molly. Indeed, after she had slapped the boy, he had pushed her away with a shove to defend himself. Some people had defined his behaviour as "too kind". Nevertheless, the neighbours - who were gifted with strong imagination - reported that the couple's quarrel had gone on for over a week, and that Gavin had threatened Molly with death.

None of this was true.

Gavin almost got himself arrested several times, although he had always been released as his crimes were considered petty. Indeed, he had been accused of drink-driving and theft of a bike. When he was a teenager, he was also caught in the act of heroin possession. That stunt had costed him dearly. Indeed, he had been sentenced to probation and rehab. Eventually, he had redeemed. Gavin didn't look like a criminal *back then*, nor *now*, he was far for looking like a murdered. But appearances are deceptive. He wasn't aware that the testimony he had provided the day before on the Boyton case would have backfired. He had said that he had only greeted little Wendy, and that he had given her a little bag full of lemon candies, those with sugar grains on top. They had eaten them together - exactly like brothers do - before the guy finished his shift.

That was his mistake.

It was the imperceptible leftovers of sugar on Wendy's lips that had betrayed him. Indeed, few grains of sugar were found on her neck marks along with genetic material. For some unknown reasons, Richard Walsh - the Coroner who usually takes ages before providing results - had already analysed every evidence in a short time. Only the result of the biological specimen wasn't ready yet. "Good job, Welsh", one might say. His record-breaking research had astounded everyone, even the London Road headquarter, and even Margaret who was struggling to accept that news. That day was a memorable one for the Police Station's employees. That would have been Slohan Oak's first gory case solved in less than twenty-four hours. It would have made the history, and it would have been written in all modern criminology textbooks. The citizens of Slohan Oak would be to safety from the imminent danger of the monster, the *child-eater*.

Gavin, lawyer Brian Russel, the Inspector and Margaret were seated in the interrogation room. Since the beginning of the voice recording, Russel had continued to repeat to Gavin which were his rights, as if he had to pass an exam at the *University of Leeds*. Cole upset lawyer Russel, who had finally calmed down when he had realised that the guy was condemned to his fate. Then, silence fell in the room.

"Your friend his wasting his time because of you" – Cole said, mocking Amilia. "You could take the pressure off if you tell us why you had decided to snack on Wendy's body."

"I've already told you, you're wrong" – Gavin replied.

He drank one more glass of water, as his face was on fire.

"You mean that a four-years old girl bit her neck herself?" – Cole asked him.

"What I mean is that you are detaining an innocent man. I know you have always wanted to put me in prison, but now it's time to stop harassing me and my family! I have nothing to do with all of this. The DNA test will prove it!"

McCarthy entered the investigation room. He was holding a folder, which contained Gavin's clinical tests. The moment of truth had arrived.

"Now, read."

Fear took over on Gavin. His eyes were wide open, while sweat lit up his forehead.

"I've been framed!" – Gavin shouted furiously. "You set me up!" – Then he jumped up on Cole like an enraged beast.

Suddenly, two officers entered to stop him from attacking Cole and to handcuff him.

"You bastards! I want to be tested again. I didn't kill Wendy!" – He repeated.

The Inspector concluded the interrogation, "Gavin Amilia, you're accused of the murder of Wendy Boyton. You will be taken out of this room. Charges will be read out to you, and you will be in preventive detention."

XXVIII

The discovery of Wendy's body was the main news of the local TV, and it was debated even on the national one. In the blink of an eye, Slohan Oak was populated by satellite dishes, journalists who wandered around the town holding microphones and followed by cameramen. They tried to interview the residents to acquire information. The sudden chaos, as well as the citizen's concern for the *child-eater* - aroused the anger of deputy mayor Burton Burch, who had unwillingly become Mayor. The journalists had already interviewed Mayor Burch after Brickenden's death and - even in that case - the journalists had acted arrogantly, as they had stopped in front of Burch's house for days. Unfortunately, the reporters had become even more brazen, to the point that the policemen had to intervene and remove a television crew who had also started interviewing the neighbors.

Cole had called off Oliver Danton's deposition. Such news left everyone stunned, as the man was supposed to be the first to testify, while now his testimony was no longer needed. Thus, it could be thought that there had been a turning point in the investigation. Anyway, Oliver had thought to go back in town to take his son to visit his grandmother's grave, and then he would have gone to the Police Station as he had announced the night before.

Marta - who was getting boring at Blagdon Lake - greeted Ashley and decided to go to the Police Station with Mr. Danton. She wanted to talk to Inspector Cole to steal some further information.

"Stay inside the car, I'll be back soon" – Mr. Danton told to his son once they had arrived at the Station. Marta caught up with him shortly after, but as she hadn't notice that Reece was all alone inside the car, she walked to the building. That thought had haunted her for years, and - throughout her life - she had wondered over and over again how things would have gone if she had acted differently that day.

Reece saw his father enter the building and - after few seconds - he saw also Marta, who was very nice with him. However, he didn't say hello to her as he was busy playing a video game. His parents rarely allowed him to play with the old *Game Boy*, which belonged to an older cousin of him. Thus, he locked himself inside the car and took advantage of that moment. He made the blue porcupine run around in search of gold rings. According to Reece, there was no better way to spend time. Every now and then, he tried to get warm, and emitted a few puffs with his mouth, creating small clouds of warm breath. Then, he resumed playing.

"Cole, there you are. I was looking for you. So, you caught him!" – Mr. Danton exclaimed.

"Are there further updates?" – Mrs. Murray asked shortly after.

"Yes, there are, but I can't tell you anything now. There will be a press release in less than an hour. The beast is in his cell. Now, I have to go. Please, apologise me."

Cole went through the metal detector, got his things back, and left Station to head for headquarters.

Margaret didn't do the same. She was standing in front of the coffee machines to drink the umpteenth coffee. Something of that matter didn't add up. Gavin had seemed a good person to Margaret. She was also surprised to discover that his DNA matches the one found on Wendy's body. It seemed to her a witch hunt, where - in order to find a culprit - an innocent is condemned. Margaret had carried out murder cases in the past, and for this reason, she considered herself competent in such field, as she had also inherited her critical abilities from her father. However, she knew how much Cole had cared about that matter. He demanded order in the town, like everyone else. Margaret also knew that Cole would never act for glory, as he cared more for the safety of the citizens.

Margaret suddenly felt a caress on her shoulder. It was Mrs. Murray who wanted to say hello to her, as they hadn't seen each other for a long time.

They hugged.

"How is your father?" – Marta asked.

"It seems he's getting worse day by day. But I know he will get better."

"You have to stay strong for both of you" – Marta said. Then, she took off her coat and touched her forehead. "Is it always this hot here? You should adjust the thermostat" – She exclaimed. Then, Marta asked Margaret if she had carried out the case with Cole.

"Yes, I did, but only partly. I let Cole carrying it out as he took to heart the whole affair" – Margaret smiled – "What about you, Marta. Why are you here?"

"Mr. Danton was supposed to be the first to testify, but then the schedule had been changed. I came here to talk to Donovan."

"I get it, these are busy days. I fear you have to put off your conversation with him. especially since we can't reveal the detail of the case."

Thus, the two women said goodbye.

Marta thought that Wendy Boyton would have never received the justice she deserved, although having caught her killer in such a short time would still have been a consolation, albeit a small one.

She put aside her thoughts, telling herself that once she got home, she would do anything to try to forget that story. Nevertheless, once they left the Station, Mr. Danton realised that his life was about to change.

The car door was wide open, while a pair of glasses were lying on the wet asphalt. Little Reece had gone missing.

XXIX

The officers checked footage from the Station security cameras. Reece had not been kidnapped, he had just run away, and he had ended up who knows where.

"That little bagger…!" – Oliver said.

The policemen were confused.

"It's not the first time he did so. As if we don't have enough problems!"

"Do you have any idea where he may have gone? Maybe he caught up his mother to the store. Or maybe he went home" – Margaret said.

"My wife is in our house at Blagdon Lake. So, I doubt he had gone there."

"Well, in the meantime, describe your son to my colleagues. Call the Station if there's any news. Officers will soon start to look for him. Don't worry" – Margaret put an end to that conversation, hoping that such a horrible day would come soon to an end.

XXX

The Murray brothers had gone back to Shelley House in the morning, after having spent the evening at Urielle's apartment. They had distracted themselves from the latest upsetting event by simply chatting. The tragic news of Wendy's discovery and Gavin's arrest had distracted them from their personal problems only for a few moments.

Indeed, Philip - indignant - kept whispering, "Miserable", convinced that he himself was doomed to prison. The thought of the ample fortune they enjoyed being squandered by strangers, scared him. He was thinking of money, of his father's presumed financial troubles, of the numerous legal procedures and of the lawyer who had tried to help them. That meant more money vanishing. Philip thought about what he would have said to the judge to persuade him that his father hadn't had nothing to do with that matter, which had changed is family's perception of the world. The Murrays would have lost all their comforts, and Philip wasn't ready for that. Furthermore, he thought about the issue of his engagement to *Brunhilde*, of which - sooner or later - have talked to his mother. He knew that his mother would be back home earlier than planned. Indeed, Marta had called Alice to inform the daughter of her return and to tell her about Wendy. Nevertheless, Alice hadn't told her mother that her beloved brother hadn't gone to Switzerland. Philip was aware that he needed help. Pandora's box would have soon exploded, revealing all the evils trapped inside.

"You have to tell mum what you have told me" – Alice objected. "I know it's not the best choice, but she must know about Brunhilde. She couldn't wait for your wedding to come."

"No, I can't tell her all the truth."

"Why not?"

"You know how she will react."

"I don't understand."

"Her Italian genes… she's a traditionalist woman. A deadly combination. Do you have any idea what her reaction might be? It will keep her up all night."

"I think you're overestimating her" – Alice replied frowned. "You've just broke up."

"You'll see, Alice."

Philip didn't tolerate those *Italian ways*. Despite looking calm, his mother got straight to the point. She never beat around the bush. He had often told her to be more discreet, but she had always ended up saying that her behaviour was the result of being born in a Tuscan family. After all, Marta had always proudly shown off her origins. Thus, Philip was getting ready for that fight. He would have told his mother that his relationship with Brunhilde wasn't working anymore, and that breaking up was the wisest thing to do. As they say, *sooner rather than later*. It would have been a white lie. He didn't want to tell his mother about Detective Bassett. Philip would have followed the script, and Alice would have covered his back.

When Mrs. Murray came home, she wasn't surprised at all to see Philip. She had deduced that he had his own reasons, of which she didn't care at that moment. After what had happened to little Wendy, Marta knew that it would take much more to surprise her. Furthermore, after having learned about Gavin's detention - *the child-eater* - she only needed to rest. The mixture of information, injustice and violence had astounded her. Marta was on the endurance's edge. Thus, she didn't waist more time there. She hugged both Alice and Philip and the took her suitcase and went upstairs.

After having stepped on the fourth step, she said

"Whatever life has in store for us, we will never be prepared". Then, she headed to her bedroom.

That statement had worried Alice. What did her mother mean? Marta, more than anyone else, seemed to be aware of her husband's secret affair. However, Alice couldn't ask her, not now that Marta had decided to go away. She could feel paranoia growing inside her and taking the form of her father, of the coven, and of the subterfuges. Then, she remembered that - sooner or later - she would have to go to the cemetery - the Hades - to look for the rune. That whole story was wearing herself up deal in her bowels. It would end up destroying her.

Philip had foolishly focused only on Marta's indifference, as the fact that she had gone resting would have saved him a lot of trouble. Even so, his pride hurt. It was uncommon that *his* mother had decided to isolate herself. She had always fought by his side, and had taken up the cudgels for him, even going against her husband. The fact that she had never asked why he was at home upset him. It was time to accept the truth:

the Earth revolves only around the Sun, there is no place for him and the other planets.

He glanced at Mabon. He was the only one who couldn't realise the world's problem.

"*I envy you, kitty!*" – He thought.

The cat hadn't moved since Philip had come home; he was lying on the floor next to the studio's ventilation grille. His fur was thick and shiny, he didn't look wasted away. It seemed that in the last few days he had even become sturdier and taller! Soon, he would have become a lynx or any other large feline.

"What do you feed him? Looks like a different cat" – Philip said hinting at a smile.

"Leftovers" – Alice replied, then turned to the cat and frowned. "Actually, he barely eats. There's always food left in his bowl."

"I would never have guessed. Look how much he's grew."

"Also, he never sleeps."

"That's impossible!"

"Trust me, it is."

"A cat that doesn't sleep nor eat, it's not a cat!" – Philip laughed.

Alice stared at the animal and saw its hostile gaze. Mabon was perhaps the only cat who didn't behave as such. He used to spend his days watching over the studio, and when someone got close to it, he got annoyed and began to shake his tail. He had unexpectedly become its keeper. Alice thought that perhaps it was time to feed him with kibbles rather than leftovers. Better yet, she would have called the vet, Dr. Ward.

"Imagine if he had worms." – Philip said, disgusted at the only idea.

"How can you even think it?"

"Before Aleister found him, he had left home alone for who knows how long. Maybe he had picked up internal parasites."

"It doesn't look like he could have worms. He has only some obsessions!" – She stated.

Therefore, Alice tried to trick him with some grounded beef covered with cheese. Unless Mabon went hunting only when he was alone - which is unlikely for any animal that has been fasting for days - he would have eaten it.

The cat's hunger strike wasn't a good omen. Although he could have scratched her, Alice thought that the only solution was to shut the cat in a cage to take him to the vet.

She slowly had gotten closer to him, then she crouched down. The first attempt was a failure, as the cat had pushed her away emitting sinister meows.

Philip's phone rang, distracting his attention from Mabon. His enthusiasm was the same as those who got the umpteenth advertising call. He nodded, then mumbled "Ok" for countless time, as he wanted to hang up the phone.

Alice was wondering who he was talking to but tried to focus again on Mabon. However, as she leaned over, he shown his sharp canines, bit her hand and run upstairs. Alice held her scream of pain and fear back. Only swear words came to her mind. She was almost writhing in pain, as if a cobra had bitter her, rather than an ungrateful cat.

"*Mannaggia a te!*[16]" She thought in Italian as she pressed the injured back of her hand. "*Fetente di un gatto!*[17]".

Her eye was caught by the ventilation grille that the pet had watched over. It was made of iron and loose screws. Alice took a coin to remove the screws. Little movement had been enough

---

[16] Damn you!
[17] Rotter!

to remove the four screws. She put the grille and the dusty filter on the ground. Then, she lowered her head to the side to look inside the duct. She glimpsed something, even if she can't tell exactly what. She thought that it could be a piece of the ventilation duct. She looked more closely and saw a dark fabric.

In the meanwhile, Philip had hung up the phone. He had decided to inform Alice of his departure to London for some matters related to the family's assets. Nevertheless, he noticed the door of the studio ajar and entered it.

Philip saw Alice, who had her back to the door, motionless crouched on the floor. The pack of ground meat was placed next to her. She was in a cold sweat; and he could hear her heart beating like a drum in her chest. Alice was holding a gun in her cupped hands, as if she was about to receive the Holy Communion[18].

---

[18] Catholic ceremony.

XXXI

"Who stands with wars and weapons will be doomed to hell." That is how Father Arun Dilshan's homily had started.

Father Dilshan had come from Sri Lanka to indoctrinate young people. "I ask you to think about the commandments, in particular about the fifth one: you shall not kill. Killing is a sacrilege, it is an act against God. Killing tarnish permanently the soul of men."

Alice was nine years old when she attended that endless Sunday Mass. She didn't know if she admired his ability to spread the good word, or weather to believe that he was only stating the obvious. During the previous Sunday Mass he had talked about keeping the Sabbath Day. Alice knew she had always respected that commandment: she had always awaited for the Christmas day with trepidation. However, that day Father Dilshan had remembered people not to kill, because killing blemish people.

"*Of course*" – She had thought. Her mind - covered with red hair - had thought of more practical sins. Killing not only tarnish one's soul, but it also stains other things. Indeed, she had imagined blood stains on the ground, on hands and even blood encrusted under one's nails.

"Ew! That's so gross!" – A little boy sat next to her had said, as if Alice had thought aloud. They had both chuckled, until it become contagious and other kids begun to laugh at that phrase.

Although Father Dilshan's speech was valid, Alice hadn't been able to take his words seriously. The only violence she was ware of was that of her brother's video games, where he killed zombies and shot *flesh monsters*. Her mother didn't even tolerate verbal violence. As far as Alice knew, the only blunt objects her father owned were barbecues knives and golf clubs. Thus, during that old Sunday Mass, Alice had laughed and would have continued to do so, sure that she would always be safe.

The memory of Father Dilshan - a cheery memory - came to her mind in a flash, but it had vanished as soon as she touched that gun. The weapon was a semi-automatic gun, a 9mm short *Smith & Wesson*, efficient for personal defence. At least, that was what Philip had said. It seemed that had passed ages since Father Dilshan's sermon. Who knows what he had thought of the Murrays that day. Although Alice didn't care at all about that, she was sure that there will have been some share thoughts.

Philip moved close to her and urged her. "Put the gun on the ground, Alice!"

He knew that Alice would have never shot, but since the gun was without safety, he wanted to prevent any accidental shot. Philip took the gun from the ground, holding it by the barrel, then he wrapped it in its cloth.

He sighed in relief.

"Well" – He said, trying to stay calm. "Now we will get rid of, and we won't talk about this story ever again."

"It belonged to dad, didn't it?" – She asked frightened.

"It's certainly not mum's, and I don't want you to think it could be mine" – Philip told her. "We better get rid of the gun, as we don't know how far this affair can go. Before it's too late."

He inhaled and exhaled before speaking again. He stared at the fabric with incredulous, perplexed eyes, as when he got into trouble as a child, aware of the consequences.

"So" – He resumed – "We have to get shot of it without lose sight of it. Let's not doing bullshit, such as throwing it from a bridge or long driving's to bin it in the middle of nowhere."

"I totally agree" – Alice replied – "In a few hours I'll meet Aleister to talk about the Hades matter. Maybe..."

"What?"

"Maybe we could give him the gun in custody."

"To Aleister? Why not? After all, why not committing an accessory to the crime?"

"I don't want to get rid of it completely. I'm sure that this gun will play a crucial role in the affair."

Philip laughed mockingly, then he whispered "Alice, its role will be to send us to jail. But okay, let's do what you want."

"We don't have many other choices, beside telling mum or leave the gun where we found it. If the police will ever search the house, we'll have to explain why we have a gun in the house" – Alice said, observing the ventilation duct, while Father Dilshan's face came to her mind.

She imagined him waving his finger in warning, as to remark that they would have been doomed to hell, supposing that place really exists. Although Philip looked lucid, he was thinking about something else. He could only think about a lawyer discussing his family fate with a public prosecution. Philip had not even wondered if the possession of that gun could be justified for self-defense. Or was the weapon ascribable to reasons still unknown to them? He took in consideration the first option, but then he thought, "*In defense of what? In defense against whom?*"

He could not imagine his father in the role of a gangster, in the role of *John Dillinger*[19]. That thought could have been funny if only Arthur Murray hadn't denied for all those years that he was corrupted.

Amen.

---

[19] American gangster of the Great Depression.

XXXII

Entrusting the firearm to Aleister was apparently the only valid choice, as that wouldn't have included foolish actions. On second thought, giving the custody of a gun to an almost stranger was an equally insane and dangerous decision. On the other hand, the whole affair was insane.

In the middle of the morning, Alice rushed to Manor Falkenberg earlier than planned. Before getting out of the car, she had thought for a few minutes of what would happen shortly thereafter. The rain fell relentlessly on the car, and produced a pleasant sound, although it was enough to cover up her thoughts. She looked at the dark cloth that enveloped the gun emerging from the passenger seat, and that smelled of cordite. Giving the gun to Aleister would have been a real sign of trust, although dangerous. She was aware that no matter how that matter ended, their friendship - if it could be defined as such - would change. She sang the chorus of a song playing on the radio.

«Oh, ohh c'mon
you had a sweet, sweet childhood

but now you got your hands dirty with blood.
You told your mama,
monsters live beyond the wood»

Alice tried to contain herself from screaming in distress and began to laugh nervously until her face turned red and tears rolled down her cheeks. Finally, Alice burst into a liberating cry. She cried, not caring at all that someone could have seen her. Then, she wiped her face, took a deep breath, and finally got out of the car carrying the firearm under her arm.

She knocked at the door twice, then, Madame Dutrieux opened it. The governess invited Alice - whose shiny blue eyes contrasted the cloudy sky - to come in. For a moment, Alice had forgotten that Aleister lived with other people. There was no time for pleasantries, thus - after having adjusted the gun under her arm so that the woman couldn't see it - she only said,

"Thank you, Madame. But I'll wait for Aleister here."

"Are you sure you don't want to come in? You'll get a cold?" – Madame said worried.

After Alice's second refusal, she didn't insist. She went to call Aleister, leaving the front door ajar, as she hoped that the girl could change her mind.

While waiting, Alice looked her soaked shoes, which had become darker due to the water. Indeed, she had worn a pair of suede boots for the rush. She remembered when her mother used to scold her because she neglected herself. Then, she looked to her hand - the one Mabon had scratched - which now had an inflammation. Alice had disinfected it, but the bandage hurt her, and so she had removed it. She had noticed four dark red dots on her skin - perfectly equidistant from each other - which could have been joined to form a square.

Aleister reached the entrance hall, slowly opened the door. For some unknown reason, his hand was inexplicably aching, even if he grabbed small object.

"Why don't you come in? Do you want us to go to Hades right now?" – He asked Alice while smiling at her.

However, even before Alice answered, Alice's injured hand caught his eye.

"What happened?" – He asked.

"Mabon bit me" – Alice shook her head – "it's not a big deal. We just have to take him to the vet. He isn't eating anymore."

Then she looked at Aleister's hand, apparently healthy, although he opened and close it with mechanical movements.

"What happened to yours?"

"I accidentally shut it in the drawer."

Aleister had found himself lying again. He had thought that Alice was responsible for his hand pain, which had started hurting all of a sudden while he was painting in the *Scarlet Room*. The brush was softly sketching on the canvas when out of the blue the pain made him drop it. He had felt as a spur had ripped up his skin. Yet, he didn't mention that to Alice.

Aleister inspected Alice and noticed a fabric coming out of her arm. Then, he looked at her face, realizing that something was upsetting her.

"Alice, is everything okay?"

She swallowed, "I need to talk to you."

"Tell me."

"Actually... I have to ask you a favour. Not here, let's go elsewhere."

Unconcerned of the pouring rain, they walked to the stable.

Epos hardly noticed them; she was calmly sheltered under the roof.

"Now, you can talk" – Aleister told Alice.

"I just want to tell you that Philip would have taken care of it if he hadn't had to go to London ..."

"Are you at home alone? Why did he go away?"

"Assets matters… that's what he told me. Anyway, I don't believe him, I rather think it has something to do with Bassett." – Alice turned her gaze away and then resumed – "I swear I'm sorry to ask you that, as I know this can make things more complicated."

The guy slowly stretched out his arm to grab the fabric Alice was handing out. As soon as he touched the cloth, he realised what was inside it.

"Do you want me to deal with it?" – He asked her.

Alice nodded her head, then whispered, "Yes, please."

"Okay. I don't care where this gun come from."

"We can…" – She begun – "we can both decide where to hide it… if you want."

"No" – He replied – "The only thing I want is that you stay away of this gun. Wait for me in the car."

Aleister thought that it was unfair that such a pure person like Alice had to suffer the consequences of other people's choices. Her being was still uncontaminated by the human cruelty. He could saw in Alice what other people have lost. The *Erheiur* had overwhelmed him once again.

Then, he had managed to get into the house without leaving his wet footprints on the floor. There was only Madame at home, as Orpeco was at the bookshop. They should never have learned about the gun, as it would have endangered them.

Aleister begun to look around him, as to recreate the planimetry of the Manor. Aleister had to choose the best place to hide the firearm. Common rooms - such as the *twin rooms*, the library, and the studio - couldn't be take into consideration, as well as the kitchen and the sleeping area. Very few places could host that weapon, although he had to make sure that no one would have found it. Then, he headed to the pool room: he would have hidden the gun there. He walked to the pool table, looking for the small opening where he could place the arm.

Click. The fabric perfectly fit into one of the side pockets. Aleister had made it; he had managed to conceal the existence of that evidence.

Murmurs - similar to a female soliloquy - came out from the adjacent room. Nevertheless, Madame Dutrieux wasn't in the kitchen. Aleister knew that Madame would see him if he walked out the pool room. Thus, he went to the door to greet the governess, who was sitting on the floor with her hands placed on her lap and her head bowed. It seemed that she was praying.

"God Almighty, you have given me hope three times, you have supported my care three times, you have helped me guiding myself three times. Now, I humbly ask you that they receive the same protection, as you have done for us long time ago. I ask that you watch over them."

Aleister didn't interrupt that intimate moment, as he had learned of the existence of something - or someone - on whom the governess relied on. Madame Dutrieux was definitely praying, although it was her spiritually devoted heart that spoke.

Aleister quickly grabbed his coat and went outside. The rain was about to end. It softly fell on the ground, as if it had accomplished its task of washing away the evils. Suddenly, the smell of the air changed, turning into a less stinging scent. Then, snowflakes begun to fell onto the wet ground. He rushed into the car, then blew on his frozen hands to warm them up. His fingers had turned red, while his skin had cracked.

"Do you think this is normal?" – He asked Alice, who glanced over the steering wheel.

In the background, a radio speaker was telling a funny marital anecdote.

"You know Paul... my wife, Jenna, took this seriously. So, she told me... Alex, take Propolis in the morning and in the evening, so your blood pressure will lower! It will also lower the risk of infections! So, I looked at her worried, very worried and then I said... Jenna, it will also sag my..."

Alice turned off the radio, opened the glove compartment and took a pair of gloves that once belonged to her father. "Put them on."

Then, before starting the engine, Alice looked at him, taking advantage of the fact that he was distracted. His unintentional messy look was aesthetically pleasing to her eyes. His breathing was heavy, while his rosy cheeks contrasted with wet and messy hair. Alice smiled at him and waited for him to fix himself up. Then, she started talking to him.

"Aleister..."

"It's all settled."

"Well... I think the firearm belonged to my father. I didn't want to..."

"Alice..." – He grabbed both her hands – "It's all settled, let's forget about it."

The snow had also paved the Hades. The image of its streets covered with cotton candy softened that sad place.

As soon as Alice and Aleister crossed the entrance, they realised that finding the rune would have been impossible and pointless. Indeed, they weren't even sure that James Harvey had referred to *that* cemetery.

Eventually, they had found shelter under a porch. Aleister kept wondering while Alice hadn't stayed in the car, as her shoes were soaked and not suitable for snow. Indeed, they could have gone to Shelley House and returned to the cemetery another day.

"I'd need a ciggie... it's a pity that they've been making me sick lately."

"Alice, I saw something very weird today" – Aleister said – "For the first time, I saw Madame pray."

"Why do you think it's strange?"

"I didn't think she was a believer."

She lowered her head and hinted at a sneer. She was probably thinking to some faded memories. Hearing Aleister's words had reminded her of some anecdote.

He resumed, "I was wondering ... If none of your family believe in God, why did you bury your father in this cemetery?"

"It was one of his last wishes. He was the only one who still believed in ... all of this."

"What made you change your mind?"

"*Joseph McWorn.*"

The girl sat down on one of the stone steps. Then, Aleister sat down too.

"When we were children, we used to play together, we attended the same school and even the same church. He was my best friend. He had two other brothers, but they were younger than him. They were so ... so similar to the point that the seemed twins. They both had blond hair, and reddish cheeks in both summer and winter. Joseph smelled of freshly baked bread. I've always wondered if his mother used to bake it for breakfast."

Alice tried to hold back her tears. Her lips began to shiver, sadness had subdued, and her eyes became wet. There hadn't been a single day during which Alice hadn't thought of Joseph. She had thought of his tragic disappearance every single day.

"His father worked as a delivery man. He used to transport fresh milk every morning. Joseph had always been fascinated by his job, to the point that when he was ten - few days before Christmas - he had asked his father to go with him. The night before it had pouring rained, so the road was slippery. They had a terrible car accident on the morning of December 19th, 2004... the van went off the road and crushed on itself. His father survived the accident, while Joseph... he was found dead in the nearby field only few hours later. Since then, I hadn't believed in any god. How could a God be so selfish? There is no God, Aleister. I wish Joseph had received a second chance, just like I did. What comfort me is that his soul will live forever in peace, among the stars."

Aleister sighed. "So, you believe in souls."

"I have a very uncommon point of view on that. I think that only souls are capable of surviving death."

"What do you mean with 'uncommon'?"

"My idea of soul isn't religious, but scientific. Philip always tells me that souls are made of quantum energy, which put us in contact with the whole universe by simply producing light. Thus, the more souls shine and the more they reunite with the cosmos."

"What if someone doesn't have a soul, or has fewer souls than other people?"

"Fewer? I don't think it could be possible... bodies coexist with soul. Without it, bodies would only be doomed to death. The prospect of a long life is the only thing capable of making me reconsider the concept of death itself. Actually, each of us will live forever, each of us is destined for eternity in the cosmos. I firmly believe in it, and I'm ready to pursue this promise."

"A promise..."

"What?" – Alice smiled, then looked at Aleister as to encourage him to talk.

"The biggest promises are those made by those who gave part of their soul" – He said. However, as soon as he noticed her confusion, he put an end to that conversation.

It seemed to Aleister that Alice was aware of having received a second chance. He wasn't able to say the right thing, as humans couldn't considered that rescue fair. He continued wondering if one day Alice would have ever understood the *Erheiur*. Even him himself couldn't understand why Altors let most humans dying, and Joseph incident was the proof. Their actions were due to the belief that they were acting in the name of good, as they were omnipotent beings able to love unconditionally. Perhaps they were impostors who had stolen people's souls, taking advantage of their free will. Alice didn't know that, but her soul was split in two, like the sharp difference between good and evil, between mortal and immortal. However, they both would be mortal on earth and in the immaterial life. At that very thought, Aleister felt ashamed. He felt ashamed of being an Altor because he had denied Alice' soul of eternal life.

The snow had begun to strongly fall on the ground. Snow-flakes had lied on the stonegraves of those who had been denied the chance to live, *for now*. Also, the statue of the winged genius had been covered by the white snow.

Aleister carefully watched the statue; it reminded him of himself, except for its wings and its innocent face. It looks like the Altors. Even if he needed to hear Alice's voice more than ever, he thought that it was better not to tell anything about her friend's death.

Suddenly, Mrs. Beans entered the cemetery, indeed, despite owning her flower shop in Maddox Street, long time ago she had been allowed to use a small building of the cemetery as a flower shop. She walked through the back door, muttering and complaining about something. Then, she bent on her plump knees, looking for *something* in the snow.

Alice approached the woman to ask her what was happening. Witnessing that scene would have made anyone believe that Mrs. Beans was out of her mind.

"My dear Alice!" – She stood up to greet her, but Aleister's beauty amazed her to the point that she was almost fainting. "I lost one of my earrings!"

"Are you sure you dropped it here?" – Alice asked her.

"I'm very sure! Look, it's like this one" – Mrs. Bean showed Alice sapphire set in a white gold. "It's a gift from my husband, one of the few that I have deserved after forty years of marriage! *Ah, men*! I'll have to go home without earring. It is not good to wear just one, it is not good for a woman of my age! It would look like one of those piercings youngsters have. Anyway, I'm sure I dropped it here."

Alice kindness made her crouch on the ground to help her, while Aleister watched them from under the porch.

"No, honey, come on! Go to your *friend*!" – Mrs. Bean told her. Then she whispered a sentence that made Alice blush and smile at the same time. "Thank you anyway, my dear. I don't want your help. I'll inform Edmond. *Ah, men*! If he will find it, I'll tell him to store it in the lost and founds box. I hope he'll understand how I care about the earring. You know, he has always his head in the clouds. Otherwise, it will be impossible for me to deal with my husband. *Ah, men*!"

They took their leave. Then, the woman resumed her business. For the first time Aleister and Alice learned about the lost and found box, and such news was a turning point for their research.

Thus, they headed to the gatehouse.

Aleister suggested Alice to go to the caretaker's office alone not to attract attention. *Cerberus* was too focused on reading and - as her presence wouldn't have distracted him - he would have continued reading.

The LOST AND FOUNDS wooden box was located at the back of the office, on a dusty table full of empty vases. Nevertheless, the smell of mortuary flowers permeated the room. In the box there were lost keys, stuffed animals, gloves and even a boot. How can you lose a shoe? But more importantly, there was a non-working watch equipped with a chronograph. The rune was set in the strap.

At first, Alice hesitated, but then she took the watch and put it in her pocket, as if she was a novice thief. Then, she went out the room excitedly.

On the back of the metal case, the name of the owner was engraved. Unfortunately, she knew him. it was Hamond

Prestcote-Hill's watch, the Prosecutor General. In Harvey's diary he was the owl who had lost its time where silence reigns forever.

Prestcote-Hill hadn't appeared in the photo group yet.

He was still alive!

Mr. Hamond was still alive!

XXXIII

That same afternoon, Aleister and Alice had decided that the best thing to do was going to *Nightingale House* - the Prosecutor General's house. However, Aleister had thought that Alice didn't need his help in that circumstance, as his presence would have turned that meeting into an interrogation. Thus, he had gone home after Alice had reassure him that it would have been a brief and informal conversation. Nevertheless, Aleister knew that the meeting wouldn't have been brief at all.

Ms. Solovyov - the governess - welcomed Alice, who was intrigued as she had never had anything to do with her before. The governess had asked Alice who she was, and then, with her strong Russian accent, invited Alice to wait for Mr. Hamond in the living room.

"He won't take long. He's finishing his bath" – The governess said while offering Alice delicacies and freshly baked butter bread.

Nevertheless, Alice asked for a warm drink. She looked around the modern corridors and the low ceiling wide rooms.

The rooms were furnished with only basic furniture. The building - which had often appeared in many magazines for its special contemporary minimalism - was designed by a well-known Egyptian designer. In the past, that house embodied the spirit of the British pop art. Monochromatic wallpapers and colourful decoration adorned its rooms. Nowadays, those decorations had been replaced by wide rooms and handrails, which made the house look like a rest home. Alice ignored all those alterations the house had gone through. Indeed, the last time she had met Mr. Hamond was the year before she went to *Durham*, when he still held the office of Prosecutor General and regularly went to Shelley House. As far as she remembered, Marta hadn't ever mention her of Mr. Hamond's health problems. Therefore, the only thought of discovering any possible disability of Mr. Hamond made her feel completely numb. Indeed, she had broken into his house, expecting that he would have told her about that watch.

Thus, Pop art style objects and colourful decoration had given way to minimalism decorations. In fact, silence reigned in the house. The clock hand marked the seconds, producing the only detectable noise in the whole house. That noise resembled that of drops falling into a bowl of water.

The governess brought a teapot and poured some tea into Alice's cup. Then, she started talking. Her conversation was actually a monologue about the climatic changes in England, about her husband who fled to Costa Rica and then about her, who had to move to Wiltshire in search of a better life. Ms. Solovyov's attempts to kill time ended up boring Alice.

"So, you know Mr. Hamond? No one comes to visit him anymore, except his daughter and a *handsome, tall, rich, and green-eyed man*. It's been a while since the last time I've seen the man, while his daughter comes almost every week" – The governess told Alice.

"Yes, I know him. He's a family friend. He encouraged me to continue with my studies in law" – Alice was trying to figure out who the *handsome, tall, rich, and green-eyed man* described by the governess could be. Those few words had been enough to intrigue her.

"So, you are a lawyer?"

"No, actually I work at the plant nursey."

"What a pity! I wanted to ask you for your help with the divorce with Sergei."

"*There she goes again!*", Alice thought.

"Ms. Solovyov, can I ask you a question?"

"Sure, you can ask whatever you want about Sergei."

Alice hesitated before resuming talking. Then, she looked around herself and lowered her voice.

"I don't want to ask you about Sergei. Forgive my insolence, I didn't know Mr. Hamond was... sick."

"We don't know much about his illness. He just seems... lost."

"Lost?"

"His mind got sick."

"Has he been sick for a long time?

"He has gotten worse since November. He barely speaks, and when he does it, he confuses people. He always mistakes me for his daughter. You should see Miss Margaret's face when her father mistaken her for me! 'Ms. Solovyov, do this, Ms. Solovyov, do that'. We always say that when Mr. Hamond speaks, it is because he is in a good mood." – The governess said laughing. Alice thought that Ms. Solovyov had the nerve, so she had decided not to laugh.

The sliding door behind them opened.

An attendant entered the room pushing a wheelchair, on which Mr. Hamond was sat. The attendant, whose name was Maksim, was talking to the man with a reassuring, yet jokingly voice. He looked at Ms. Solovyov with a knowing look, which made her blush. Then, they talked in Russian, and Alice didn't understand anymore.

"He's in a bad mood today" – Maxim said as he walked towards the living room.

He had a dazzling smile, so white that it could blind. He introduced himself to Alice with a firm handshake, then he arranged the wheelchair in front of the girl so that she could speak to Hamond.

"We'll leave, so you can talk to him. If he doesn't remember about you, just ignore it. If any problem occurs, use the remote control on the side of the wheelchair" – The governess said, then she left the room, leaving the doors open. She headed to the kitchen to catch up with Maxim, who - as soon as saw her - pinched her butt.

Mr. Hamond was taciturn, while his eyes were staring at the floor. Alice noticed that his eyelids were moving slowly, almost as he had forgotten how to blink. She soon realized that talking about the watch would have been impossible, as well as telling him about the Divum Deus. She would have kept him company for a little while and then she would have joined Aleister.

"Do you know who I am?" – She asked softly.

However, Hamond's gaze was still focused on the floor. She looked around herself thoughtfully, then glimpsed the clock face on the fireplace. She wouldn't have stayed there any longer.

She rummaged inside her pocket to take the watch. Then, she touched the surface of the strap, thinking aloud.

"How fool I have been. I came here thinking that you could tell me more about this matter, but you can't even speak." – Alice stood up to leave the house.

"Yes" – The man nodded weakly.

"So, you can… you can understand what I'm saying?" – She asked surprised.

Maksim was wrong, it was a beautiful day for Mr. Hamond! Maybe…

The man didn't answer immediately, he only looked to the sliding doors. Thus, Alice walked to the door, waiting for the man to say something. However, he only blinked twice; he would have talked to her, but only behind closed doors.

"Alice, I know who you are."

"So, you remember me."

Then, Mr. Hamond stood up on his own legs, while Alice's were shaken. She headed to the windows and closed the curtains.

"What does this watch mean?" – Then, she looked at him scared and added. "You don't look sick."

"Alice, where you got the watch."

"Why are you pretending you don't know? Are you hiding from the Divum Deus?"

"Okay, okay. One question at a time. They've tried to give me a tranquilizer and I feel my mind almost asleep. First answer my question."

"I found it in the cemetery, as it was written in James Harvey's diary. Hamond, it was you who had hidden it, right? I came here only to know the truth."

"James did it. I asked him to hide the watch."

"Why?"

"Alice, you're shrewd. But remember, sometimes ignoring the truth can save your life. Be careful, this matter will get you into trouble."

"My father is dead. And many other too. How can you say that?"

Alice took the photo group from her jacket and pointed out the faces not yet appeared on the photo. "Who are they?"

"The Divum Deus coven began with the ancient Attenborough family, and has been passed down to us, the worthy students of Oxford. Success and the desire to stand out brought us together. One day, a stranger woman joined the group. She gave a rune to everyone as a sign of belonging, reminding us to hide them also from our roommate. The runes would have led us to a life of fortune, and they actually did it. We became the men who had dreamt of, people of power and respected by everyone. However, we had to pay for it… we had to pay with blood."

"Blood?"

"Sacrifices. Those who owned the rune had been called to arms. They had been asked to kill, otherwise their beloved ones would have suffered the consequences. Your father, James and Timothy escaped the oath by taking their lives."

"So, have you already killed someone? Is the *woman* you were talking about the one with the powder-coloured dress?"

"Alice, one question at a time, have mercy on me. I'm not a killer, not directly. For Margaret's sake I refused it. That's why I'm playing the part of the old, crippled, and sick man. After your father's death, I faked my illness. James's complicity was essential, because - beside Arthur - he was the only loyal friend I had. As I expected, he chose the most common place to hide the watch. Damn! I should have expected this. The Harveys have always been too contorted" – Then, Mr. Hamond looked at the photo, "Yes, she's the woman. She defined herself as the Phoenix, she was a conceited villain. She said she was the chosen one, but she was just a witch."

"Why did Dorothy die?"

"She took her own life. She was aware that otherwise, someone else would have killed her. After Timothy's death, she wanted to leave the town, she wanted to run away. She had probably witnessed the scene, and it must have scared her. However, I strongly doubt that jumping off the bridge was her initial thought."

"What about my father? Why did he keep all this matter secret?"

Alice was clearly sorry. She wasn't ready to accept the truth. "The runes are not lost. We can destroy them and put an end to this insane matter" – She said.

"Arthur wanted to protect your family. He defied cruelty and look that turned out. Runes can't be destroyed. You must hide them in a safe place, where *she* can't find them" – Then, the man leaned his body towards the girl and whispered, "All, but *one*."

"Which rune are you referring to? Who's hiding behind all of this? Speak clearly, tell me his name!"

"If I tell you that, all my attempts to protect Margaret would have been in vain. I can't let any other innocent people dying. I've already lost my daughter forever, now, you'd better leave."

Alice detained herself on the chair. She demanded more information, she wanted to know more about the congregation. Nevertheless, Mr. Hamond pressed the button of the remote control, making Maksim rush breathlessly, while closing the zipper of his trousers, exactly like a *bad guy*.

Thus, she was forced to stand up.

"Has something happened?" – The assistant asked out of breath, then he looked around, noticing that the curtains were closed. He looked at Alice as if she was the real bad girl in that room.

"We talked about the good old days. Now, it's better if he rests a bit. Bye, have a good day!"

Alice left the house in great agitation. The tall, handsome man with green eyes was James Harvey who had been appointed to hide the runes. The governess hadn't seen him anymore because he had taken his own life.

She quickly walked the flight that separated the walls of the house from the garden. Walls... like those who separated her from her loved ones. She could feel death loom over her. It was only a matter of days, or even of hours.

Before getting on her car, her gaze met that of Margaret Prestcote-Hill, who was visiting her father.

XXXIV

Gavin's corpse was found that same night by an officer. His mouth was wide open like the man portrayed on *The Scream*, while his lips had become blue, blue like those of little Wendy. Someone had dropped a ballpoint pen in his cellar - as if it was on purpose - with which he had torn his forearms. Blood had gushed from his veins. Purple blood, like childbirth liquids, like anger, like shame. He had dipped his finger in it to write on the gray tiles:

IT WASN'T ME.

XXXV

Wednesday, 3rd of January 2018

Margaret's morning turned out to be as unpredictable as the Russian roulette game. Each day could be compared to a round: she inserted the shot, turned the drum, and pulled the trigger. That day, the suicide of Amilia had been the variable of the game. In addition, the fact that little Danton hadn't been found yet, upset her. She hoped that the *child-eater* matter had ended with Amilia's death, hoping that the police hadn't arrested an innocent. Thus, it seemed that destiny had already been written by someone. She couldn't do nothing but accept it. Working, sporadic visits to her father and a lot of sex were her daily life's keywords. She had woken up at the side of a strong man, whose skin scented of Monoi. Margaret loved spending her nights with different men. That need intensified at least once a week, meaning every time she visited her father.

The muscular man - who was still laying on her bed - saw Margaret getting out of bed, after having heard her speak on the phone. She had run into the bedroom only to ask him to go home.

"Come on! It's still 6 a.m.! Come lay with me" – He urged her.

"Listen, Mick…"

"Spencer… My name is Spencer."

"Right, Spencer. You'd better go now, or I'll be late for work."

"What do you do? You didn't tell me last night."

Margaret detested his attempt to stall as it made him seem even more annoying. She sighed. She found telling stranger about her private life irritating. After all, they had shared only a night of pleasure. Margaret would have never revealed her real job to none of her night conquests. She couldn't tell him that she was a Chief Inspector, thus, she had to lie.

"I'm a teacher."

"Oh, I thought you worked as a policeman. Last night you 'threatened' to handcuff me if I hadn't obeyed you" – Spencer said laughing.

Margaret didn't answer. She stared at him menacingly, while she was trying to remember how many tequila shots she had drunk to tell him such words. *"Ten? Maybe even fifteen…"* she thought, then she got dressed.

"So… you're leaving?" – He asked her.

"Yes, Mick… Spencer! and you'll leave as well."

Margaret grabbed his clothes - which smelled of Monoi and testosterone, exactly like his skin - and threw them to him.

"Can we keep in touch? What if you give me your phone number?" – Spencer asked as he was getting dressed.

Margaret was wearing a gray sheath dress, and - as soon as he asked that question - she turned her look to him, saying,

"Nah, but you can still be helpful. Come zip my *Armani dress*… Spencer!"

After having literally kicked Spencer out of her apartment, she put on a pair of elegant dark boots. They were the only shoes she had compulsively bought and that didn't hurt her feet. She quickly looked at the sky through the window and noticed that snow was quickly falling on the ground. She grabbed the keys of her *Volvo*, parked in front of the house, and drove to Slohan Oak Police Station.

Margaret would have recognized Cole's voice a mile away. Every time she looked at him, she ended up feeling both melancholy and the desire to tear his clothes off. The nature of those contrasting feelings was unknown even to her. The only thing she knew was that reminding of her happy childhood and her mother's premature death caused her melancholy, which could be healed only by the pleasure the man gave her. Perhaps she was unconsciously in love with him. However, as she was his superior, she knew that her rigid behaviour was required.

Cole was talking with Walsh in front of the vending machines. Before she reached the gatehouse, Margaret had heard them talking about the Premier League and the football match that had been played the night before between Manchester City and Watford.

As soon as the woman stepped into the room, the atmosphere became tenser. Indeed, after having heard the noise of her heels on the floor, they began to talk about safety criteria of the Station.

"Good morning, Margaret" – Cole greeted her, then, he selected a bitter coffee from the vending machine. Cole knew her morning rituals, thus, he didn't even ask her if she fancied a coffee.

"Any update?" – She asked assertively.

"Amilia… he took his own life with a ballpoint pen. At least, he was enterprising" – Walsh muttered from under his reddish beard.

"What about his livid lips?"

"The first examination reported that it was probably due to bleeding and hypothermia."

"Well, I think we should watch the footage recorded last night" – Margaret replied.

The Inspector did not say anything about what had happened. Cole just looked at the woman and hinted at a smile that she ignored. Then, he solemnly placed a hand on Walsh's shoulder - as one does when swear on Bible - and asked him to wait for him in his office.

They were left alone.

"Margaret, we caught the man responsible for Wendy's death" – He reported. Nevertheless, the woman couldn't keep her eyes on him. "Maggie…"

It was only at that moment that he got her attention, although she could barely tolerate his confidential tone during working hours.

"It's over. Brutally… but at least it's over. Justice has been done" – Cole said.

"You can't call it justice. A man has died under our custody. I would like you to send me the footages."

"Okay, I'll take care of it."

"Have you already informed Amilia's sister?"

"Breanne Amilia? No, not yet."

"I'll ask Officer Lewis for her home address. I'll informed her of what had happened in person.

Margaret didn't mean to justify Gavin's brutality, nor she wanted to sugarcoat it to his family. She just thought that informing Breanne in person was the only right thing to do. Being sympathetic and talking to the criminals' family were part of her work.

Margaret overstepped the guardhouse, asked for the address of the Amilia's house and headed to the car, taking care not to slip on the wet road. She had tried to arrange a brief and compassionate speech to give Breanne. Thus, before starting the engine, she tried to tell it as she looked at herself in the mirror. Then, she remembered a detail that could have justified the austerity she had shown to her colleagues. Walsh had claimed that the boy had died of bleeding and hypothermia. However, it could have been very strange that Gavin had dead of hypothermia. Indeed, as Mrs. Murray had noticed, the Station was very warm. Thus, hypothermia was to be excluded a priori. Even Margaret considered the heat in the Station unbearable, as well as Gavin, who had complained about the heat the day of his interrogation. Therefore, she decided to go back inside the Station, reporting Officer Lewis that she had forgotten her wallet in front of the vending machines. She hoped to see Cole there, taking his morning dose of caffeine. Unfortunately, he wasn't there. Margaret glimpsed his pocket watch on the ground, the one Cole used to pass between his fingers. She took it and went to his office. She was about to knock on the door, but suddenly hesitated. Although she was very enterprising, insecurities always take over. Her life didn't evolve only around wild sex, it was only a front for her real personality. Indeed, she was still the introverted little girl who - when she used to play hide-and-seek - she apologised when she couldn't run back to 'home base' to save the other players.

"*I can do it*" – She told herself. However, when she reached the wooden jamb, she realised she couldn't help listening to the conversation between the two men.

"This matter must quickly come to an end!" – Walsh burst out worried, and almost on the edge of fainting.

Unfortunately, Officer Lewis appeared exclaiming her name. Believing she had done her a favour, she ignored that Margaret was eavesdropping.

"Have you found you wallet, Chief? – Lewis asked.

"Yes, Officer."

Margaret firmly knocked on the door twice. Cole welcomed her sitting on his chair.

"Forgive my interruption" – Margaret said embarrassed – "I just want to point out something."

She continued, looking at Walsh with disappointment. The Inspector encouraged her to talk by nodding his head, then, he adjusted his tight jacket and finally crossed his arms as a sign of boredom. His gaze was that of a father annoyed by his daughter's insolence. He was her subordinate, although he didn't act like that. Margaret was fully aware of this, which is why she had hesitated before knocking: after all, she was able to show her supremacy only under the sheets.

"Walsh, your report wasn't accurate. Even my father's care-giver could have conducted a more thorough one. How the story of the hypothermia came out is still a mystery to me. The Station is as hot as hell. Instead of wasting time here, chatting with Inspector about Watford, you'd better take Amilia out of the cold room and do the autopsy all over again. Our duty is to provide explanations as plausible as possible to the deads' family. It seemed to me that you have carried the whole case too superficially."

"Sure, I'll do the autopsy again" – The Coroner replied. However, as his look suggested, he probably hadn't grasped the urgency of that request.

"Is there anything else?" – Cole asked annoyed.

"Yes. Any updates on Reece Danton?"

"Officers are carrying his search forward. I appointed Morris to sift through basements, houses, and sheds of the *Suburbs*. Moreover, his mother had asked the community to join her to look for her son during the night" – Cole told her.

Finally, Margaret handed him the watch, "I think it's yours. I found it on the floor. You must have dropped it."

Then, she left the room. She tried to focus only on the speech she would have given to Amilia, wondering if the two men were keeping her in the dark from other truths.

Amilias' home was located at the north side of Slohan Oak, nearby the suburbs. The house once was a small building made of red bricks and surrounded by a neglected country yard infested by weeds. In the garden, there were a small tool shed and an old swing. The snow had hit the *Suburbs* so much so that it made those areas look like a ghost town.

A light smoke came out from the chimney of the house, hinting that there was someone in the house. After Margaret knocked on the door, the sound of the door unlocking could be heard.

"Why are you here again? You've already broken into my house yesterday" – Breanne said with disappointment. Her brown hair was tied in a bun, while dark circles marked her eyes. She was leaving to Melksham, to reach the *Antico Caffe*, the café where she worked, which was run by two Italian friends. However, Chief Inspector's visit had suddenly made her reschedule her day.

Breanne let Margaret go into the living room only because she had informed her boss of any possible delay. She had only granted the minimum wage of hospitality, putting aside all kind of pleasantries. Margaret would have left the house soon, and Breanne - who was carefully observing the enemy - was impatiently waiting for that moment to come.

The living room was furnished with second-hand furniture. A weird floral-patterned wallpaper covered the walls, while stains of mold came out from the corners of the room. Yellow lace curtains covered the windows, while a wooden crucified Christ was hung on the fireplace. An acrid scent of burnt wooden and ash could be smelled in the room. However, the house was overall clean and well kept.

Margaret sat next to the sofa and kept her gaze down on the floor. Her inner introverted little girl had come to light again. What would have she said to Breanne? The whole truth? The ballpoint pen issue could have led Breanne to a bitterest truth. Had Gavin been forced to kill himself? She couldn't accept that truth. Gavin had taken his own life, which could be considered a fair death for a *child-eater*. Nevertheless, the matter of his livid lips was still inexplicable. Yet, reconstruction of that case was hadn't been very accurate. Although her conscience suggested her to tell the truth, she knew that she had to cover her colleagues at any cost.

As Margaret expected, omitting the details of Gavin's death hadn't been easy. Breanne burst into tears, grabbed her red face in her hands. She was filled with anger.

"You killed him!" – She kept repeating. – "You have taken my brother away from me and killed him. When will you stop tormenting my family? You've visited him... you've accused him just for the sake of killing him, right?"

"Who has visited him?"

"Ever since Gavin had seen that man standing by the tool shed, he was aware that it would end badly. I told him to report the matter to the police, otherwise he would have taken a beating. But he thought that *merciful God* would have protected him and shelter him from his past. Now, he got death!"

"Breanne, who are you talking about? Did Gavin know him? Have your brother ever told you his name?"

Breanne's face became red with tears, then she said sighing, "Cole, his name is Cole."

The woman slowly stood up, as if she was feeble, and finally looked at Margaret. "In this life, you're as cursed as all of us. Now, get out of my house" – Breanne whispered.

Margaret left the house, aware that Amilia's case couldn't be dismissed. She had proof that the Station knew about other details, and piece by piece, she would have made that puzzle. The first thing to do - without any hesitation - would have been to involve her colleagues, one by one. Nevertheless, when she took her phone to call Cole, she realised she had eight missed calls from Miss Solovyov.

Margaret had rushed to Nightingale House, but when she arrived, it was too late. The governess told her everything in detail, to the point that confusion and fright made her begin that conversation with few Russian words. She told everything to Margaret, except that she had flirted with Maksim the whole time, which had distracted her from noticing that Mr. Hamond had gone to the bathroom on foot. She had found him dead in the bathtub three hours later, after having seen his wheelchair in the living room. The man had taken all the drugs he had collected over the time and then he had swollen them. There were stains of vomit on the floor. Indeed, he had ended up throwing up some of the pills, while others had reached his hearth causing his death.

Until his last heartbeat, he had tightly held two photos in his right hand: the first one portrayed him with his five-years old daughter in his arms, while the second one portrayed a pale blonde woman. That was *Maggie's* bequest: unsaid words that hid unconditional love. Of all those years, she would bring the memory of their hard times, his debilitating *illness*, his death, and the last afternoon they had spent together.

Looking at her father's corpse inside the tub, Margaret began to recall those moments, which were now imprinted in her mind. When the afternoon before she hugged him, her father cried, wetting her cheeks with his tears. She would have known that it was a farewell.

XXXVI

The alarm clock - a strange eighteenth century invention that reminds humans to get up - had immediately intrigued Aleister. Madame Dutrieux had placed that useless object on his night table. Indeed, Aleister didn't need an alarm to wake up. He had an inner biological clock perfectly synch with the stars that lit up above the heartly sky. At any time of the day, if someone would have asked him the time, he would have answer accurately.

On that cold January morning, Aleister had woken up at around eight o'clock. He laid in bad staring at the blue ceiling of his room, thinking of how many shades of that colour he had seen since he had arrived on earth. Indeed, that colour - which was able to replace the grayness of his loneliness - had different shades: *indigo* blue like Alice's car; *Rörstrand* blue, as that of porcelain; *sapphire* blue like Orpeco's eyes; *klein* blue; *cobalt* blue, like the sky; *sideral* blue, like the star that had created Aleister. If that colour had ever had a scent, it would have been that of Alice's. He was sure of it.

In order to liven up that day - which would have soon turned into an apocalyptic one - he had planned to watch the VHS of *To Kill a Mockingbird* with Alice. Bad weather had forced them to stop from their research on the *Divum Deus*. In any case, a brief two-hours break wouldn't have caused any major slowdown. After all, the BBC had spoken clear: Hurricane *Eleonor* and its strong gusts of wind would be only one of the many atmospheric disturbances that would have hit the Country. The newscast had invited its viewers to be cautious and not to undertake long-driving journeys or taking planes. A stronger Siberian cold snap would hit the Country in February. By then, the Great Britain would be in state of weather alert, causing huge general inconvenience.

Aleister frightened to hear the news report. No one had ever been frightened like him. He regretted of having reached such a cold country. Nevertheless, he realised that he could have been worst if he had reached Alaska, for example.

"You know, last night before I fell asleep, I thought of something ..." – Alice told him as soon as they sat on the sofa in the living room.

"Something about Mr. Hamond told you?"

Alice shook her head.

"No, I've already ruminated on it. I was thinking about... about the question you asked me, the one about souls. Why do you think that someone can have a lower amount of soul than others? Or even not having it at all?"

"Quantum physics assumes infinite possibility; you should know that. In any case, I really don't know how you can face certain topics with lucidity in the early morning."

Alice smiled and turned on the VCR.

Aleister had decided to put an end to that matter, otherwise he would have ended up telling her of his real nature. On the other hand, Alice would have continued asking more question if he hadn't folded his arms.

"These are just theories, aren't them? – She asked. "Exactly like the exoplanet you come from." – Alice added.

Her rumbling stomach put a stop to that conversation. Thus, Alice went into the kitchen to take some food. Despite there was enough food to eat for breakfast - and despite the fact that the streets were covered with snow - her mother had decided to go out to buy more. Indeed, Marta had hung on the fridge for yellow post-it notes, aware that Alice wouldn't read the messages she had sent her phone. On the first note, Marta had written that she would have had dinner with Slohan Oak research team and that she should have liked that Aleister, Urielle and Alice joined her. The second and the third ones informed Alice that she was going to the convenience store and then she would have taken Alice's blue car to the mechanic. On the last post-it notes, Marta asked when the *prince* would have come back home. Alice could even imagine her mother's disappointment in writing that note.

The four notes were disjointed one from the other, just like day and night. Some of them embodied her role as mother, other marked her duties. After all, Marta would have never backed out of her responsibilities. Alice had probably missed that detail. Despite what had happened in the past weeks - namely deaths, disappearances and unpleasant truth - their lives would always find a way to follow their own course. She had to look up to his brother, who pretended to be in London for financial reason. Or even to Urielle, who was enjoying that cold snap in her apartment, probably reading a book. Alice knew it: if she had learned to divide things, her life would have been easier.

Marta's decision to go to the mechanic was an act of love for her daughter, as well as a good idea. The repair shop was run by Mr. Harris, the skier - as Philip used to call him, because of his big feet that reminded of two skis - who would have soon closed the business permanently. Indeed, the man had fallen ill with a rare pulmonary syndrome that doesn't allow him to work as a mechanic anymore. It was him who had fixed Alice's car after her accident, before he was diagnosed with that syndrome. Despite Mr. Harris had always been authoritarian - almost like a father - he really cared about the girl.

Alice's car tyres needed to be changed. Not because there was a specific decree, but because it would have been safer to change them in view of the arrival of the Siberian cold snap.

That morning, a handsome young man covered for him. His long and slender legs and his emeralds green eyes didn't get unnoticed. He claimed that he knew Philip as they had both studied engineering, although Marta didn't remember him. After having finished, he listed all the checks he had carried out. He reminded Marta to have the drive belt checked at the end of the season, and to make sure that the car battery wasn't turned off for more than two weeks in a row. In that regard, he advised Marta to remove the battery and store it in a dry place, so that the cold wouldn't compromise its functionality.

Marta smiled. Not because she or Alice would have destroyed his expectations, but also because the guy reminded her of Philip. After having checked the car, he had looked at her with a pure and almost familiar smile.

"Mrs. Murray, wait a minute" – He walked to the back of the shop and returned with a small purple cloth bag.

Inside it, there was a heavy metal ball engraved.

"Do you mind give it to Philip? I found it in my attic, but it belongs to him. He must have lent it to me for a classroom experiment."

"Of course. But if you prefer it, you can give it to him in person. I can ask him to come over one of these days."

"It's not necessary. I'm going to move to the north given those hard times. You can give it to him."

"Can you tell me your name? I don't think I've already asked you."

"My name is *Bor.*"

"Okay *Bor*, I'll send him your greetings then."

Marta left the workshop. Although she was suspicious, she didn't think of that matter more than she should. Her son always met new people; thus, it wasn't strange that he knew a *Bor* who feared those hard times.

After having started the car, she slowly headed home. She tried to pay attention to the snow-covered roads. The windscreen wipers dragged heavy heap of snow. Winter in Slohan Oak would have hit hard that year, mercilessly and without restraint. And if Reece really was as far away from home as they all believed, the freezing storm would be fatal for him.

Slohan Oak is a small town with four thousand, three hundred and sixteen inhabitants, located southeast of Erlestoke. Generally speaking, many ironically perceive the weather fair at the right point all the year round. While cold and humidity were a constant, it couldn't be said the same for the name of the town, which had been changed several times throughout British history. Originally, the town was name after a woman committed to occultism - *Silohan* - whose existence was rejected with the advent of the Catholicism in the southwestern region. Silohan practiced esoteric rituals in the service of the community. It was said that she nourished her energy with the sap of a century-old oak. Everyone loved her, both adults and children. However, not much in known about the *witch*. She died of old age, after having decided to live in the woods, hiding herself from the Norman conquerors who destroyed the village.

From the 11th century, a large part of Wiltshire territory passed into the hands of the Catholic Church, except Slohan Oak. Indeed, the town was relinquished to the laic Osborne Giffard, the knight who invaded the English lands by the order of William the Conqueror. The former name of the village - which in the meanwhile had become a small rural town - was replaced with *Grandchesne*. After the destruction of the Norman castle by order of the English Parliament in 1648, the town took the name of *Fallenoak*, in memory of the soldier who died in the war in Devizes. When inquisition practices and witchhunt spread all over Europe, the name of Silohan Oak disappeared from the records. People who talked about the period before the Christian domination were convicted in public. Only from the nineteenth century - thanks to the unification of Great Britain and Ireland and with the assignment of the ancient and prestigious Attenborough family - the name of Silohan reappear. Following a phonetic contraction, 'Silohan' became Slohan. Compared to the surrounding areas of the Wiltshire, the town was just a tiny dot. Ruins of the ancient romans could be seen in the nearby countrysides, while a sense of peace and tranquility flooded the town. Even nowadays, the centuries-old oak stands on the slopes of the wood. The legend has it that during the night, a female voice singing could be heard before the sun rises. Some people also claim that, going to the oak when one is facing an hard period is a good omen, especially in the spring, when the *myosotis* covers the ground. And that will be when Silohan could offer help to those who ask for it.

Mrs. Danton had lost hope. Nevertheless, she asked the community to meet up at the feet of the oak. She thought - somehow - that gathering the whole Slohan Oak community would allow her to find her son. The meeting time was arranged at 6 p.m. and, although the storm was still raging on the town, people took part to give their help and support. A long procession started from the church yard up to the centuries-old oak.

Just before the procession reached the slopes, the sight of a dead body on the ground caused horror and screams. It was Reece. He was still wearing the clothes he wore the day before, the same jacket in which he had been caught by the police security cameras. His pale face was covered with a flux of crusted blood. His lips were blue, while his lively eyes had been tearing off and his empty eye sockets had been filled up with mud.

Someone must have taken his eye.

Someone must have *eaten* them.

XXXVII

Thursday, 4th of January 2018

Following the discovery of Reece's corpse, shock took over among the inhabitants of the County. The thirst for justice could not overcome the deep concern of having a killer on the loose. This time, London Road would have handled the case, to remedy the shortcomings and negligence revealed by the Slohan Oak Police Station.

Everyone went back to their homes, and so did the Murray women, more astonished than ever. Marta had cried so much that she had run out of tears and tissues. Alice, on the other hand, was speechless. She only promised her mother that she would stay by her side for as long as necessary. Assuring her mother that things would work out was a lie, a lie to Marta and to herself.

Nothing would return to normal. The death of such many people had released a kind of fear similar to a pestilence, which couldn't be easily eradicated, and not even time could do anything about it. Slohan Oak was now to be considered a cursed place where an evil hungry for pain and suffering had ended up plaguing the town.

That morning the doorbell rang at around ten. Alice hesitated before opening it, as she knew that every time the bell rang, misfortune showed up. Nevertheless, it was Margaret. As soon as Alice saw the woman, she didn't know whether to calm herself down at the idea of seeing the Chief Inspector, or to discourage herself. Although their family used to be friends in the past, Alice didn't really know Margaret, as the latter had always found a way not to attend the meetings. However, Alice noticed that the *beautiful* thirty-years old woman - with her reddish cheeks, well-marked cheekbones and blue eyes - now looked even older and wasted away. A desire of revenge could be perceived in her gaze. Margaret had gone to Shelley House to talk to Alice, as the girl had been the last person who had visited Nightingale House and to have visited Mr. Hamond. Thus, they talked about Alice's visit, although the girl was still unaware of Mr. Hamond's death. She knew she didn't have much to lose, except the opportunity to the whole truth and be heard by one of the most important people in London Road. Alice told her everything. She also told Margaret about her lack of confidence in the police, which had exacerbated after Philip's assault in the woods.

"Your father told me that he couldn't reveal the name of whoever delt with all of this. But I ask you to trust me. I've never thought he could do such an extreme action" – Alice said.

"You mean that he also took part in those sacrifices you're talking about?" – Margaret asked. She was seating on the armchair in the living room, and while she asked that question, her gaze turned to look out the window firmly.

"No, he wasn't that kind of man. He had faked his disability to protect you. I suppose not to be targeted. Unfortunately, that's all I know."

Then, Alice showed Margaret her father's watch and the group photo, exactly as she had done with Mr. Hamond. The girl explained how and why the people portrayed on the photo had dead. Alice hope that the Chief Inspector could found out more about the Divum Deus.

"Look, your father had appeared in the photo too. As regard those three people, I don't know them" – Alice told anxiously, pointing to two blurred faces and to the woman in a powder-coloured dress.

Unexpectedly, Margaret took from her bag a photo. It was the polaroid his father had held in his hand until his last breath, and which portrayed a blonde woman.

"Alice, do you think they are the same person?"

The girl looked at the photo Margaret was showing her and gave a start. "It's her!" – Then Alice plunged into the sofa.

Margaret sighed.

Alice - after a short silence - resumed speaking "I hope the case of Wendy Boyton is not connected to this story."

"Why should there be a connection?"

"If we consider what your father said, the Divum Deus works through sacrifices."

Exactly when it seemed that the conversation was over because of Margaret's scepticism about the role of the occult in that affair, the woman suddenly turned pale. She took the group photo shaking. Her blue eyes had become wet. The two faded faces begun to lighten, revealing that the two men were Donovan Cole and Richard Walsh.

The group photo was now complete.

None of them had survived.

Margaret quickly notified the Station. She reported that the two men were in danger and that it was urgent to track them down. She would have provided the Station with further explanation afterwards. Looking for them was the real urgency. The officer on duty, in fact, told her that both the Inspector and the Coroner had not been seen since the night before, and that, Walsh hadn't shown up to examine Reece's body.

That news confirmed Margaret's fears. Thus, she decided to go to Castle Combe - the Inspector's house - without waiting for her colleagues. Overwhelmed by confusion, the woman had allowed Alice to go with her, as the protocol claims that any civilian could witness the scene of a crime.

They left Shelley House in a hurry and reached the Inspector's house two hours later, as the storm had made them slow. During the journey, Margaret prepared herself for the worst scenario. She hoped that Cole wasn't at home or even that the photograph was wrong. Indeed, she wanted to think that it was only a resolution error, rather than an esoterism as Alice had said. The only certain was that she would have allowed the girl to enter the house. She would have told Alice to stay in the car to *keep watch*, and to prevent her from any unpleasant encounters.

Margaret parked her car. Then, she headed to the front door realising it was ajar. Her breath became heavier. With a lump in her throat, she pulled out the gun and turned to the car, while Alice was fearfully staring at her from the windows.

"Cole?" – She said.

Then, she shouted again. "Donovan?"

She walked cautiously, approaching the jambs of the rooms lit by the reflection of the snow.

As soon as she entered the studio, she couldn't believe her eyes. She had to rally all her forces before warning her colleagues. She briefly swayed on the heels of her expensive boots, then inhaled the cold air of the house and called the Station.

"It's Prestcote-Hill at *Barrow Cottage*, at Castle Combe. I found them, but they're both dead."

She tried to hold back the tears, but a river begun to flow from her eyes over her warm face. She sobbed, covering her mouth with her hand not to be heard by someone. She could feel her heart exploding, confirming that she was madly in love with Donovan Cole.

Cole and Walsh lay on the ground lifeless. Donovan had a large cut wound in his abdomen, while Walsh's femoral was severed. His mouth was livid and full of clotted blood, as if someone had cut off his tongue to prevent him from speaking even in a *postmortem* life. The murder weapon was still there. A scalpel was put through the Coroner's mouth. Cole had been spared that horrific mutilation. However, the pocket watch he used to pass between his fingers was placed inside his mouth. The watch crystal had been shattered.

Margaret fell on her knees and, while she tried to wipe away her tears, she noticed that Walsh had somehow tried to communicate. With his index finger stained with blood, he had written a name of which only two letters could be read.

BR

"It was a brutal act, premeditated and devised by a twisted mind" – Margaret told Alice what she had seen. However, she hadn't allowed the girl to reach the crime scene, and she had merely reported what she had seen. In any other circumstance, her professionalism would have taken over her emotions, preventing her from reporting any details.

Alice grasped that there was something more than just a working relationship between Margaret and Cole. Indeed, as the woman said Cole's name, her voice broke abruptly.

They both remained locked in the car waiting for reinforcement to come. Margaret's perplexity about the link between the Divum Deus and the murders of her colleagues became evident. According to her, revenge could have pushed someone to kill them. The bloody letters Welsh had written on the floor led her to suspect about Breanne, Amilia's sister.

"Alice, I trust you. I shouldn't even talk to you about these. Unfortunately, the situation is abnormal. As you have probably grasped, inside the house there is one of the most important people in my life. I feel emotionally exposed. You mustn't talk to anyone about it until this case will be made public. I'll call you in the next weeks, but only if strictly necessary. As concern the photo group, we'll deal with that later. Until then, I'd like you to keep my father's watch along with the runes you have. Gather them in a place that only you know."

Finally, Margaret asked one of the Officers arrived to take Alice to the nearest train station, the one in Chippenham in that case.

XXXVIII

Friday, 5th of January 2018

For a long time, the main topic of conversation at Shelley House had been about esotericism and quantum physics. According to Philip, *science* was the set of codes that ruled both the known and the unknown. Annihilation processes had always amazed him. Indeed, his successful university career had allowed him to take part in the IZP in Bern, where his work was appreciated and constantly developing. The team of scientists he collaborated with was led by Dr. Lipika Sharma, who held the boy in high esteem. Philip loved talking about the research conducted at the IZP with his sister, while she listened to him amazed and eager to learn more about that. Yet, she couldn't grasp all those concepts. It could be said that scientific anecdotes were Alice's favourite bedtime story, which she could listen to over and over again. Marta, on the other hand, believed in karma. She thought that for every negative action, there was another one of greater intensity. Her thought almost resulted into superstition, which was typical of the Italian culture. Marta was sure that if people had worked in the name of empathy, any possible disaster would have been prevented.

On January 5th of that same year, the storm seemed to calm down over the whole Country. It calmed just for one day to allow the inhabitants to catch their breath and regain their strength, as if they were soldiers who had to get ready for the imminent second wave of bitter cold.

That morning, Mr. Hamond's funeral was also held. The news had been made official with a press released broadcast on all the English newscasts. Even most of the unwelcomed acquaintances of the Prestcote-Hill family - including some of the Ministers of Parliament and senior police officers - had took part in the ceremony of the late Hamond. Despite her father was well-known for the position he once held, Margaret would have preferred to receive support from a few trusted people rather than a multitude of strangers.

Marta attended the funeral as formalities required it. However, at the end of the liturgy she didn't take part in the procession to the cemetery accompanied by the choir of white voices. Indeed, she remained in church, sitting deep in thought in the lateral nave. The marbled checkerboard floor was as cold as her husband's body had been few months ago. A straight line of footprints from the entrance up to the altar could be distinguished on the floor. They were the steps of those who had unconditionally accepted the sacred Eucharist. Marta had quietly observed it, superstitiously thinking that perhaps, the misfortunes that had befell her family were due to her lack of faith. She continued to wonder about what divine punishment would be due to those sceptical like her.

A sudden cough from the left aisle distracted Marta from her thoughts. Seated on one of the benches and wrapped in a cloak, the slander figure of Madame Dutrieux was praying in front of the altar. Her bony hands were placed on her tired legs.

Marta slowly approached her, while her long coat rustled on her boots.

"Madame" – Marta murmured. – "I didn't expect to see you here today."

"*Un dernier adieu*[20]. Come join me."

Marta smiled and sat down next to her. The governess was holding an object in her right hand; it wasn't a rosary, nor a cross. It was a metal pendant with a moon and owl in relief. It could be said that the pendant was particularly important to her, as she kept rubbing her index finger on it with an increasing movement, almost as if that comforted her.

"Do you often come here to pray?" – Marta asked her.

"It's the first time. I'm not *His* follower, are you?"

"If I come to church often?"

"No, I'm asking you if you consider yourself a believer."

"I don't know what to believe anymore, Madame. All these deaths…" – Marta murmured. Then, she looked again at the pendant with the owl. "Could it ever be that this pain falls over us because of our lack of faith? Probably, all we have to do is find the right path."

Madame instantly stopped running her finger over the pendant. Then, she slowly raised her head and looked at the altar.

"The path has already been mapped out for each of us, Marta. But evil has pierced the canvas like a sharp stinger of a hornet."

---

[20] One last goodbye.

Then, a clatter of boots headed from the central nave to Mrs. Murray. It was a woman, with locks of blonde hair shining of reflected light and hung down on her gray coat.

The conversation between Marta and Madame Dutrieux ceased. Indeed, Madame stood up to take her leave, stretched out her arms to grab Marta's gloved hand. Only after having looked Marta straight in her eyes, Madame whispered, "*Fais attention*[21]."

In only Philip had known before that day about the Altors and the ultra-dimensional laws that allow them to come on the earth, he would have probably reformulated old theories and stated new ones. Although Aleister's appearance on earth had produced enough positive energy - the *Øbernin* - it had generated a directly proportional negativity energy, the *Osernns*.

The bright blue star that had enveloped Aleister had inevitably created a slit in the dimensional space; an imperceptible gate that would have allowed souls trapped in the limbo to come on earth. Those evil and envious souls that had long waited for the ultra-dimensional veil to wear thin in order to pierce it and loom over our dimensional universe.

---

[21] Be careful.

XXXIX

The runes were carefully gathered and separated from their shells. While observing them, a shiver run down Alice's spine. Then, the girl put them in a small fabric bag she had found in Marta's sewing box. It was made of delicate muslin that Marta and her mother had embellished with a floral pattern when the woman was eight years old. Alice regretted haven stolen that sentimental bag for such a sinister aim. However, as the saying claims, the *ends justify the means*.

Alice hadn't taken part in Mr. Hammond funeral ceremony. Thus, she took advantage of the apparent calm of that Friday to go to the house on Lake Hoarmere and hide the runes. Several times she had wondered about the very nature of the runes. However, what had been troubled her in the last few days was the thought of understanding which animal represented her father, Arthur. However, the hardest part would have been telling her mother everything about that affair. Alice considered every possible reaction of her mother, including that Marta, in dismay, would have asked her tons of questions for days.

The gun Alice had found in the ventilation conduct made her doubt about what Mr. Hamond had said; namely that her father's extreme action had been moved by the wish to protect his family. The girl - just like Philip - feared that her father had gotten involved in some illegal activity which could have justify the sumptuous belongings and their high standard of living. She had begun to doubt that all their possessions were due to her father's entrepreneurial ability and his successful antiquarian business. Alice and her family had to get ready to face the possibility of paying the consequences of Arthur's mistakes, both economically and in term of their reputation. Who knows how the usual scandalmongers of Slohan Oak would have laughed in knowing of their failure. Who knows...

Despite that apparent calm, once she arrived at the lake, faith began to play tricks on her. Indeed, her phone suddenly switched off while she was about to pick up to her mother; as if that wasn't enough, the landline was still out of order. She inspected every single place in which she could hide the runes, but she couldn't find one.

A sudden noise distracted her. That noise reminded her of the meringues Marta crushed when she made the *Eton Mess*. Thus, Alice immediately hid the small bag in her bra. She began to act like a thief, trying to hide herself. While she was scrutinizing from the window, her eye was caught by a semi-angelic figure standing under the porch; a woman whose blonde locks hung over her gray coat. It was Brunhilde, with a clear look of guilt on her face. She had probably regretted of having broken up with Philip.

The young woman knocked at the door twice, and then said with her Swiss accent, "Are you home?" – She asked.

Alice was almost frightened. However, pretending not to be inside the house would have been foolish, as her blue car was parked in the garage. She wondered why Brunhilde, the *perfect Hilde,* had come, and if she was there to meet with Philip. To be honest, she wondered how she had managed to cross the English Channel without being halted, since hurricane *Eleonor* was raging. The only thing Alice could be sure of, was that the sooner she got Brunhilde out of the way, the sooner Alice could dedicate herself to hide the runes.

Once Alice opened the door, she was astonished. Indeed, not only Brunhilde hugged her, but she even smiled at her. All of that was very uncommon. *"So, she has teeth too!"* – Alice thought ironically.

Brunhilde, the *perfect Hilde*, was in Wiltshire to reconcile with Philip. She had found out about Mr. Hamond's death and the numerous people who had attended the funeral of the Prosecutor General. After having met Marta, and after having asked about Alice and Philip, she had been invited to have a tea at Shelley House. Under that circumstance Brunhilde was informed that Alice was at the lake. Thus, it had been an endless word of mouth. Then, the young woman tried to apologise herself with her usual cold-heartedness.

Brunhilde claimed that her decision to split up with Philip had turned out to be ignoble and impulsive. Brunhilde feared love, just like Alice and Urielle. Certainly, she couldn't be blamed for that, although she could be blamed for having lied to Philip about her job. As Alice realised that their conversation would have last longer, she invited Brunhilde to come inside the house and gave her a glass of water.

During their conversation, Alice had tried not to talk about her brother. On the contrary, she had even tried to change the subject, but she failed.

"What about you, Alice?" – Brunhilde suddenly asked her.

"There's not much to say."

"Have you found the love?"

Alice widened her eyes, which shone like headlights. The charming Swiss thought that maybe she should have encouraged Alice to answer that question.

"What about the guy who attended your father's funeral?"

"Oh, Aleister" – Alice replied.

A sequence of frames appeared in her mind like flashes: the cracking of some glass shuttered under the shoes, then the roar of some thunder.

Then, that vision ended.

"Does Philip know that you're here? When could I meet him?" – Brunhilde asked impatiently.

"He's in London. I have no idea when he'll be back since the storm in sill raging."

Alice wished that as soon as Brunhilde finished the glass of water, she would have leave. Suddenly, Alice had an epiphany. Fear rose up in her. Brunhilde began to appear threatening in her mind, rather than the angelic girl once betrothed to her brother. She wondered why Brunhilde was at the lake house, despite having been informed that Philip wasn't in town.

Brunhilde - unaware of Alice's thoughts - took off her coat, suggesting her will not to leave the house. Alice couldn't help observing her slender and elegant neck, typical of an *étoile*. Her eye was suddenly caught by the necklace she wore: a golden pendant held within it a tiny stone, a small white rune. Alice felt dizzy, while her vision suddenly blurred. Thus, she stood up and told Brunhilde that she needed to go to the bathroom.

She grabbed the cordless phone, but soon remembered that the landline was still out of order; she began to silently swear, sweat beaded her forehead, and her chest began to beat like a drum.

Did Brunhilde have anything to do with the photo group?

Had Brunhilde stolen the rune from a coven member?

Was Brunhilde a killer?

Who was Brunhilde really?

As soon as Alice left the room, a white handkerchief was placed on her mouth. That was the last thing she saw. Then, she fainted.

White, the symbol of purity, of creation. The only one that encompasses all the colours of the colour wheel. When she was a child, Marta used to dress up Alice with ivory laces clothes which - matching her pale face and contrasting her red hair - marked her innocence. White reveals grace. It is the symbol of elegance, capable of arousing pure feelings.

But white is also the almost achromatic colour.

White symbolises also emptiness, like the one that suddenly invaded Aleister in the middle of his morning readings. The book fell from his hand, his head suddenly bent down for a few seconds, while his mind and limbs went numb. He dreamed of sideral and cold spaces, and for a moment, he rejoined the cosmos. Then, a good-natured soul brought him to Lake Hoarmere, where he saw Alice trembling with fear in front of the house developed by a dark mist. Aleister awoke with a start and looked around himself, realising he was home alone. Anguish overwhelmed him and, as soon as he heard the door open, he rushed towards it. It was Madame Dutrieux who had come back from the funeral in her snow-covered cloak. The woman noticed Aleister's agitation and asked him what was happening.

"I must go to Lake Hoarmere" – He told her.

"Okay, Aleister. I'll go getting the car keys."

Alice's awakening was abrupt and unusual too, after she was knocked out with ether. Although that scene could look like that of an action film, Alice didn't find her wrist tied, nor did she found herself trapped in a coffin. The girl could still move, could still talk. She was cold and confused. The only clear thing in that situation was the *white* snow under her body.

It had been Brunhilde, the *perfect Hilde*, who had treated Alice like that. The perfect Hilde had now become a *kidnapper* who maliciously watched Alice's tiny body from the lake shore. She was holding a gun and, as soon as the girl opened her eyes, Brunhilde ordered Alice to get up and slowly walk towards the centre of the Lake. In that very moment, Alice realised that any rash movement would sentence her to death.

"I'll only ask you once. Where did you hide them?" – Brunhilde asked.

"Why are you doing this to me?" – Asked Alice in a daze, but Brunhilde did not answer.

"Give me the runes, and you won't have any other troubles."

"How do you know about them?"

"I just know. Give them to me immediately."

A car noisily parked near the house. Philip and Urielle got out of it. Brunhilde looked at them, loaded the gun and pointed at Alice, ignoring Philip's screams calling for Alice.

That same day, Marta had called Philip - who was returning from London with Urielle - to inform him about Brunhild unusual manners, as she was roaming around Shelley House rummaging everywhere in search of God knows what. Philip had asked his mother where Alice was, and once he learned that his sister was at the lake house, he hung up the phone and rushed to Hoarmere. Thus, Marta had sent Brunhilde away who had turned to look at Marta with a threatening gaze. Then, the woman had tried to call her daughter to inform her of Brunhilde's visit to Shelley House.

"Who owns the rune on your necklace?" – Alice asked.

"It belonged to my mother, Olga Richter."

"The woman in the powder-coloured dress in the photo taked at Oxford", Alice thought.

"Do you know why your boat is named Amor?" – Brunhilde asked Alice.

Alice shook her head in exasperation, the cold began to numb her.

"These are my parents' initials: Arthur Murray and Olga Richter."

An acid regurgitation went up her throat. Alice began to think that Brunhilde was a psycho. She yelled that to her, so laud that drops of saliva fell on the icy surface, remind Alice of the precariousness of that ground.

"If you've read that idiot Harvey's diary, you will also know the names of the animals and their correspondents. Brickenden was the crow, Harvey the horned snake, Hamond the owl, Walsh the tortoise ... He was even so slow to die!"

Those words terrorised Alice.

"Cole was the dragon. My mother the phoenix, and our father the fox. They had chosen their names."

"You're lying about everything" – Alice objected without much conviction.

"I am the heir of my mother, I'm the new phoenix. I must gather the runes of those cowards who haven't observed the oath. They were only able to take without ever giving anything in return."

"Did you cause all those deaths?"

"Yes and no. It doesn't make much difference ... Donovan and Richard helped me to some extent in this, but terror played tricks on them. I know that animals and children are hard to digest, but *she* needed them. After having killed the second child, Cole didn't feel like killing anymore. So, I had to get rid of them as soon as they asked me to go to Castle Combe to tell that they were out of this affair. They even gave me their runes spontaneously, underestimating the gravity of their precarious position. Even in that circumstance, *she* guided me. Trust me, it hadn't been hard to kill them."

"She? Who?" – Alice asked.

"The *omnipotent*" – Brunhilde whispered – "My master, my guide, the one who will lead us to the glory. Whatever you ask will be given to you as a sign of devotion to the ancient *Heridean* scriptures. We praise you! Come to us and lead us to the glory. Come to your servants as the *Heridean* scriptures demands! Give me the runes Alice, tell me where you hid them. If you care about those two" – She said pointing out at Philip and Urielle – "You'd better talk. I had the chance to kill your mother today, but I didn't. I had mercy on the one who stole my father's love from me, relegating me to an existence of solitude and emotional deprivation. As you know, I grew up in an orphanage. So, consider it as an act of generosity."

Alice, frightened to death was about to land the loot. She put her hand inside her sweater and took off the tiny back that she placed on the icy surface of the lake. Nevertheless, when she was about to slide it towards Brunhilde, she pulled the bag back.

"At least, tell me why you need them" – Alice yelled at Brunhilde.

"Their conjunction will allow her to return beyond the veil."

As Alice heard those words, she opened the bag and scattered the runes, throwing them away.

What happened after that was just chaos.

A faded voice shouted from the distance, "Watch out!" Then, a sequence of gunshots, a white glow, and suddenly the darkness came.

Someone once said that when one is on the verge of dying, but still conscious, the mind is the first to fight for survival. The images of memories became clearer in the head. They are sequences shown by the eyes like reviews of a film that we will watch for the last time. The heartbeat is unstoppable, and the muscles stiffen. While memories come to mind, escaping from pain and compulsion is the only thing that can save us. Every fragment of life lived becomes a necessary foothold to overcome death: the gaze of a mother at her daughter, the greyness of a sky full of clouds, the sound of rain, the reading of a good book, the scent of sweets, flowers in spring, the faces of the people we love.

Thirty... Thirty-one... Thirty-two... Every extra second we manage to count before reaching the end of life always seems insufficient.

The last image that came to Alice's mind was *Aleister's* face.

It was a succession of lightning-fast events, which outcome changed only thanks to the arrival of the Altor, who had arrived in a beam of light. Aleister stepped between Brunhilde and Alice. The bullet sank into his flesh, at shoulder height, while he tried to push Alice away. The ice cracked and suddenly shattered under their foot.

Aleister barely managed to emerge from the lake bottom, rescuing Alice. He felt a kind of push coming from the bottom. His body had become uncommonly warm, allowing him to break through the ice formed again on the surface. When the lightning stopped and visibility returned to normal, Brunhilde was gone, she was disappeared.

Alice's face gradually turned pale, while the water flowed endlessly from her mouth. Philip rushed to her terrified, trying to reanimate her. If tears at his disposal had had a limited number, it could be said that Philip cried all his tears.

"Alice, wake up!" – Philip screamed.

Heart massage.

"Alice, please! Please wake up!" – Philip was desperate.

Heart massage, followed by a series of punches in the center of her chest.

Alice finally threw up the water but fainted a few seconds later.

"Philip, calm down. She's fainted" – Urielle said shaken.

Then, they both looked at the dying Aleister, who was lying on the ground with his clothes soaked and stained with blood.

"You have to take her to the hospital" – Urielle told him – "Now!" – She screamed.

"He's hurt too" – Said Philip.

"Urielle, you have to take me to Orpeco. He will know what to do" – The Altor said suffering. Then, with a gaze full of bitterness, he watched Philip and added, "Save Alice, and you will save both of us."

XL

Snowflakes started to fall again. The forecast cold storm from the East brought snow and gusts of wind that caused inconvenience across the Country. In the *Suburbs*, some houses had been damaged; tiles fell from the roofs, threatening people's safety. Passers-by commented on the unexpected damages with bewilderment, while many people were rushed to nearby hospitals. The time spent in hospital is governed by different physical laws. The rooms host the concerns of those hospitalised and lying in white uncomfortable, yet clean, bed. The length of their stay in the hospital is unknown.

Alice had managed to escape hypothermia. Even so, the elderly and bald specialists decided to hospitalise her until she was fully recovered. Philip had told the doctors - the *bald ones*, as he said - about the incident that took place at the lake, omitting the detail of the shooting. At first, Philip had also told Marta that Alice had accidentally fallen into the icy lake. However, after a couple of days he had decided to tell his mother the truth. Even today, Marta prefers not to remind herself of that event, but when it happens, she finds comfort in smelling Alice's scent from her clothes.

Alice was diagnosed with a slight form of amnesia; she had woken up with an inexplicable stabbing pain on her shoulder, and she could hardly remember what happened that day. When the doctors suggested Philip to help her remember, the guy objected, and angrily demanded them to leave Alice alone. The first night of convalescence was a kind of psychedelic journey of hallucinations, as happens to those who are under the influence of mescaline; nevertheless, only saline and painkillers flowed through the IV.

After two days, Alice's hospital room was permeated with colours and cheerfulness. Uncle Lory called from Florence to find out more about Alice's health condition and announced his daughter's birth, Iris, who was born few hours before Alice's accident. He had waited to tell the news due to the commotion the incident had caused. It seemed that the good news had had perfect timing. Flowers embellished the whole room, picking up everyone's spirits. In the village, many expressed their support to the Murrays. The children of the refuge gave Alice some sketches; Madame Dutrieux and Orpeco paid homage with an apple crumble; Mrs Beans' gift was regal as always. She had attached a note that reads "I can't also find the other earring, but everyone will get their memory back! *Ah, men!*"

On the third day of her hospitalisation, Alice - not remembering what had happened - asked her brother why Aleister and Urielle hadn't visited her. After having hesitated for a moment, Philip told her to be patient. What can it be said about Philip? Shake, he was shaken. After all, who wouldn't be? What Brunhilde had done was dramatic, but Aleister's arrival had aroused infinite doubts. Philip still couldn't understand what had really happened. He had asked Urielle for confirmation, but she had refused to give any explanation in that moment. Nevertheless, as an older brother and family man, he had to keep his calm, although that situation had become abnormal.

Alice's memory came back thanks to Philip's reluctance. The girl suddenly remembered of Brunhilde, the gunshot and everything that had occurred before she pulled the trigger.

"You knew about our father, and you lied to me" – Alice told him.

"I would have told you everything once I get back from London. I hadn't told you before because I didn't want to alarm you. Detective Bassett had summoned me right before you found the... the *gun*" – He whispered. – "He informed us about that during our last meeting. He pulled her backgrounds and managed to track down the owner of the French bank account... it was our father who paid her a monthly amount from Passy. Following this lead, Bassett found an old letter from her mother, Olga Richter, along with a photo portraying both of them."

"Where did he get this?"

"He found it from the records of the orphanage in Bern, where Brunhilde grew up. *Erid...Waisenhaus* or something like that. She wasn't lying about Harvey's diary. Believe me when I say that it wasn't easy to accept even for me. I was supposed to marry her!"

"I don't understand why you lied to me, saying that you were going to London to talk about financial matters. Also, why did you brought Urielle with you?"

"Until the very end I hoped it was bullshit. I hope Brunhilde had cheated on me. Selfishly, I even hoped I could feel better away from here" – Philip run a hand over his face to hide his bitterness. – "I told our mum everything."

Alice eyes widened, but she didn't say anything.

"She needed to know it" – Philip said.

"How did she react?"

"Better than I thought. She has decided that our father's studio will become a fabulous walk-in wardrobe. As soon as you get back home, she will go to Florence to talk to her trusted interior design and to visit Uncle Lory."

They both laughed at their mum's decision, then, they hugged. "I'm glad you're alive" – Philip added.

Margaret Prestcote-Hill entered the hospital like a widow, to visit Alice the morning of the fourth day. Alice told the woman the whole story in detail. During her stay, Margaret updated Alice on Breanne Amilia, adding that, after the incident on Lake Hoarmere, she issued an arrest warrant for Brunhilde. Such verdict put the last deal to the investigations on the Divum Deus and the death of its member. As regard the runes, Alice dropped them on the bottom of the lake, where they would remain forever.

No one had heard from Aleister and Urielle, except Philip, who had said that they were at home and that they were fine, continuing inviting Alice to be patient.

Five monotonous long days passed, seven thousand two hundred minutes. A slight numbness had replaced her initial pain on the shoulder. That afternoon would finally be the last - after boring days spent receiving visits and doing nothing - Alice would finally leave the hospital. Thoughts had aroused in her mind during her recovery like never before. The doctor hadn't even allowed her to change room or ward.

As the day went by, the dynamics at the Hoarmere, of the gunshot, and of her fall become clearer in her head. She had even begun to think that Aleister wasn't as fine as they wanted her to believe.

That same day - while Philip was telling her about some new events in Slohan Oak - the guy had to leave the room, as someone wanted to talk to him. After few minutes, he briefly entered the room to wave at her, then he left again with a smile on his face.

Someone knocked on the door, and immediately Aleister appeared, holding a bouquet of *Ausmas* on his right hand, while he wore a brace on his left arm. Shortly after, Urielle entered the room with a smile.

Alice was happy to see them, although she was disappointed that they hadn't visited her before. The thought that Aleister was injured, and that Philip hadn't told her, had pestered her. Overall, Aleister seemed to be fine, except for his look, inexplicably agitated.

Alice thanked him for the flowers.

Looking at her, Aleister thought how vulnerable she was, with her pale skin and her red hair red hair framing her tiny face. Alice was carefully observing him, in search of clues about their mishap.

"Oh, many have already brought you flowers" – Aleister said, looking around the room. "How do you feel, Alice? Your brother told me about your blackouts."

"I feel better, thanks."

Then, she asked them to seat down. Urielle sat on the armchair, while Aleister sat by her bed.

"It took you some time to come visit me, Urielle" – Alice scolded her friend, who shrugged without saying anything.

Alice sighed. Their visit had turned out to be stranger than she thought. The more she looked at Aleister, the more he seemed sad, although she couldn't figure out why.

"It was complicated for everyone" – He said.

"How are you? Is your wound healed?" – Alice asked the guy. She noticed that, even if his arm was bandaged, he could easily move it. She thought that any gunshot wound couldn't heal so quickly. Suddenly, she thought of what had happened the day of the demonstration at Maddox Street: the wounded on his forehead had turned into a discolouring stain.

"Show it to me" – Alice ordered him.

"I can't, I have the bandage. Isn't it enough for you to know that I'm fine?"

"No, Aleister. It isn't enough, not anymore."

At first, he didn't say anything, he just looked at her, aware that the truth would come out. He bared his chest unwillingly, where he had been shot. There was nothing, no bandage, no stiches, only a slight discoloration of the epidermis.

"This is ... impossible" – Alice said, while Urielle groaned like a wounded animal.

"It's complicated to explain, but if you want to listen to me, you'll understand everything."

"Who are you really?"

That was the sentence Aleister was afraid to hear. How would he start the story, and how would he conclude it? Although, the several pros and cons of that revelation, Aleister came to the conclusion that - even if he hadn't told her - Alice would eventually realise that he didn't belong to this world.

"I'm not human in the way you interpret it" – He paused.

"Are you ... alien?"

"I'm an Altor."

Alice was speechless. For a moment, she though it was a lucid dream, and that Aleister wasn't really there.

He touched her hand. Aleister was there, in that room. He took a deep breath and told her everything from the beginning, without omitting anything.

"This explains many things. Has it always been you to influence my dreams and my night apparitions?"

"Your memories, your joys and your pain lay on me. Wherever you are, every emotion you feel, is able to reach me. I tried to limit the flow of my thoughts so as not to reveal my true nature to you ... For this reason, you have lucid dreams."

"Is this how you managed to find me on that day at Lake Hoarmere?"

"Yes, I had what you humans call 'vision' and I realised you were in danger."

Alice looked to Urielle, who nodded. It was in that moment that the girl realised that her best friend had always known it.

"Alice, please, say something" – Aleister said.

"Does Philip know about that too?" – She asked.

"As a man of science, he has reacted quite well. He found answers to many of his questions, which will be the basis of his research at work" – Urielle reported.

Alice was shocked, her eyes wet with tears and full of uncertainties. She needed time to process what Aleister had just told her.

"Now" – Alice said – "Now, I need to be alone for a while." Aleister left the room, aware that it could be a farewell.

XLI

Thursday, 11th of January 2018

Philip had push Alice on a wheelchair to the car to bring her home. His face was relaxed than he'd been in a long time. He had started bearing Brunhilde affair and her deceptions. That wasn't a happy ending story. Philip would have always worn the scars of that incestuous and illusive relationship. Even so, he had managed to turn those disappointments into motivation that made him feel alive and with a real purpose to pursue. After all, all their pain, anguish and fears hadn't been useless.

"So, he's an Altor" – Alice said as she sat in the seat of the Mercedes.

"Yes, an Altor!" – Philip replied. – "We are not alone in this universe. I knew! I told you so! This certainty really excites me! I'm high on adrenaline. We should all scream Eureka! But we can't. Humanity is not ready to accept a phantasmagoric event of this magnitude. It would break down all the religious dogmas that people have always believe in. Aleister would become a freak."

Alice said nothing. She was dazed and confused by that truth. She tried to understand her brother's enthusiasm towards

Aleister. According to Philip, Aleister was a hero without fear and without reproach, just like in knightly sagas. He wasn't human, but after all, he had proved the most human of all.

Alice's first rescue had caused her soul to halve, but according to Philip, that loss was more than admissible. Without the intervention of the Altor, she would have died, and elfishly speaking, none of them could ever have accepted Alice's death.

"So, Aleister is pure *Øbernin!*" – He said almost shouting. – "What once were only hypotheses, they are now scientific truths. I will finally be able to demonstrate the energies that govern our universe."

One of their favourite childhood songs played on the radio. They would have listened to it over and over again and again, regardless their mood. That track evoked the memory of a concert they went to the last June. Alice smiled and looked at Philip as he continued to explain his theories.

Once they arrived at Shelley House, Urielle welcomed them. Embarrassment was inevitable at the beginning. Alice knew that Urielle had hid the truth. *The truths.* Looking at her, Alice wondered if she really knew her friend. She could see Urielle's soft brown hair, her genuine and contagious smile. But probably, this wasn't enough.

"Philip talked to you about science, but I..." – Urielle sighed, as she turned her eyes on the ground – "I'm gonna talk to you about esoterism, Alice."

Thus, they spent hours and hours talking in the living room and sipping tea from time to time. Urielle revealed every single detail about esoterism. She began by telling Alice about her paranormal gift, the long night chats in the three-room apartment with his grandmother, and that she could see people's halo. Then, Urielle told her friend that she could communicate with the spirits, and that this gift had led her to hate herself when she was younger. However, she had managed to grasp the positive side of it, just like Aleister and Orpeco. Human's small and dull minds would have considered such diversity as an intrusion into their world.

"The only worrying aspect of this story - which sees the meeting of science with esotericism - is the *Osernns* generated in parallel with Aleister's *Øbernin*. Now, we know that Brunhilde was operating to carry out a task. But her disappearance is not comforting. It would have been better to have known her dead" – Urielle said.

They all agreed not to mention the complicity of Cole and Walsh in the murders of little Boyton and Reece Danton. They didn't have enough evidence to support Brunhilde's statements. Thus, the guys decided to leave the resolution of the case to the police.

Urielle's explanation filled the gaps of the complex plot reported by Philip. As soon as Urielle finished talking, Alice grabbed her friend's hand.

"Riri" – She said – "We are your family, why have you waited so long to tell us about your gift?"

Tears begun to flow from her eyes, shining like glitters. Alice thought she had never seen her friend so upset and, even on that occasion, she ended up infecting herself with deep sadness.

"You are my family" – Urielle said suffering.

Later that afternoon, the weight of responsibility manifested itself in Alice. It was the weight of Aleister's life that was connected to her by an invisible thread. Even if there were miles away from each other, that cord would be strengthened day after day. Then, she thought to an expression her mother used to say when she felt laden with responsibility. "Everyone lives, not by chance, but for a greater ultimate goal. Life itself is the greatest goal that we are allowed to pursue." Although at first Alice thought that a life spent like that was to be considered like a doom, she eventually realised she was wrong. Some things can't be understood without first experiencing them.

That symbiosis between them - similar to that between a mother and the child in her womb - highlighted that they were meant to be together. They were the predestined, and she no longer had any reason to dwell on the suffering experienced and the sense of helplessness of the situation. Now, Alice could see it crystal clear: light was coming out of those wounds.

She grabbed the key of the blue car and left the house, without informing anyone.

She saw him in the distance, sitting on the snow-white ground in his dark coat. In June, that meadow is covered with cerulean *myosotis*. Although it isn't well kept, spots of blue and green flowers alternated on that lawn, creating a contrast with the *blue* sky. Now there was Aleister as a dark dot in the muffled white. Restless, he desperately tried to find peace by looking at the sky and recalling his home in the solitude of cold space.

Aleister heard the wheels of Alice's car creak, but he didn't turn around. Even when the sound of her footsteps on the snow became closer, he kept staring at the void. Alice walked through the garden to the not very deep, yet dangerous, overhang. Then, she sat on the ground in silent. For the first time, they both were heedless of the humidity that would eventually wet their clothes.

"The weather has graced us today" – Alice said with a smile.

"I just want you to forgive me" – He replied.

"You don't have to ask for forgiveness, you didn't do anything wrong. I was scared, that's why I react badly. Sometimes fear makes you act foolishly."

"I am scared now."

"You shouldn't be."

"I thought I could deserve the light, *your* light, Alice. I have deprived you of half of your soul. How shouldn't I be scared? I would deserve oblivion."

"I think you are too hard on yourself. There is a reason behind all of this, Aleister. You and I can't change the past, but we can build our future."

The boy looked at the horizon that was turning into a pale blue.

"The *Erheiur*, this is the strongest feeling. Not fear" – He told her.

"I've finally figured out what you meant when you said you knew me better than anyone else. I will never be able to experience it, but I can sense it."

He hinted at a smile.

"My mother is going to leave for Florence. I hope that the storm will end soon."

"What are you going to do?"

"I was thinking I could go with her" – Alice saw Aleister's face becoming sad again. – "I won't be away for long, just enough to get used to this new life. I need to go back to my origins."

"How can I know you'll come back, and this isn't a good-bye?"

"You once told me that the strongest promises are those made by giving the soul. Thus, you have to trust me. My soul belongs to you now. My soul is now yours too. This won't change, Aleister.

Alice rested her chin on his shoulder, between his neck and the soft coat. She could feel his heart beating accelerating.

"Why me?" – Alice asked.

"When a blind sees the light for the first time, he's overwhelmed. He yearns for it, he falls for it, and does whatever he can to protect it. It's the same for me. Now that you are by my side, the light of the dawn makes sense."

They both had a completely spontaneous reaction.

Crying.

An evil presence remained hidden in the dark and silent Shelley House and waited to be alone. Precisely in the garage, an *entity* which had brought a little confusion revealed his real devilish nature. Mabon, the cat, bigger and even more haughty showed himself to be a creeping nightmare. He had finished dining his fellow cat. Gray tufts were what had left of Rommie's carcass. His thunderstruck petrified gaze could still be seen on the remains of his head, as if Rommie wanted to beg for Mercy.

Only after having violently torn to pieces his guts, Mabon left the house. But there was something unusual in his pace. Not only he had visibly grown, but his shadow had also taken human form.

Big thanks to:

Sara Mazzarello, a very talented translator, and collaborator who took part in the realisation of this book, a little great success. Thank you, my friend.

My beloved little brother, *Simone*, who has posed for the cover and drown the illustrations with care and dedication.

My mother, *Sandra*, my biggest friend. Thank you for all the laughs and for all the nights we have spent talking about this novel. You have never stopped supporting this project.

My father, *Paolo*, who has always listened to my ideas (even to the most bizarre ones) with interest and curiosity.

My friend *Samantha*, for the time she has spent with me and my imaginary friends without losing her enthusiasm.

Printed in Great Britain
by Amazon

77877014R00187